CONFIDENTIAL MEMO

Badge No. 0407—Bran McCall

Rank: Lieutenant

Skill/Expertise: Adept decision maker, able to quickly assess a situation and act on it. Well respected and cool under fire.

Reason Chosen for Assignment: As the arresting officer of the escapee, McCall has rank in the case, and *intimate* knowledge of the suspect's prime target—his estranged wife. Protecting her will be easy; ignoring the temptation to kiss her senseless may be harder.

Subject: Victoria Dewitt McCall

Profession: Private Investigator

Skill/Expertise: Tough, stubbornly independent, able to bluff her way out of risky situations.

Reason Chosen for Assignment: Her talent for undercover work makes her the perfect partner for her husband on this case. But can she resist the heat that flares between them in close quarters?

Dear Reader,

The holidays are here, so why not give yourself the gift of time and books—especially this month's Intimate Moments? Top seller Linda Turner returns with the next of her TURNING POINTS miniseries. In *Beneath The Surface* she takes a boss/employee romance, adds a twist of suspense and comes up with another irresistible read.

Linda Winstead Jones introduces you to the first of her LAST CHANCE HEROES, in *Running Scared*. Trust me, you'll want to be kidnapped right alongside heroine Olivia Larkin when bodyguard Quinn Calhoun carries her off—for her own good, of course. Award-winning Maggie Price's LINE OF DUTY miniseries has quickly won a following, so jump on the bandwagon as danger forces an estranged couple to reunite and mend their *Shattered Vows*. Then start planning your trip Down Under, because in *Deadly Intent*, Valerie Parv introduces you to another couple who live—and love—according to the CODE OF THE OUTBACK. There are *Whispers in the Night* at heroine Kayla Thorne's house, whispers that have her seeking the arms of ex-cop—and ex-*con*—Paul Fitzgerald for safety. Finally, welcome multipublished author Barbara Colley to the Intimate Moments lineup. Pregnant heroine Leah Davis has some *Dangerous Memories,* and her only chance at safety—and romance—lies with her husband, a husband she'd been told was dead!

Enjoy every single one, and come back next month (next year!) for more of the best and most exciting romance reading around—only in Silhouette Intimate Moments.

Yours,

Leslie J. Wainger
Executive Editor

Please address questions and book requests to:
Silhouette Reader Service
U.S.: 3010 Walden Ave., P.O. Box 1325, Buffalo, NY 14269
Canadian: P.O. Box 609, Fort Erie, Ont. L2A 5X3

Shattered Vows

MAGGIE PRICE

Silhouette®

INTIMATE MOMENTS™

Published by Silhouette Books

America's Publisher of Contemporary Romance

SILHOUETTE BOOKS

ISBN 0-373-27405-X

SHATTERED VOWS

Visit Silhouette Books at www.eHarlequin.com

Printed in U.S.A.

Books by Maggie Price

Silhouette Intimate Moments

Prime Suspect #816
The Man She Almost Married #838
Most Wanted #948
On Dangerous Ground #989
Dangerous Liaisons #1043
Special Report #1045
  "Midnight Seduction"
Moment of Truth #1143
*Sure Bet #1263
*Hidden Agenda #1269
*The Cradle Will Fall #1276
*Shattered Vows #1335

*Line of Duty

Silhouette Books

The Coltons

Protecting Peggy

MAGGIE PRICE

is no stranger to law enforcement. While on the job as a civilian crime analyst for the Oklahoma City Police Department, she analyzed robberies and sex crimes, and snagged numerous special assignments to homicide task-forces.

While at OCPD, Maggie stored up enough tales of intrigue, murder and mayhem to keep her at the keyboard for years. The first of those tales won the Romance Writers of America's Golden Heart Award for Romantic Suspense. Maggie is also the recipient of *Romantic Times* magazine's Career Achievement Award in series romantic suspense.

Maggie invites her readers to contact her at 416 N.W. 8th St., Oklahoma City, OK 73102-2604, or on the Web at www.maggieprice.net.

For my editor, Susan Litman,
who knows what a good story is all about.

Chapter 1

Coming up empty-handed after spending hours searching for her brother who'd commandeered her car didn't make Victoria Dewitt McCall feel like an ace private investigator.

Instead, she felt like a volcano waiting to blow.

Now, minutes after a fellow P.I. had dropped her off, Tory stalked upstairs to her bedroom. She tossed her purse on the upholstered chair near the floor-to-ceiling window, stripped off her black leather jacket, then shoved back one side of the heavy drapes. Mouth set, she stared out the frosted pane, her thoughts as dark as the January night.

The eighteen-year-old brother she'd raised had clearly been in the popcorn line when common sense got handed out. Danny was out on bail, his license suspended over unpaid parking tickets. If he got stopped by a cop while driving, he'd be back in a cell for failure to pay those tickets.

And her car would wind up in the police impound lot—
a complication she didn't need.

Tory huffed out a breath, leaving a small foggy circle
against the window. In truth, it wasn't just Danny's latest
stunt that had her grinding her teeth.

Life sucked. *Her* life, specifically.

She hadn't turned on the bedroom light, so when she
glanced across her shoulder, the bed, bureau and chest of
drawers crouched like shadowy forms in the weak light
spilling from the hallway. The heavy, dark wood furniture
wasn't to her liking, but then, little in the house was. It
wasn't *her* house, after all.

It belonged to her husband.

Estranged husband, Tory corrected. Her own common
sense had taken leave one evening nearly a year ago.
That's when Lieutenant Bran McCall gave Danny a break
and hauled him to her doorstep instead of booking him
into juvie hall for illegal gambling. With a hand clenched
on Danny's upper arm, Bran had sent her a slow, reckless
grin which she'd instantly decided was the sexiest thing
she'd ever seen. Two nights later she and the cop were in
bed.

Even now, those first heady weeks she'd spent with the
rugged widower were a blur of searing lust and hot sex.
As was the weekend she and Bran both lost their minds
and eloped.

Huge mistake. *Huge.* No way could a union based pri-
marily on physical attraction and set-your-hair-on-fire sex
survive long. Not when the parties involved were both
independent, take-charge and used to running the show.
Bran's walking out three months ago proved that he, too,
believed they'd made one hell of a mistake.

A sudden shift in the shadows at the far side of the front
lawn snapped Tory's senses to alert mode. Narrowing her

eyes, she leaned closer to the window. With the quarter moon ghosting through fat gray clouds, it was possible the movement had been nothing more than wind rustling the thick copse of evergreens.

Seconds later the shadow oozed fully out of the trees. An alarm shrilled in her head.

In full P.I. mode now, she assessed the figure clad entirely in black, including a baseball cap pulled down low. A man, she determined, watching him move. Tall, judging by the way he dwarfed the spiky hydrangea bush he crept past.

Adrenaline jolting her system, Tory jerked on her leather jacket while watching the man skulk toward the east side of the house. Her pride might have taken a hit with Danny eluding her, but she could still deliver any number of well-placed kicks that would take down some sneaky prowler.

And if her varied self-defense skills didn't do the trick, she had backup. She stabbed a hand in her purse, pulled out her trusty Sig-Sauer P226.

Leaving the lights off, she pounded downstairs. It took only seconds to cut through the dark living room and cross the expansive kitchen. At the back door her finger flipped off the Sig's safety, then floated to the trigger. Twisting open the deadbolt, she eased outside. A slap of freezing air hit her face.

Her mind had already settled on a plan. She wanted the advantage of surprise, so she would approach the man from behind.

The Sig hidden against her thigh, she veered west, moving soundlessly in the dark across the winter-dry grass.

Bolting around the house into the backyard, Bran McCall had no presentiment, no intuition, no flash of cop instinct warning him of another presence. He never even sensed the black-clad figure until he plowed over it, toppling it backward as he lost his footing and stumbled forward.

Bran landed with a jarring smack on top of the figure. In the glow of a neighbor's backyard light he caught a glint as something metallic flew through the air. *Gun.*

There was no way he could draw his own weapon, not with whoever was beneath him flailing and twisting violently while trying to knee him in the groin. Fists punched the sides of his head; the curses spewing against his parka were so muffled he wasn't sure if they came from a male, a female or a plague of angry wasps.

Even as he clamped a hand around one thrashing wrist, then another, a scent as subtle and alluring as moonlight hit him—*Tory's scent*—and he knew his wife was the kicking, spitting demon trapped beneath him.

"Tory, it's me."

When he felt her hesitate, he braced his forearms on either side of her shoulders. He eased his chest off hers. The next instant she pried one booted foot out from beneath his leg and delivered a stunning kick to the side of his shin that had stars springing into his head.

"Get off me, you jerk!"

Expelling an explicit curse, he locked his leg back over hers. "Dammit, woman, it's me."

"I heard you the first time," she hissed.

As if accepting she was outweighed and out-muscled, she stopped squirming. Rays from the far-off streetlight slanted across her face, picking up the flashing anger in her green eyes as she glared up at him.

"I looked out the bedroom window and saw some prowler skulking in the dark. I thought you were on the other side of the house."

"I doubled back. Decided to look through the garage window for your car."

"You ought to know better than to prowl around at night. I came out prepared to take you down." She jerked her chin in the direction the Sig had flown when she crashed to the ground. "Shoot you, if I had to."

Bran set his jaw. Her reaction was typical Tory—grab a situation by the throat and deal with it. In contrast, his first wife would have stayed safely indoors, phoned the police and reported the prowler. But Patience was long dead, and at this instant the woman squirming beneath him was the primary concern of both his mind and his body.

His hands tightened around her wrists. "When you spotted me, you should have called the cops. Let them take care of things."

"No self-respecting private investigator needs a cop's help to take down a measly prowler."

He hooked a brow. "This coming from the P.I. presently smashed beneath said measly prowler."

Her eyes narrowed. "What do you want, Bran?"

"If you'd returned one of my phone calls you wouldn't have to ask."

He stared down at her for the first time in three months, inspecting her with intensity. Her thick blond hair was still long, looking like polished gold in the faint light as it flared across the dry grass. He didn't have to wonder how it would feel to stroke that soft cheek or settle his mouth on those lush lips. Despite his parka's thickness, he was aware of the long, lean lines of her warm, supple body. The sparks they'd forever generated in bed had made for register-on-the-Richter-Scale sex. Problem was, they always had to come up for air and that was when their clashing personalities and opposing needs sent everything to hell.

The heat swarming into his blood had him clenching his teeth. Dammit, he hadn't come here to sate his physical needs. Not when an escaped killer had threatened revenge against him and three other cops.

Bran thought back to the panic that had hit him when he'd glanced through the garage window and seen that Tory's car was gone, which was unusual this late at night. Fearing that bad-ass Vic Heath had beat him here, then left in Tory's car, he'd bolted around the side of the house, intending to use his key to get in the back door and check her welfare.

Instead, he'd collided with her.

Relief that Heath hadn't gotten his hands on her seeped into him like water soaking into sand. "Where's your car?"

"Being worked on." She squirmed. "Dammit, Bran, let me up."

He nearly groaned when he felt himself stir. "All right." He pushed to his feet. "Look, I'd like to come inside. We need to talk."

She sat up, flicked a look at the hand he offered, then rose without his help. "About?"

Not us, he thought, feeling the same wariness he saw in her eyes after she scooped up her Sig and turned to face him.

"A cop got killed this afternoon."

"Not someone in the family, right?" Her free hand flew to her mouth in shock, then dropped. "Bran, tell me it's not—"

"It's not." His grandfather and dad had retired from the Oklahoma City Police Department. He had two brothers, three sisters and several soon-to-be brothers-in-law currently serving on the department. Whenever word of a cop getting hurt came down, the entire McCall clan held its collective breath.

Reaching out, Bran brushed a blond wave off her cheek. "We're all fine." He had never questioned her love for his family. Her feelings for him were a different matter.

As if to prove that, she took an instant step back, forcing him to drop his hand. "Good. Okay."

He looked across his shoulder past the shadow-laden side of the house toward the front yard. He saw nothing. Heard nothing. *Felt* nothing.

"Is someone out there?" Tory's voice was a whisper on the freezing air.

"My gut tells me no," he said, keeping his gaze trained on the sliver of front yard he could see. "But there's a bad guy loose who'd like to ambush some cops. Which is why I parked a couple of blocks over and walked here. *Skulked,* as you call it," he added, looking back at her.

He'd never thought of Tory Dewitt as easy on the eyes. There simply wasn't anything easy about her. She was tall—nearly his height—model-thin, with a face as angular as her body. A pointed chin, sharp cheekbones and sensual mouth combined to create a tough, stubborn, sexy face. At the moment, though, she looked more dangerous than sexy, standing inches away in her black jeans and worn leather jacket, one hand gripping the Sig while her breath made quick puffs of steam in the frigid air.

He dipped his head. "The dead cop was a corrections officer. You didn't know him, but there's a chance the bastards who killed him might come after me. They could show up here. You need to know what's going on."

Her mouth thinned, and he sensed her fingers tightening on the Sig. "All right."

She led the way along the shadowy cobblestone walk that Bran and his brother-in-law had laid during a sweltering summer five years ago. Now, Ryan Fox was dead, the only cop in the McCall clan who'd died in the line of duty. Bran hoped to hell there would never be another.

He followed Tory inside, closed the door and set the deadbolt. He realized the house had looked uninhabited from the front because the only light came from the one she flicked on when she walked through the door.

He missed this house, Bran thought as he glanced around the homey kitchen, its soft yellow paint setting off deep blue counters. When he and Patience had bought the place, they'd done so with a sense of permanence, of putting down roots, building a life together and raising a family. Growing old together. That dream had ended three years ago on the day his high-school sweetheart went off to play tennis. She'd suffered a brain aneurysm on the court, and she'd come home in a coffin.

Bran closed his eyes, opened them. He was keenly aware that the air in the kitchen held no lingering aroma of delicacies fresh from the oven. Unlike Patience, who'd nearly lived in the kitchen, Tory didn't cook. Other than the refrigerator, the only appliance that got more than a passing glance was the espresso maker he'd bought her to brew the lattes she seemed to exist on. He'd surprised her with the espresso maker last Valentine's Day, right after they'd eloped.

Now, eleven months later, their marriage was circling the drain. Bran walked to the long bank of windows on his right and began closing blinds, thinking he and Tory sure as hell wouldn't be spending the holiday made for lovers together this year.

"Want a latte?" she asked.

He turned, shrugged out of his parka. "Sounds good."

He studied his wife as she abandoned the Sig on the nearest counter, then peeled off her scarred leather jacket.

Her jeans, ripped at one knee, hugged her narrow hips and endless legs. The long-sleeved T-shirt tucked into the jeans was plain white cotton, and her unhampered breasts pressed nicely against the soft fabric.

The sudden image of himself greedily feeding on those breasts while she writhed beneath him speared heat through his system. But it was loss that hollowed his chest as he draped his parka over a chair at the small wooden table near the windows.

He glanced up to find Tory studying him with cool, measuring eyes as she poured milk into a metal pitcher. "When I saw you out the window, I didn't recognize the parka."

"Got it for Christmas." He pulled out a chair and settled at the table. "From Grace." Bran relaxed enough to smile. "Speaking of Grace, an FBI agent she once had a thing with is back in the picture. Name's Mark Santini. He's working out of the Bureau's local office. It's looking like they're together for good this time."

"He was all Grace talked about when I met her and Carrie for the first fitting on our bridesmaid dresses." Smiling, Tory carried the metal pitcher to the espresso maker. "Grace is crazy in love with Santini."

"Yeah," Bran agreed, thinking how quickly Tory had bonded with his three sisters. That the youngest, Morgan, had asked Tory to be a bridesmaid *after* the split underlined just how deep that bond went.

He pulled off his baseball cap, shoved his fingers through his hair. It suddenly hit him that his baby sister's wedding to Sergeant Alex Blade was on Valentine's Day. Dandy, Bran thought. He and his estranged wife would spend a portion of that made-for-lovers holiday together after all.

The sound of beans grinding filled the kitchen. A few

minutes later, the espresso machine began spewing steam, sounding like an angry, hissing snake.

"Tell me about the corrections officer," Tory said a minute later, carrying two oversize white ceramic mugs to the table. "And why whoever murdered him might show up here looking for you."

While she settled into the chair opposite his, Bran sipped his latte. A welcome zing of caffeine shot into his system.

"Did one of my sisters mention the shootout I was involved in a little over a week ago? What happened today ties to that."

"Your mother called to let me know you were okay. Roma didn't want me getting upset when I saw your name in the newspaper the next day." Tory met his gaze over the rim of her mug. "Tell me about it."

"Dispatch put out a silent alarm at a credit union," he began. "I arrived first, three other patrol cars pulled up behind me. We heard a shot inside the building, then the front doors flew open and two guys wearing ski masks rushed out. I ordered them to drop their weapons. Instead, they started firing. Five seconds later, they were dead."

"Sounds like they asked for it."

"They did." He shrugged. "We figured they chose to go out in a blaze of glory because they'd murdered one of the credit union clerks. Tox tests showed both had been flying on meth, so that screwed their judgment."

"What do the dead robbers have to do with the corrections officer who got killed today?"

"The cop died *because* of them." Bran set his mug aside. "Andy and Kyle Heath were the do-wrongs who hijacked the credit union."

"Brothers?"

"Cousins. Andy has an older brother named Vic. He's

spent the past three years in prison for conspiracy to distribute methamphetamine. Turns out I'm the cop who nailed Vic on those charges.''

"Small world, that you wound up on the call at the credit union.''

"I doubt Vic has missed the irony in that.'' Bran frowned. "He's been a model prisoner, a real poster boy for scumbag good behavior. Because of that, his request to attend his brother's and cousin's joint funeral was approved. This afternoon he was put in leg irons and cuffs and driven to a Tulsa funeral home by a corrections officer named Perry Paulson.''

"Is he the cop who got killed?''

"Yes. When Heath got there he asked to view the bodies. The funeral director showed him and Paulson into the room where the caskets were, then left. When he came back about fifteen minutes later, Paulson was dead. His wrists and ankles were duct taped together and his throat cut. Tulsa cops did a ground search and house-to-house check for Heath, but came up empty.''

"Handcuffed and shackled, he would have had a tough time doing that on his own without someone hearing the struggle,'' Tory pointed out. "Where'd the duct tape come from?''

"It wasn't the funeral home's. Neither was the knife that killed Paulson.'' Bran leaned in. "The theory is that Heath had at least one accomplice.''

"Any idea who?''

"Not yet. Our vice guys are talking to snitches to see if they can get names of Heath's associates.''

"You said he might show up here. I take it you think Heath wants revenge for you arresting him? And for your part in killing his brother and cousin at the credit union?''

"Right.''

"Is that cop instinct or did Heath make that threat?"

"A threat was made, but not by Vic," Bran answered. "His mother was at the funeral. She spouted off about how 'her Vic' was going to get back at the cops who killed their kin. One of the Tulsa cops overheard her and called OCPD. Since I was ranking officer at the credit union, the chief okayed our chopper to fly me to Tulsa this afternoon."

"Did you talk to the mother?"

"You bet." Bran shook his head at the memory of the hard-faced woman with skin the color of cold oatmeal. "Mamma Heath is a foulmouthed old crone with mean eyes. She took pleasure in telling me that Vic's coming after all the cops who'd been at the credit union. That Vic's going to eat our hearts out."

"Lovely family," Tory murmured. "Do you believe her?"

"I believe in not taking chances. The address and phone numbers for cops are unlisted, but if you've got a computer, some skill and enough time, you can find anybody. It's been over a week since the shootout and we don't know what information Heath has, if any. If the threat is real and he finds the addresses of the cops who were at the credit union, the logical place for him to start looking for us is at home. Which is why I'm here. And the reason I tried to call you for hours. And sent my brothers by here, too," he added.

"I've been out." Bran almost missed the elusive shadow that flickered across her eyes. *Almost.* "I got home about fifteen minutes ago."

He waited a beat, watching her. "Where's your car?"

"In the shop, remember? Sheila Sanford picked me up," Tory said, referring to a P.I. she often teamed with on jobs.

Bran felt his frustration surface; he'd spent hours trying to contact her and getting no results. Worrying about her.

"What about your cell? In addition to the machine here, I left messages on your voice mail. Said they were urgent." He leaned in. "I realize we haven't spoken to each other for three months. We've got issues to deal with. But when I call and say it's important that you get back to me, I'm not playing games."

Her chin came up. "I left my phone in the car." She shoved back her chair, walked to the V in the counter where the answering machine sat. "It doesn't show any messages waiting," she said, turning back to face him.

"Well, darlin'," he drawled, "I sure as hell left one. And I'll make a wild stab at what happened. While you were gone, Danny dropped by and checked to see if any of his pals left him a message. Brother dear just couldn't go to the trouble of leaving you a note to call me. Sound familiar?"

Thinking of his reprobate brother-in-law put knots in Bran's gut. He couldn't blame the breakdown of his marriage on Danny. But the way Tory had dealt with the kid's screw-ups had magnified the problems in their marriage and ignited the final blowup that prompted him to pack his bags.

Tory's chin went up another notch as she gripped her hands on the counter behind her. Her breast-skimming blond hair was still tousled from their rolling around on the ground and his comment about her brother had color rising over her cheekbones. Watching her, Bran felt his chest tighten. How many times had he seen her look much the same after a long, searing bout of sex?

Standing there, just *standing there* she was getting to him, filling him with need he didn't want to feel, stirring

up images of her that he'd spent days, weeks, months trying not to think about.

"We aren't going to talk about Danny," she said in a
voice that had gone very low and very cold. "Ever again."

"Seems to me we have to," he countered, feeling his
own face heat as three months of pent-up anger kindled
bright and hot. "Because your story doesn't add up, and
I figure it's because of Danny. You depend on your cell
phone for your business. If you had forgotten and left it
in your car while it was being worked on, you'd have gone
back and picked it up. Of course, that'd be a little hard to
do if you didn't know the whereabouts of your car." He
narrowed his eyes. "Danny took it and disappeared. That's
where you and Sheila have been, right? Cruising around
looking for your brother and your car? Think maybe I
ought to track him down? Remind him his license got
suspended when he *chose* not to pay all those traffic tickets
he'd racked up? Remind him of what happened to him
after he got tossed in jail?"

"I doubt Danny needs a reminder of that. Any more
than I need one about the questionable choices *I've*
made." She used her hand to make a sweeping gesture of
the kitchen. "Not when they're all around me," she added
in a voice that sounded like chipped glass.

"You don't like the house, you can always move out."

"I plan to, as soon as you sign the divorce papers my
lawyer sent you."

"*Sent* me? Your slick attorney didn't just send them.
He had a process server track me down at the briefing
station and slap the damn papers in my hand." A muscle
ticked in his jaw. "Every cop on the shift knew what was
going on."

"I didn't know." The flicker of surprise in her eyes

verified that. "I had no idea my attorney planned to serve you that way."

"Well, now you know."

"I talked to him yesterday. He said he hasn't received them back from you. Why haven't you signed them?"

Bran curled his hands into fists. He'd sat in his ratty apartment, staring at the document for hours, telling himself to just sign the damn thing and be done with it. The fact he had no clue why he hadn't was like a splash of alcohol on his rekindled anger. And, hell, maybe he was ticked because she'd beat him to the punch and served him first!

"I'll let you know when I sign them."

"Why wait?"

Rising, he sent her a caustic look. "Why hurry?"

She lifted a palm, dropped it. "Look, we made a mistake. We ran off and got married when the only thing we knew about each other was how good we were together in bed. If we'd just stayed there, we would have been much better off. Instead, we've spent the past eleven months trying to force each other into molds in which we'll never fit."

She stabbed a hand through her hair, closed her eyes. When she reopened them, an aura of weariness had replaced the agitation.

"You left, Bran. You walked out. You belong in this house, I don't. I've found a condo I want to buy. Legally, it'll be a lot easier to do that after our divorce is final. Why won't you do both of us a favor and sign the papers?"

He damn well wished he had an answer for that. Since he didn't, he flipped the topic. "Let's get back to the reason I'm here," he said, closing the space between them. "Vic Heath."

"Fine." She thrust her tumbled hair behind her ears. "Fine."

"His mother might be right about Vic being in eye-for-an-eye mode. And my having put him in prison gives him even more reason to come after me. If he shows up here, I don't want him to find you. You can bunk with Morgan, Carrie and Grace until he's picked up."

"You're the one who should stay at your sisters' place. Heath's after you, not me."

"True. But if he can't find me, he might settle for my wife. I don't want you hurt, Tory."

"I don't want you hurt, either," she said quietly.

"Well, that's something we agree on. You can pack a bag now. I'll drive you over to my sisters' place."

"Has Heath been spotted since he left the funeral home in Tulsa? Does anyone even know if he's still in Oklahoma?"

"No, to both questions."

"If the threat was to me, I'd go."

Bran caught her chin in his hand as she started to move away. "Victoria Lynn, this is serious. Life and death."

Beneath his fingers he felt her soften. Something like regret, only more complex, flickered in her green eyes. He eased out a breath. When it came to standing on her own the woman never gave an inch. "No one's going to view you as dependent if you bunk at my sisters' house for a few days."

"I carry a gun for a living, too," she said, shaking off his touch. "I know how to take care of myself."

"The corrections cop probably thought the same thing. We'll never know since he's on a slab at the morgue."

"I appreciate you letting me know about Heath." As she moved to slip past him, her shoulder brushed his. He felt the instant connection. The pull. She was right, he thought dourly. They should have just stayed in bed having mind-blowing sex and bypassed the wedding.

When she reached the counter opposite him, she turned. "I've got three active cases going right now. All have surveillance involved, which means I won't be spending a lot of time here over the next week or so. When I am here, I'll activate the security system. Keep my guard up." She patted the Sig she'd left beside her leather jacket. "I'll keep my eyes open. If you have a picture of Heath, that would help."

"His picture's all over the television by now."

"I'll turn it on. Memorize his face. You'll let me know when you find out who helped Heath escape?"

"The minute I know, you'll know."

He gave her a considering look. As long as she chose to stay here alone, there wasn't much he could do about it. And, he conceded, when she'd gone with him to the police pistol range she'd proven she was his equal with a gun. She also held her own in hand-to-hand combat—he might have had her on the ground outside, but the way she'd moved had kept him from going for his weapon. Yet knowing all that, he still wasn't satisfied.

"I've arranged for extra patrols of the neighborhood by both uniformed cops and plainclothes," he said.

She slanted him a look. "Is one of those extra patrols going to be you?"

"Not officially. Everyone involved in the shootout is on desk duty until the review board completes its report." He lifted a shoulder. "That doesn't mean I can't drive by, simply as a concerned citizen checking the safety of a neighborhood."

"I'll be careful. You don't need to worry about me."

A vicious case of frustration had his head pounding. He

wished to hell he had even an ounce of control over the situation. *Over her.*

"If something happens, call my cell. Even if you get a bad *sense* about something, I want to hear it. That goes for everyone in the family. You need us, we'll be here for you. You know that."

"I know." Her eyes softened. "It's nice to have dependable backup who all carry badges."

"Yeah."

She wouldn't call *him,* Bran would stake his life on that. She'd spent the entire time they'd been married showing him how independent and take-charge she could be. It was ironic, he thought, that his innate nature was to protect, comfort and soothe and he'd married a woman who wanted no part of that.

Patience had. She had always considered him her protector.

Turning, he walked back to the table. He jerked on his parka, wincing when the age-old injury to his right shoulder kicked in.

He had always figured he and Tory would get around to dealing with their unfinished business. After tonight, he wondered if the smart thing to do was just to let things go. Make the break before they heaped more emotional debris on what they'd once had.

He crammed his black ball cap low on his head. Maybe when he got to his apartment, he would sign the damn divorce papers and be done with it.

That would be the smart thing.

Chapter 2

"It's just a ding," Danny Dewitt said after he returned Tory's four-door Taurus to her garage the following morning.

Her gaze razored from the vehicle's right rear to her brother. He was tall and lean with a lopsided smile and black hair worn in a stubby ponytail. His face was angular, and his eyes a dreamy shade of green. His looks, combined with a glib tongue and the cocky sense of self-confidence that accompanied youth, often had females falling over their own feet.

Females other than his sister.

"It's a *dent,* Danny," Tory pointed out. "The size of a dinner plate."

He gave the Taurus another look. "A *small* dinner plate."

She pressed her lips together. "You took my car without permission. All of my equipment is in there. *My cell phone.*"

"I didn't mean any harm." He shrugged. "A friend dropped me off here yesterday afternoon. You weren't around—"

"I was helping Sheila on a case. It's called *working*."

"Figured you were doing something like that," he said, ignoring her jibe. "I came out here and saw your car. I decided the least I could do was buy you gas, a wash and an oil change."

"Gas, wash and an oil change take about an hour. Tops." She wrapped her arms around her, gathering Bran's Oklahoma Sooners red-and-white football jersey closer to ward off the cold. The jersey still carried the musky scent of his cologne and made her feel even more unsettled. Hollow. "If I had intended to let you drive my car, I'd have given you a key."

Danny grinned. "You keep an extra set in one of those magnet things under the front bumper."

"Not anymore." She wiggled her fingers. "My keys."

He handed them over with an amiable shrug. "When I got to the gas station I ran into Rocco," Danny explained. "He had a line on a poker game, so I left your car at the fast lube. Jewell was at work, and I planned to hang at the game until time for her to get off, then pick up your car and bring it back. But I started winning and couldn't leave. This morning, Rocco took me to get your car. The manager at the lube place said it got hit in their lot. Their insurance'll cover it. He gave me a form to fill out. In triplicate. It's over the visor."

"Don't take my car again. Ever."

"Sorry, Tor. I was trying to make things easier on you."

How many times over the years had she heard that? And always, Danny's good intentions took a left turn, leaving a mess for her to clean up. In triplicate.

"Want to hear how I spent last night?" she asked. "After I wasted hours looking for you and my car, Bran dropped by."

"Bran?" A hopeful look sprang into Danny's eyes. "Are you guys talking again?"

"Oh, we talked," she confirmed. "First about an escaped killer who might be gunning for Bran. Then about the messages he left on my answering machine and cell. Messages I never got."

Danny winced. "Yeah, I checked the machine. I meant to write you a note about Bran's message, but forgot."

"Too bad. That lapse of memory just got you barred from the house when I'm not here." She held out her hand. "House key."

"Geez, Tor, you're being kind of hard, aren't you?"

"I wouldn't have to be if you'd act like a responsible eighteen-year-old."

After Danny handed her the key, she continued. "Bran and I also discussed your driving my car." Her stomach knotted at the memory of how their tempers had flared. "You went to jail because you racked up so many tickets and didn't bother to pay them. The judge who granted your bail suspended your license. If a cop had pulled you over last night, you'd be in a cell right now. Did that beating you got in jail teach you nothing?"

He arched his dark brows. "Taught me I don't want to go back there a second time."

"Then why take my car? You've got one week left until your license gets reinstated. Why chance driving now?"

"I didn't think. But at least I won playing poker." He grinned. "How could I not when I had the best teacher in the world?"

"I taught you to play when you were ten years old. We

used toothpicks, not chips. I never intended poker to become your main source of funds.''

He pulled a layer of bills from the wad in the pocket of his jean jacket and handed it to her. "Here's the first installment on the bail money you and Bran fronted me.''

Tory glanced at the bills. The bail had not come with Bran's blessing. She'd told him after the fact she'd used a thousand dollars of their savings. In her mind, her doing so without telling Bran first had been justified—she'd *had* to bail Danny out of the jail's infirmary. He'd been beaten so badly she was afraid he would be permanently scarred without good, fast medical care.

Even now she could still feel the heat of Bran's anger over what she'd done. Still hear the harsh words they'd exchanged. Still see the grim look on his face as he packed his bags.

Water under the bridge, she thought. Right now she had Danny to deal with. She jammed the bills into the front pocket of her jeans then leaned a hip against Bran's workbench.

"Listen up, pal. If you get arrested again, the money I used for your bail goes down the drain. That happens, it won't be Bran who comes after you, but me.''

Danny looked at her car. "I guess you're plenty steamed right now.''

When she didn't answer, he rocked back on the heels of his scuffed running shoes. "I was hoping you'd give me a ride to Jewell's apartment. She's probably mad, too, over me being out all night.''

"You think?'' Tory asked. All she knew about the woman Danny had moved in with was that she danced at some bar under the billing "exotic performer.'' Stripper was more like it, Tory suspected. "You want a ride, call your pal Rocco.''

"Yeah." Danny moved to the door that led into the kitchen, then paused. "Tor, I didn't mean to make you mad."

"You never do."

She fisted her hands as he stepped into the house. Considering the way he'd been raised, she couldn't totally fault Danny for assuming he could forever shirk responsibility.

Their mother had been brought up by overindulgent parents who had never seen the need for their only child to learn to deal with whatever complications life tossed at her. They'd just handled them all for her. And unwittingly raised a daughter who was codependent in every aspect.

Tory had no trouble picturing their mother clinging to their father, the air of helplessness hanging around the woman almost palpable in the air. Just as easily she could see her father's face, transforming over the years until the only thing left was unbridled disgust for his wife's pathetic weakness. He hadn't even stayed around long enough to see his son born.

Tory had been nine years old when her father walked out, a young girl to whom her mother transferred as many burdens as possible. It was Tory who'd been saddled with making decisions about everything from finances to meal planning. Tory who'd learned everything there was to know about responsibility while their mother raised Danny into the mirror image of herself.

Then, when Tory was eighteen, their mother had died in a car wreck. Their father had passed away several years before. Since they had no blood relatives to turn to, Tory had stepped in to raise her then nine-year-old brother. *That's* who she also saw when she looked at Danny: the grief-stricken boy who'd clung to her while sobbing over their mother's grave. The boy who'd collected and recycled tin cans and bottles to help earn enough money to buy a stone to mark that grave.

No one had questioned Tory's ability to raise her brother. After all, she'd been shouldering responsibility for years and had grown into an independent young woman. A woman who'd vowed never to make herself the kind of burden her mother had been. Growing up, it had taken all her energy to deal with the people who needed her, so she'd never let herself *need* anyone. Not even the man she'd run off and married.

How ironic that she'd lost her head over a cop for whom it was run-of-the-mill to deal with other people's problems. A broad-shouldered, gorgeous man very willing to let her shift her burdens onto those impressive shoulders. A dream made in heaven for most women, Tory conceded, but not *her*. Never her.

And that was the crux of her and Bran's problem. According to his youngest sister, his first wife had been a slim, shy brunette who'd welcomed having a husband who shielded and protected her. She'd been happy to have him manage the problems life had to offer. From all accounts, Patience McCall had lived contentedly in Bran's shadow, quiet, deferring to him without conscious thought.

A visceral little pang of envy for the happiness Bran had shared with another woman tightened Tory's heart. As did the knowledge that Bran had spent the entire time they'd lived together comparing her to his first wife. Oh, he'd done so in silence, but Tory was well-versed at reading people, and she had seen the comparison being made in Bran's face often enough. Just as she'd seen it last night in the kitchen when his expression went distant with what she knew had been memories of another time, another woman.

A happier time with a woman who'd shown him in every way how much she needed him.

A woman whom Tory knew she could never come close to emulating. She just didn't have it in her to allow herself to lean on a man. On *anyone,* for that matter. Not when just the thought of her mother's clinging neediness put a sick feeling in her stomach.

Her gaze settled again on the workbench, sweeping over the tools that had gone untouched for months. Before she could block it, her mind flashed a picture of Bran standing there, his hands and muscled arms covered with a fine mist of sawdust, a lock of sandy hair falling over his forehead as he worked with the tools.

She felt the ache of loss through every bone and muscle. She'd felt that same sense of loss last night, lying crushed beneath his weight while everything that was female in her responded to the feel of his corded biceps, his hard chest against her breasts, the scent of his musky cologne. The damn chemical signals that sizzled through her whenever Bran got near had started nerves and needs pulsing through her in fast, greedy waves.

For the first time she allowed herself to open the door in her mind that she'd locked tight when Bran walked out. Even at the beginning there had been more between them than just that basic attraction. That physical pull. There'd been a shared affection, and what she thought had been love. All those feelings had gotten swept into the background by the conflict that had so quickly developed between them.

A bright, swift pain twisted in her heart, and the mental door she'd opened slammed shut. It hurt too much to think about how swiftly their marriage had crumbled. It was over. *They* were over.

Outside, the muffled honk of a horn sounded, and she

figured Rocco was there to pick up Danny. Seconds later, the front door slammed.

Shoving away the memories, she glanced at her watch. She had paperwork to deal with and equipment to check before starting what would probably be a week of night-time surveillance on one of her new cases.

While out tonight, she also planned to connect with some of her street contacts. Most of the individuals she knew who fell into that category would rather eat dirt than talk to a cop. It was possible one of her contacts had heard something about the killer who might possibly come gunning for Bran.

The thought of that happening sent a twinge of icy premonition drifting through her. Just the thought of Bran getting hurt made her throat go dry. So, while he watched her back, she intended to watch his.

One week later, Bran steered his patrol car into the driveway of the house he'd shared with two very diverse women. One calm, serene and elegantly quiet. The other wouldn't know calm, serene and quiet if they kicked her in the head.

It was that woman he'd come to see. The fact he wasn't sure *why* had him scowling.

Sure, he needed to update Tory on what the cops had found regarding Vic Heath's associates. It was vital she have the latest info in case the escaped killer sent a pal by to exact his revenge. But Bran had already e-mailed her some of that information. And he could have driven by and slid the paperwork he'd put together last night into the mail slot. Instead, he'd called to make sure Tory was home.

So, why was he here? he wondered as he sat in the idling black and white, staring at the two-story Victorian white frame house with green shutters and a wraparound porch. After he'd walked out, he and Tory had gone three months without any contact. He hadn't even called her on Christmas Day when thoughts of her were weighing heavily on his mind.

Their latest encounter had changed things, he conceded. It wasn't the dismal state of their marriage that had clung like a burr in his brain over the past week. It was how it had felt to have her lying under him again. Granted, his plowing her over in the dark and her winding up beneath him had been an accident, still, it had reignited a fire inside him he had thought dead. Had wanted dead.

He dreamed about her now. Every night since then, he'd dreamed of her. Smoky, erotic visions in which he felt her soft skin and slim body under his. Saw her desire-filled green eyes gazing up into his. Felt her shudder while their sweat-slicked bodies mated and they took each other over the edge to heaven.

Those nightly carnal fantasies had left him itchy and unsettled and irritated. Like a drug, he could feel Tory seeping into his system again, and he wasn't sure how to deal with that.

Wasn't sure if he even *wanted* to. Dammit, why the hell did the woman have to be such an exact match for him in bed, and so unsuited for him in every other way?

The thought of how she had never hesitated to debate him when their discussions turned to music, politics, TV shows or even at what restaurant they should eat dinner had him shaking his head.

That wasn't why he'd left, though. In truth, he admired the way she could hold her ground and take him to the wall in a debate. What he couldn't handle was a wife who would rather choke on her stubborn independence before she turned to him for anything. A wife who'd totally shut him out when it came to handling problems about her brother, leaving Bran battling feelings of impotence and hot fury. Their final confrontation over her bailing Danny out of jail without giving one thought to calling her husband—*a cop*—had led to the type of verbal argument that could be broken up only with a fire hose.

Dammit, her concern over her reprobate brother hadn't been the issue. *He* had understood her need to get Danny out of jail fast—in the holding cell, the kid had gotten on the wrong side of a skank drug addict and gotten the fire beat out of him. Bran would have done whatever it took to get his own brothers or sisters out of there and into the hands of a doctor. What he'd no longer been able to swallow was that he had a wife who refused to turn to him. To *need* him. So he'd walked.

That had been three months ago, but the thought of what had transpired between him and Tory still stirred his temper.

As he had so often in the past, he gritted his teeth against those stirrings. No matter how he felt about what had happened between them, she was still his wife. Because of that she could wind up an unintentional target of Heath's vengeance.

So, here he was, Bran thought as he climbed out of the patrol car into the cold bite of the January day, coming to see the woman he'd married in a sexual haze, then months later walked out on.

And still tugging at his mind were those damn divorce papers, sitting on the coffee table in his shabby apartment. Maybe the fact he had yet to sign them wouldn't be such a constant irritant if he could explain *why* the hell that was.

His breath cloudy on the freezing air, he hunched his

shoulders beneath his insulated uniform jacket and took the steps up to the porch two at a time.

He bypassed ringing the doorbell and slid his key into the lock. When he'd called earlier, Tory had told him she'd likely be in the garage checking her surveillance equipment and for him to use his key to get in.

He strode down the hallway, its dark oak floor scattered with colorful rugs. Veering right, he moved through a living room that resembled a comfortable, cluttered English study. He and Patience had picked out the leather furniture, the thick wooden tables, the brass accessories, the artwork. Sweeping his gaze around the room, Bran determined that Tory hadn't changed a picture or moved a chair.

He was glad of that, he conceded. Although he'd clung to his grief, it had faded under the demands of everyday living and the passage of time. Memories of Patience now brought more pleasure than pain and he found comfort in having a visual reminder of the wife he'd planned to grow old with.

His spit-shined black uniform boots sounded like gunshots against the kitchen's ceramic-tiled floor. As he neared the door leading to the garage, the air began to pulsate with music. Or with what Tory termed music. To him, the stuff she blasted out of speakers was nothing but unintelligible noise that slammed the eardrums.

Blowing out a breath, he tossed his hat and leather gloves on the nearest counter. He pulled open the door to the garage, wincing against the blast of head-pumping rock and roll.

When his gaze landed on Tory, he froze midstep. His last cognizant thought before the blood totally drained from his brain was that he had never seen a more erotic sight than the leggy blonde leaning under the open hood of her car, her jeans-clad hips performing a bump and grind to the pulsing beat.

When the music swirled into a crescendo and her bottom did a quick, snappy twitch, his mouth went dry. His gut clenched. And instantly he was swept back into the erotic dreams that had plagued him over the past week.

Dammit, he wanted to touch her so badly that the ache in his body spread all the way to his fingers. Fingers that wanted to shove into that long blond hair so he could tug her head back and feed on the mouth that had taken him to heaven more times than he could count. Yet he held himself back. He'd had good, sound reasons for walking out on their marriage. Too bad those logical reasons couldn't stop him from wanting the woman worse than he wanted to breathe.

At first, Tory thought it was the hot, pulsating soundtrack that had shifted her nerve endings into vibrate mode as she attacked the corrosion on her car's battery cables with a wire brush. Seconds later, a flash of awareness hit her. With her instincts blaring the warning she was no longer alone, she jerked her head up hard enough to thud against the hood of her car.

"Easy!"

She heard the shout at the same time she whirled, the wire brush raised like a weapon. Her heartbeat faltered when she saw Bran. She'd known he was coming by. But for the past week she'd schooled her thoughts toward the possibility of Heath or one of his pals showing up. Going into defense mode with the wire brush had been knee-jerk reflex.

She swallowed hard. "I didn't hear you come in."

Bran cuffed one hand behind an ear. "What?"

Turning, she leaned across the span of the car's engine toward the portable CD player propped on the fender.

When she flipped the switch, silence dropped on the garage like a stone.

"I didn't hear you come in," she repeated.

"Go figure." Unzipping his insulated jacket, he hooked a brow at the wire brush she still held defensively. "You planning on making a run at me with that thing?"

In his sharp-pressed uniform, he looked much the same as he had on the night he'd stepped into her life, hauling Danny home from a shadily-run poker game. Whipcord-lean and ramrod-straight, chiseled jaw and thick, sandy hair, Bran McCall had quite literally made her mouth water. Now, without warning, a lot of complex sensations surged up out of the past, washing over her in waves.

"You're a good guy, so you're safe," she said, pleased that her voice sounded cool and calm. "But this wire brush would do a wicked job on some bad guy's face."

"True."

Hoping to jettison her jangling nerves, she turned back to the battery and tackled a small spot of corrosion still left on one terminal. Maybe the sight of Bran in his uniform wouldn't have had such an effect on her if she hadn't spent the past week trying to rid her mind of maddening thoughts of how it felt to lie beneath him again, to look up into his face while his body molded against hers, to feel his sure, firm weight while the musky scent of his cologne filled her lungs.

When he stepped beside her and stuck his head under the hood, her belly tightened. Blood warmed. The slouchy red sweater she'd pulled on that morning was suddenly doing too good a job at keeping her body heat contained.

"Did your battery give out?" he asked. "Or are you just making sure it doesn't?"

"Making sure." He smelled wonderful, like soap and something musky and male that hinted of sleep and sex.

While a rivulet of sweat trickled between her breasts, she continued scrubbing, even though the corrosion was gone. "I'm working a case involving nighttime surveillance at the downtown library learning center. The guy I'm watching is a slime. Last night when I left there, my battery barely kicked in."

She was babbling, but couldn't make herself shut up. "It's supposed to get even colder tonight. Didn't want to risk the battery giving out. Decided to do some maintenance."

"Good idea."

When he leaned in for a closer look at the engine, the knots in her stomach tightened.

He gave a hose a testing squeeze. "This feels a little hard. You might want to replace it."

"I'll put it on my to-do list." She slanted a look at his profile. Hero-perfect with a hint of rugged. Why did just looking at him cause those damned chemical signals to zip through her? Flash red alerts?

A second later he had the oil dipstick out. "Oil's a little low."

"I planned to check it."

Nodding, he replaced the dipstick, then leaned in farther. "How about your power-steering fluid?"

"You know, I really don't need...." Her voice caught when she turned her head and found they were eye-to-eye and mouth-to-mouth. Her throat tightened when his warm breath skated across her face. If either of them moved in, their mouths would touch. The heat coiling inside her belly streaked up into her cheeks.

She knew that heat had turned to a flush when his Viking-blue eyes darkened. A second later something sharp and reckless slid into those eyes and his gaze dropped to her mouth. The ache in her belly turned into a throb.

"You really don't need what, Tory?"

"I...." Oh, God. She didn't need to be thinking about her soon-to-be ex touching her in places that had frozen over during their months apart.

She jerked back. "I don't need help with my car."

"Yeah, what the hell was I thinking?"

Watching him, she could feel his withdrawal even before he stepped back.

His mouth thinned. "You've always made it clear just how little you need me." His voice was now about ten degrees colder than the air in the garage.

"Look, I wasn't trying to make a statement. I just.... Dammit, I don't need help checking the fluid levels in my car."

"Or anything else." He loomed over her, tall and unfathomable, staring at her with those hot blue eyes.

She eased out a breath. He knew about her past. About her mother. Just as she knew all about his. About Patience. He wanted a woman with a fragile side. She wanted a man who didn't view her take-charge personality as a liability. He had left because he knew their situation was hopeless. Nothing had changed.

Resigned, she laid the wire brush aside. "On the phone, you said you'd found more of Heath's associates?"

Bran watched her for a long, silent moment, then nodded. "Somewhere along the line in his criminal career, he started a motorcycle club with ties to drug smuggling, pornography and prostitution. The club was called the Crows."

"Was?"

"It supposedly disbanded." He pulled an envelope from the inside pocket of his heavy coat. "But plenty of the members still live around here. There's about twenty names of former Crows on this list. I've included copies of mug shots and surveillance photos to go with the names. A couple are relatives of Heath's, others just running buddies. Three on the list made regular visits to Heath while he was in prison. I put checks by those names.''

''Are the cops watching them all?''

''The ones we can find.''

''Do you know yet who helped Heath kill the corrections cop and escape from the funeral home?''

''No.'' He laid the envelope on the workbench. ''The vice cops say if any of their snitches know, they're not talking.''

''I'll keep my eyes open.''

''I expect to hear from you if you spot any of them.''

''You will. Bran,'' she said when he took a step toward the door. ''Since you're here...''

He turned, said nothing.

She met his steady gaze, uneasiness drifting through her. ''There's one other thing.''

''What?''

''The condo I mentioned the other night? The owners called. They need to know if I want to buy it. I do. Their asking price is reasonable and they're selling a lot of their furniture, which is the type I like. So, if you could sign the divorce papers, I can tell my Realtor to get the ball rolling.''

''What type?''

''What?''

''The furniture you like. What type?''

''Oh.'' She knitted her brow. During their short time together they hadn't gotten around to discussing furniture preferences. Among other things.

''Sleek. Streamlined. Nothing massive.''

He studied her so long she resisted the urge to squirm. ''So, if you could sign the papers?''

"I'll bring them by tonight." He zipped up his jacket. "You said you'll be at the downtown library?"

"Starting at seven. I'll wrap up this case tonight, so I won't be there more than a couple of hours. Call my cell and I'll let you know where in the library to meet me."

"Fine."

"Fine," she repeated softly. The ache in her throat dropped to her chest and formed a lump of regret as she watched him disappear into the house.

The desire between them was as sizzlingly hot as ever— the little interlude beneath her car's hood proved that. But nothing between them had changed. They had no common ground upon which to build anything lasting.

With them, it was all about sex.

As good as they'd been together in bed, that simply wasn't enough.

Chapter 3

"**B**een a week since Heath escaped," Nate McCall pointed out that evening. "Any word on the street about him?"

Sitting across the booth from his brother, Bran shoved aside the plate of dinner-special meatloaf and mashed potatoes he'd barely touched. Around them, the small downtown diner was filled to capacity, the air thick with conversation and the warm, spicy smell of home cooking.

"Zilch," Bran said. "We've got a list of Heath's associates, most of whom were with him in the Crows gang. But still nothing solid on who helped him kill the corrections cop and escape from the funeral home. The lowlifes we've rousted claim they haven't got a clue where Vic is." He gave his head a frustrated shake. "Bottom line is, we've got nothing."

"The theory that he and his partner headed for Mexico might be on target," Nate pointed out. Like Bran, the middle McCall son had inherited their father's tall, rangy build and wide shoulders. In contrast to Bran's lighter coloring, Nate had the olive skin, black hair and chocolate-brown eyes prevalent on their mother's side of the family. Presently on duty and working out of OCPD Homicide, Nate wore a black suit, crisp white shirt and crimson tie. Beside his empty plate, his handheld radio broadcast the usual muted chatter between cops and dispatchers.

"Heath isn't in Mexico," Bran said. "He's here. Close."

Nate studied his brother over the rim of his coffee mug. "What makes you so sure? None of the cops involved in the credit-union shootout have gotten so much as a hang-up phone call." Nate's eyes narrowed. "Unless you have and haven't told me. If that's the case, you and I need to step out in the alley so I can beat some sense into you."

"You're welcome to try, bro," Bran drawled as he rolled his right shoulder in an attempt to ease the ache out of it. "I haven't heard from Heath. But I can *feel* the bastard, Nate. He's burrowed underground somewhere close. Waiting."

Nate set his mug aside. "I'd be the last person to slam cop instinct, since mine has saved my butt a few times. I just hope yours is sending a faulty message in this case."

"Yeah. Maybe."

Bran shoved back the cuff of his sweater and checked his watch. It was nearly eight. He'd gone to his apartment when he got off work, changed out of his uniform, then settled in front of the TV. Soon, his attention veered to the well-worn furniture that had come with the apartment. It ate at him that until that morning he'd had no clue what style of furniture Tory preferred. He'd never even asked. His mind had soon shifted to wondering what else he hadn't bothered finding out about the smart, stubborn, sexy woman he'd married in a fever. The woman from whom he'd wanted intimacy both in and out of bed. With those thoughts weighing on him like lead he'd called Nate and arranged a dinner meeting. He'd chosen the diner because it was a short drive to the library learning center where Tory was working surveillance.

"Nate, thanks for meeting me, but I need to take off. I have to go by the library."

Nate angled his chin. "What's there?"

"Books," Bran said dryly. "And Tory. She's working a surveillance."

Nate snatched up the check and pulled a couple of bills out of his pocket. "So, since you know where she is, you guys must be talking again." He held up a hand when Bran started to protest his paying the tab. "You buy next time. This is good, right? You seeing Tory?"

"Depends on a person's point of view. I've got the papers she served me in my parka. I'm supposed to sign them and give them to her tonight."

"Supposed to?" The trained interrogator in Nate pounced on the words. "Since you haven't signed them, does that mean you're having second thoughts about the breakup?"

"No, Sherlock. It means I didn't have a pen handy."

Nate's dark brows drew together. "Dammit, Bran, you and Tory haven't even made it to the one-year mark. Are you positive you can't work out your problems?"

"No hope there, bro." Especially not since their problems came down to different inherent needs, Bran added silently. He wanted a woman to turn to him, lean on him. Tory had shown him time and again she was too take-charge to do that. Her getting miffed that morning when he'd tried to help check under her car's hood proved she hadn't lightened up.

It had also proven a few other things.

Namely, the hunger he felt for her was as sharp as it had been from the first moment he'd laid eyes on her. He hadn't had to kiss her today to know what she tasted like— he carried her taste inside him. Still, he had damn well wanted his mouth on hers again. On a lot more places than just her mouth.

Picturing her leaning near him under the car's hood, he had to grit his teeth against the instant tightening in his gut. With their mouths nearly brushing, he had watched her face flush. Saw her green eyes go smoky. Her response during those heat-driven moments had told him her desire equaled his. The white-hot chemistry that had brought them together—and fueled their elopement—was still a churning eddy inside them both. That he'd wanted to dive back into the eddy told him his defenses were not as impenetrable as he'd thought.

That little slice of reality had convinced him it was best to let her go before they tangled themselves up again. He would sign the papers tonight. Then Tory could get on with her own life and he could regain his balance in his.

Nate leaned in. "Look, everyone in the family has been walking on eggshells over the subject of you and Tory. Since you brought it up, I figure that opens the door to me asking you a question."

"Which is?"

"What the hell is the deal?"

"What deal?"

"Why did you walk out? And don't tell me you don't care about her. I've seen the way you look at her."

Bran had no intention of examining emotions he'd clamped a lid on months ago. "We have certain issues."

"There's headline news," Nate said drolly. "You don't want to tell me, fine. But you know how good Grace is at zeroing in on relationship stuff, and more than once she's said—''

"Wait a minute. Have you and Grace been having regular conversations about Tory and me?"

"I wouldn't call them *regular*," Nate said with a shrug.

"What the hell *do* you call them?"

"Occasional. And we're not the only ones who've been talking. The sisters had a big powwow at Mom and Dad's. Josh was in on it, too."

Bran's eyes slitted. "Little brother sat in on a gossip session about my marriage?"

"To be fair, he was there because he heard Mom was making spaghetti. So he just got dragged into the discussion."

"Well, great." Bran jabbed an index finger in Nate's direction. "How would you like it if the sisters had powwows about your relationships?"

Grinning, Nate winked at a petite, blond waitress who zipped by with a tray loaded with food. "I don't have relationships, remember? I have encounters. Anyway, Grace thinks you walked because Tory's so independent. I figure the big problem you've got is that she's so different from Patience."

Bran's jaw set. "You don't think I knew that when I married Tory?"

"Maybe you thought you did. But for a guy used to being totally in charge and calling all the shots, I suspect you didn't know what hit you."

Bran's teeth threatened to grind together. Only to himself would he admit that Nate was right—not until after he and Tory eloped and the sexual haze began to lift had he seen the immense contrast between his late wife and his present one. And he'd also understood that a gap the size of the Grand Canyon separated his and Tory's basic needs.

Because the idea of pounding on his brother sounded like a good way to work off his frustration, he aimed a feral smile across the booth. "Speaking of getting hit, I'm ready to adjourn to the alley."

Just then, Nate's radio crackled to life. A patrol cop's disembodied voice notified dispatch of a Signal Seven at an address across town. *Dead body,* Bran's cop brain automatically translated.

"You'll have to give me a rain check on the alley," Nate said, scooping up the radio.

"Too bad," Bran muttered while Nate advised dispatch that Homicide was en route to the scene. "I suppose everybody will get together for another damn powwow after the divorce is final," Bran said as he and Nate rose in unison and pulled on their coats.

Nate slapped his shoulder. "Knowing our sisters, it's inevitable."

"Yeah."

The instant they stepped out into the brutally cold night, Bran's cell phone rang. He snagged it off the waistband of his slacks, flipped it open and frowned when it continued to ring. It took him a second to realize Nate's cell also had an incoming call.

"McCall," Bran said into his phone. He and Nate turned slightly away so they could each hear their respective callers.

"This is Captain Everett," Bran's boss said, his voice booming.

"Yes, sir—"

"A black and white is at your wife's house. She's not home. Do you know where she is?"

Bran froze. "Yes. Why?"

"Garcia's husband was murdered. Shot."

Bran's pulse kicked. Susan Garcia was one of the patrol cops involved in the credit-union shootout. Shifting, he glanced at Nate, saw his brother's grim expression as he listened to whoever was on the other end of his call. Bran figured Garcia's husband was the victim at the scene Nate had just been called to.

"What happened?" Bran asked.

"Miguel Garcia sold high-dollar cars," Everett began. "A guy came into the dealership late this afternoon asking for him and requesting to test drive a Jaguar. Garcia went with him, but never came back. His boss went out looking for him. He just now found Garcia, dead in the Jag."

Bran swallowed back the bile rising in his throat. "Anybody get a look at the customer?"

"We've got a vague description. Could be Heath. Could be a lot of guys."

"Tory's at the downtown library. I'm less than five minutes away."

"Get there fast, McCall. Zelewski's wife is also missing."

Zelewski. Bran pictured the patrol cop who'd arrived at the credit union a minute behind him. "His wife sells real estate, right?"

"Yes. We've got cops checking all her listings now. Let me know when you locate your wife," Everett said, then ended the call.

"Looks like Heath hit Garcia's husband." Bran barked the words at Nate while punching in Tory's cell number. "Maybe Zelewski's wife, too."

"Going after cops' families," Nate added as he and Bran dashed to the diner's parking lot. "You said Tory's at the library. Do you know *where* at the library?"

"No, but I'm damn sure going to find her."

"*We'll* find her." Nate held up his keys to indicate he would drive. "My partner can get started working the homicide scene."

Bran climbed into Nate's car while he listened to Tory's cell phone ring. Closing his eyes, he sent up a silent prayer that he wasn't too late.

Her miniature camera tucked back inside her leather tote bag, Tory slipped out of the library learning center into the freezing night. As surveillance jobs went, this one had been a cinch. A professor's wife suspected her husband was spending his evenings at the library working on more than just a research paper. The wife was right. Over the past four nights, Tory had witnessed the professor and a nubile grad student disappear into a series of cozy study rooms. It was unfortunate for the professor—and a plus for Tory—that the doors on the rooms were equipped with grates through which the small lens of her camera fit.

It was another plus that Oklahoma City's new downtown library learning center had an espresso bar.

Taking a sip of the steaming mocha café latte she'd purchased on her way out, she headed for her car. To avoid snagging the prof's attention, she had parked in a different area of the parking lot during each of her visits. Tonight, the biting wind had her wishing she'd found a spot that didn't require a hike to get there.

By the time she unlocked the Taurus's door, her nose and cheeks stung from the cold. Not to mention her fingers, since she'd forgotten to snag her leather gloves off the kitchen counter.

Tossing her tote bag onto the passenger seat, she slid behind the wheel. She nearly fumbled her latte when the cell phone she'd switched to silent mode began vibrating like a big insect against her waist.

She pulled the phone off her belt and slid it into the converter installed in the dash so she could converse hands-free. She answered, blinking when Bran shouted, "You still at the library?"

"Yes, in the parking—"

The word ended in a choked scream when something metallic dropped past her face and jerked back against her throat. Before she could react, the cold metal yanked tighter. The bright shock of pain blinded her.

The cup dropped to her lap, spilling steaming coffee across her jeaned thighs.

Choking, gagging, she clawed at the metal while fear stormed through her. *Chain* her mind registered at the same instant a second loop dropped over her head and circled her neck.

Hysteria bubbled in her blood. She used her feet to push herself up in the seat, trying to ease the pressure on her windpipe. As she dug at the chain her fingernails carved furrows into her throat. Fisting one hand, she swung behind her in a futile attempt to knock her assailant back.

"Bitch, this is from Vic," a man's voice hissed near her ear. "Gonna eat your old man's heart out," he added before giving the chain a vicious jerk.

Fire roared through her lungs. Her brain begging for air, she fought to remain conscious. *Weapon,* her senses screamed. Her Sig was in her tote on the passenger seat, far out of reach.

Darkness loomed at the edges of her vision, a tunnel narrowing. Her hand groped for the console. Her flailing fingertips brushed its lever. The chain tightened. She leaned, straining for the lever, increasing the pressure on her neck. Unconsciousness closed in. When she hit the lever the console's lid sprang open. Her hand came up, gripping the emergency rescue hammer she habitually kept there.

Terror screaming through her, lungs bursting, her throat crushed beneath the unyielding metal, Tory swung the hammer in a desperate arc behind her. Rippling pain shot up her arm when one of its sharp steel points rammed into a solid mass.

"There's her Taurus!" Bran shouted when Nate swerved his car into the parking lot amid a squeal of tires and smoking rubber.

Bran bailed out before they rolled to a stop. Glock aimed, blood boiling like a demon possessed, he went in low, advancing toward the car's rear.

The back window was fogged over, obscuring his view of the interior.

Seconds later, Nate stepped beside him, automatic clenched in his hand. "I'll take the passenger side," Nate murmured.

Dread pounded in Bran's brain. Training battered with the urge to rush to the car, but he held himself back. He wouldn't be any good to Tory if he got himself shot. Staying low, he crept toward the rear door. Over his cell phone, he had heard her scream. Heard a man's vicious, "Bitch, this is from Vic."

Bran gritted his teeth. He would hunt Heath down and kill him with his bare hands. If it took the rest of his life, he would find the bastard.

The car's side windows were less fogged than the back. Bran raised up enough to peer into the shadow-laden back seat. He saw a man's booted feet and jeans-clad legs stretched across the seat. His upper body was slumped, face-down in the passenger-side floorboard. *Heath?* Bran wondered. *His pal who helped him escape, maybe?*

Nate pulled open the rear door, his automatic trained on the man.

Bran edged to the driver's door, checked through the window. His throat tightened when he saw the front seat was empty. He pulled open the door. Tory's tote bag lay on the passenger seat, its contents spilling across the upholstery. Her cell phone was still plugged into the converter in the dash. A paper cup lay in a puddle of coffee on the floorboard.

"She's not here," Bran said, and saw in Nate's grim face that their thoughts were on the same wavelength. There was only one man in the back seat, which meant either Heath or his pal was still out there. Maybe he had Tory. Maybe he was close, waiting to ambush both cops when he got a clear shot.

Nate held his gun steady on the still figure while he pressed his fingers against his throat. "DRT," he said, using cop shorthand for *dead right there*. He angled to get a look at the man's face. "I don't think its Heath," he added before keying the mike on his handheld radio.

Staying low, Bran dashed toward the nearest grouping of parked cars. Only minutes had passed since Tory first answered her cell phone. Surely if Heath had grabbed her they couldn't have gotten far.

Bran had just reached the front of a white SUV when he heard the faint clank of metal against metal. A croaking sob followed.

Gun aimed, he peered around the SUV. Relief surged through him when he spotted Tory. One palm pressed to the pavement, she knelt between the SUV and another car. Her Sig lay near her hand. She'd fled the Taurus, he theorized, fearing another attacker might be nearby.

It took a split second for him to register the jerky movement of her shoulders. Another to realize her free hand was clawing at her throat.

"Tory!" He rushed to her, his pulse spiking when he saw the chain looping her neck. He realized immediately the metal links were tangled in her long hair. The more she struggled, the tighter the chain pressed against her windpipe.

"Stop!" He dropped his weapon, grabbed her hands. "Tory, stop."

"Get it off!" Her voice was a panicked rasp on the cold air. *"Get it off, get it off."*

"Hold on." His fingers squeezed hers. "Just hold on."

Lungs heaving, she leaned into him.

Kneeling over her, he tried not to think. About the blood that slicked the metal links. Or the precious seconds lost because his fingers trembled so badly. A lifetime later, the chain slithered to the blacktop with a clank.

While sirens wailed in the distance, he eased her into a sitting position. Barely breathing himself, he watched her body shake as she dragged in short, rusty breaths.

"You're okay," he said, for her benefit as much as his. "I've got you now. You're okay."

He took a few drags of icy air while he watched her. She was one of the toughest women he knew, yet she looked fragile, terrifyingly so. Her face was drawn and impossibly pale; her eyes bright with fear. Bloody furrows marred her throat. Already, a necklace of dark bruises bloomed around the furrows.

"Tory...." His chest tightened. Heath had come after her because of *him*. She had almost died because of him. Bran wanted to pull her into his arms, hold her, yet she was gasping for air, her body trembling. He settled for placing a hand on her shoulder. "I'm sorry. God, I'm so sorry."

As if his touch flipped a switch in her she broke, simply broke. Sobbing, she surged into his arms, her face against his chest, her tears soaking into his sweater.

"Just let it out," he said, stroking her hair. He had never seen her cry. Never seen her even close to tears. Now, the sound of her raspy sobs, combined with the knowledge of how close she'd come to dying nearly overwhelmed him.

She was down to shuddering breaths when she said, "I thought...I was...going to die."

"I know." He squeezed his eyes shut. "I know."

"Did you...get him?"

Bran realized she didn't know she'd killed her attacker. That news could wait until she was steadier. "Yeah, we got him."

Still stroking her hair, he glanced across his shoulder when a siren whooped nearby. Four black and whites and a crowd of onlookers now filled the lot. If Heath had been in the vicinity, he was gone.

An ambulance barreled into view. Emergency lights pulsed. Bran settled his hands on her shoulders and inched her gently back. "An ambulance is here. Let's get you out of the cold."

She nodded, looking up at him. Her blond lashes were spiky, her eyes swollen from tears.

He settled his hands on either side of her waist, lifted her to her feet. When she swayed against his chest, he tightened his grip.

"Let me carry you."

She raised a hand, her trembling fingers brushing his cheek. "I...can...walk," she croaked. "Need to...walk."

Even now she wouldn't allow herself to lean on him. For the space of a heartbeat he loosened control on the emotion roiling inside him: the need to protect her, to comfort her, the blind rage against Heath for nearly killing her.

She was alive solely because she was brave and a fighter. She hadn't needed him to stay alive. Didn't need him to carry her to the ambulance.

"Okay, you walk." He pressed his lips against her forehead. "I'm a step away if you need me."

Keeping one hand locked on her elbow, he swept up his Glock, holstered it. Her Sig went into a pocket on his parka. He was about to retrieve the chain when he felt her shudder.

"Forget walking." He swept her up gently and headed toward the ambulance. "I'm taking care of you, Tory. No one is going to hurt you again."

"Thanks…for the lift." When she trembled convulsively, Bran tightened his arms around her.

Gonna eat your heart out. The threat that Heath's mother had hissed at the funeral home—and that he'd heard coming over Tory's cell phone during the attack—replayed with new meaning in Bran's head. One officer's husband was dead. Another's wife was missing. Bran didn't know yet if Heath had gone after the wife of the fourth cop involved in the credit-union shootout, but he figured he had.

It was clear now that Heath had planned all along to hit the families of the cops who'd killed his brother and cousin, not the cops themselves. What better way to eat someone's heart out than to target their spouse? It was the ultimate twisting of the blade, a way to deal unending, excruciating, lifelong agony to the cops.

Grim-faced, Nate strode toward them. Bran inclined his head toward the spot where he found Tory. "There's a chain back there. It needs to go into evidence."

"A chain?"

"The scum had it wrapped around Tory's throat."

Nate nodded. "I'll take care of it."

A pair of EMTs pulled a gurney into view at the same instant Bran reached the rear of the ambulance. He sat Tory down gently on the stretcher, kept his hands locked on her shoulders. He looked into her eyes, felt the tremors that still shook her. "I'm riding to the hospital with you."

She rubbed a hand over her mouth, nodded.

He stepped back to give the EMTs room to work.

The pain of seeing her hurt was the equivalent to a razor slashing at his heart. Because that pain threatened to overwhelm, he went with anger.

He hadn't known what Heath had been planning, but he'd known damn well he would try something. Just as Bran now sensed with cold, hard certainty the bastard would make another attempt on Tory.

"Try it." The violence bubbling in his blood transformed his voice into a lethal hiss on the cold night air.

He spotted Nate, saw the blood-slicked chain dangling from his brother's fingers. Bran forced himself to take a long, measured breath. Rage, he knew, clouded the mind. So he would throttle his back. Keep it under control. Do what he had to do.

Bran stepped to the ambulance, swung up into the back.

Tory was still his wife. His to protect. *His.*

And he had just become her shadow.

Chapter 4

During the two hours following the attack, Tory's neck was poked, prodded, X-rayed, then wrapped in gauze. Now she lay in a hospital bed, her brain and body growing more sluggish by the minute, compliments of the sedative a nurse pumped into her.

Despite her hazy state of mind, Tory was keenly aware she was under the watchful eye of every McCall who lived within a hundred-mile radius. Although she cared deeply for her extended family, she felt overwhelmed with her cramped, antiseptic-scented room packed with warm bodies.

Adding to her unease was that she was still a McCall solely because Bran had yet to scrawl his name on a couple of dotted lines.

Still, whenever a McCall's gaze shifted in her direction, she saw open caring, grim concern and a glint of hard-edged fury that one of their own had come under attack.

That same deep caring shone in her mother-in-law's

eyes when Roma McCall stepped to the side of the bed. "I've shooed everyone out so you can get some sleep." Her face taut with worry, Roma placed a hand on Tory's and squeezed. "We're all thankful you weren't hurt worse."

Feeling woozier by the second, Tory managed a half smile. "Thanks...for...coming," she croaked, then winced. Her throat felt as if someone had dragged sandpaper across her vocal cords.

"Don't talk, dear," Roma cautioned. "Rest."

Roma was a tall woman, sturdily built, with dark hair, flawless olive skin and shrewd brown eyes. Those eyes flicked upward when her eldest son stepped beside her. "Brandon, you're staying close by Tory tonight?"

"I'll sleep there," he said, dipping his head toward the recliner angled into a corner.

"Good. Call in the morning to let us know how she's doing."

"Will do." Bran wrapped an arm around his mother's waist and pressed a kiss to her temple. "Thanks for being here."

After another squeeze to Tory's hand, Roma turned and disappeared out the door.

The click of the latch had Tory realizing she and Bran were alone for the first time since the ambulance had delivered them to the ER.

Gazing down at her, he brushed her hair back from her cheek. "Can I get you anything?"

She blinked. Her vision had taken on a medicated, shower-curtain haze. "Water," she rasped.

"Coming up." He retrieved a plastic cup from the nightstand. Leaning in, he slid the straw between her lips. "Slow," he cautioned when she sucked greedily.

Despite her mental fog she could see the worry in his

face. The cold, hard glint at the back of his arctic-blue eyes. Fury, she knew. Fury that she'd been hurt by a vicious escapee bent on revenge against *him*.

"Not...your...fault."

"Don't talk." He set the cup back on the nightstand. "Sleep."

His words might have been comforting, but the tone was much too controlled. She could almost feel the emotion slicing at him.

"Bran, wasn't...your...fault."

"Quiet." He pressed his fingertips gently against her lips. "The doc said you've got bruised vocal cords. Meaning, I get to tell you to shut up, and you have to mind."

Not even the sedative oozing through her system could numb the awareness from his touch that punched into her stomach. Her internal thermostat clicked up several degrees.

Great. She'd almost died a couple of hours ago. Her throat felt like a construction zone. She had enough drugs in her system to fell an elephant. Yet all it took was one touch from her sexy, soon-to-be ex and her body shifted into sizzle-and-burn mode.

She made a feeble attempt to draw her defenses together. The task, she discovered, was impossible with a brain marinated in drugs.

"You're safe." He ran a thumb over her lower lip while his fingers stroked her cheek. "No one's going to hurt you again. You have my word, Tory. Never again."

Her last thought before sliding into oblivion was that the ache in her throat had shifted to her heart.

His fingers still caressing her cheek, Bran watched her eyes flutter shut as the drug pulled her all the way under. Her long hair was a golden tangle around her shoulders, her skin as white as the sheet that covered her. This was not the Victoria Lynn Dewitt McCall he knew. *This* woman looked weak and fragile. Too weak, too fragile.

The image of her kneeling in the parking lot, the chain garroting her throat while she struggled for air scraped him raw. She was lying in a hospital bed because of him, *hurt* because of him. It was all he could do not to smash his fist into the wall.

He thought about Officer Susan Garcia, whose husband had been shot in the Jaguar. Bran closed his eyes. While Tory had been in the ER, he had checked with his captain. The body of Zelewski's Realtor-wife had been found inside one of the vacant houses she had a listing on. Tory could so easily have died tonight, too.

Cops didn't talk about the dangers of the job. They just lived with them. But not the dangers to their families. Knowing that Heath had sent one of his scum pals to kill his wife was something Bran had no intention of just living with. The need for revenge twisted into a dark, keen thirst that had his fingers trembling against her cheek.

Sensing the door behind him swing open, Bran pivoted, his hand going to the Glock holstered at the small of his back. His eyes narrowed when Danny Dewitt stepped into the room.

Tall and lanky, Tory's brother was clad in well-worn jeans, a tattered T-shirt and a scruffy denim jacket. His brown boots were scuffed beyond redemption, his black hair pulled back in a stubby ponytail. Since Bran had called the kid, he knew the sight of his eighteen-year-old brother-in-law shouldn't put his teeth on edge.

But it did. Always did.

Danny rushed to the bed, his eyes filled with concern. "Tor?" When she didn't answer, he gave his sister a long, silent examination, then met Bran's gaze. "You said she's not hurt bad, right?'' he asked, his words aching and unsteady. "She'll be okay?''

"Yeah.'' Because the kid's face had paled and there was pure fear in his eyes, Bran softened his voice. "The doc said she'll be good as new after a couple of days of rest.''

"Okay. That's a relief.'' Danny looked back at his sister. "What about the guy who hurt her?''

"We got him.'' He hadn't yet told Tory she'd killed her attacker. If she wanted her brother to know, she could tell him later. "There's one still on the run. He probably has some pals hiding him so he won't be easy to find. But we'll get him eventually.'' If it took his entire life, he would find Heath. "Until then, Tory will be with me. I'll make sure she's safe.''

"I trust you to do that.'' Danny paused, then turned. "So, Tor's out of commission for a few days?''

Bran noted that the look in his green eyes had transformed from concern to calculation. "For as long as it takes. You have a particular reason for asking how long?''

"Yeah.'' Danny jabbed his fingers into the front pockets of his jeans. "I've had some…unexpected stuff come up. Now that I've got my driver's license back I need some wheels in the worst way. *The worst.* Do you think it'd be okay if I use Tor's car until she's back on her feet?''

"Her car's a crime scene,'' Bran snapped. The question stoked the anger already simmering inside him. "Dewitt, your sister almost died tonight. Are you getting this? *She almost died.* I called because I thought you cared about her. After all, she raised you. Supported you. Turns out, all you're concerned about is getting your hands on her car.''

"I love her,'' Danny shot back. "I *get* what happened

to her.'' His face tightened with anger. ''You've already said she'll be fine. That you'll protect her.''

''Bet on it.''

''I am. It's just that....''

''Go on.''

''Tor's not the only person I'm worried about right now.''

Bran raised a brow. ''You get yourself jammed up again with the law?''

Danny stuck out his chin. ''It's not me I'm talking about. Look, just forget I asked. I'll find another way to get around.''

''Good idea.'' Bran gave his brother-in-law the dead-eyed-cop stare he had used on countless suspects over the years. ''Visiting hours are over, Dewitt.''

''You're still here.''

''I'm her husband.''

Danny's snort was accompanied by a derisive look. ''Some husband. You look at me like I don't have a brain. Fine, I admit I'm not the smartest guy around. Just remember, you're the idiot who walked out on the best woman you'll ever find.''

Bran clenched his jaw hard enough to crack fillings. ''It'd be a good idea for you to leave, Dewitt. *Now.*''

''I'm going.'' Danny moved to the door, pulled it open, then paused. ''You'll tell Tor I was here to see her? That I'll call her tomorrow to find out how she's doing?''

''I'll tell her.''

When the door closed behind Danny, Bran scrubbed a hand over his jaw. Christ, he didn't know how two blood-kin could be so different. The kid was a user. Then there was Tory, so independent she wouldn't let anyone lift a finger for her.

He damned that independent streak even as he felt sorrow for the young girl she'd been who had so much responsibility dumped on her, and then later was forced to step in and raise her brother.

Too riled to sit, he remained at the side of the bed, gazing down at his wife. He was well aware that she had survived the attack solely because she was tough and strong. *A fighter.*

They sure as hell had gone plenty of verbal rounds during their short marriage!

He swore viciously. Then again, quietly. If she was so wrong for him, why hadn't he taken that last, final step by signing the divorce papers? Put an end to things?

Forehead knitted, he studied her stubborn, sexy face with its pointed chin, sharp cheekbones and sensual mouth. He'd always believed a fast break was a clean one. Yet he'd brooded over those damn papers for nearly two weeks. Lost sleep over them. And, although he'd planned to deliver them to her at the library, he hadn't signed them ahead of time.

Using one foot, he dragged a plastic chair beside the bed and settled into it. If the events of the evening had been different, would he have signed the papers after he got to the library?

Frowning, he settled a hand over hers. And tried to come up with the answer to that question.

Light glinted in a shimmering arc when the chain dropped in front of Tory's eyes.

"No!" The word ripped up her throat. Bolting upright, she grappled at the cold links that tightened viciously around her neck.

"No!" Clawing at her throat she scrambled onto her knees, desperate to breathe, to survive.

"Tory!" The deep male voice came from a space just inches away. So close. *Too close.*

"Can't get it off!" She lashed out wildly against the hands that grabbed her scrabbling fingers away from her throat.

"Tory, it's Bran. Tory, look at me."

Still caught in the terrorizing grip of the nightmare, she saw only the chain. *Felt it.* "Get it off!"

"Look at me." Gathering her wrists in one hand, he cupped a palm to her cheek as she cowered against the bed's metal railing. "You had a nightmare. A bad dream." His voice was quiet, but firm enough to pull her out of the dark, suffocating pit.

"Bran?"

"You're in the hospital. I'm here. No one can hurt you."

"Oh, God." Her heart pounded against her ribs; her lungs burned and her face was wet with sweat and tears. She was afraid to move for fear she would crack and shatter into a dozen pieces.

"You're okay." The mattress shifted as he settled beside her. "I'm here."

Dim light from the bathroom's half-open door wedged across the bed. Blinking, she focused on his face, saw the concern in his eyes, the deep lines at the corners of his mouth.

"I...felt...that...chain." She got the words out between quick gulps of air. The pressure in her chest was unbearable. "Around my neck. So...tight. Couldn't breathe. I... couldn't...breathe."

He held out his arms. "Come here."

Shuddering, she all but burrowed into him. His arms wrapped around her. Instinctively she turned her face into his throat while the heat of his body seeped into her chilled flesh.

"I couldn't breathe." She swallowed a sob that bubbled up her raw throat. "He...wanted to kill me."

"You had a nightmare."

"A flashback," she countered, still in the grips of the fear that had overridden even the pain. "I was in my car. He dropped the chain around my neck. Jerked it. I could *feel* it." One long, sick crest of nausea rolled through her stomach. She wouldn't let herself be sick. *She wouldn't.* Her unsteady fingers explored the gauze banded over the furrows that her fingernails had dug into her neck during the attack. "I was there again."

"You're here now. With me. It's over." Bran rested his chin on top of her head. "You just need some time to level out."

Trying to absorb some portion of the strength she felt in him, she closed her eyes. They flew open instantly when she saw a flash of metal. A shiver ran through her. She realized that she'd been in shock when she'd arrived at the hospital. Then she had been suspended in an oh-so-wonderful floaty drug state that had numbed the horrors of the attack. With both the shock and the sedative wearing off, her body and her mind were now reacting to those horrors.

Reacting with a vengeance.

"I've got the shakes."

"That's to be expected. Just hold on to me. They'll go away."

She pressed against him, desperate to draw some of his rock-steady calmness into her, hold it. *Hold him.* His familiar musky scent slid into her lungs. "I...just... need...."

"Tell me." When he stroked a palm down her back she

felt the heat of his hand through the thin hospital gown. "Tell me what you need. Whatever it is, I'll get it for you."

"My balance. I need…to get my balance back." Every word burned her throat. "To deal with this. Handle it."

"Alone?" Emotions warred through Bran, anger, frustration, sorrow and guilt. He battled them back so his voice would remain calm. "You thinking you'd do best handling this alone, Tory?"

"I don't know what I think," she said, her voice a rusty whisper against his neck. "It's like the wires are crossed in my brain."

He tipped her head back to look at her face. She was as pale as death, her eyes wide and glassy. But the sheen wasn't from the drugs she'd been given. He knew fear when he saw it.

"Well, let me uncross those wires. You almost died because a piece of scum decided to get even with me." Very firmly, very gently, he cupped her face in his hands. "Do you really think I'm going to let you handle this on your own? Deal with this without me? That's not an option."

"Bran—"

"Not an option. What's happened between us in the past, whatever's going on with our relationship right now doesn't figure into this." He paused to pull in a steadying breath. "You woke up in a cold sweat, Tory. You're still shaking. That's all on me."

"The man who attacked me wasn't Heath, was it?" she asked after a moment. "I remember when he jerked the chain back, he said it was from 'from Vic.'"

Bran's hands dropped from her face, wrapped around her fingers, and felt them tremble. Her flesh was ice-cold. "Heath didn't attack you," he confirmed carefully. She might be a tough P.I., but he wanted her on more solid emotional footing before he told her she'd killed the guy. "He's still out there."

She shifted her gaze out the window into the dark night. "He wants to kill me." Her breath hitched and her hands tightened on his like a lifeline. "Might make a second try."

"He won't get close to you again." Bran struggled to keep the fury burning inside him out of his voice. "I won't let Heath or any of his scum pals near you."

When she turned her face from the window, the vulnerability in her eyes nearly undid him.

"Having a tough cop for backup doesn't sound so bad right now. I…." She lifted an unsteady hand, shoved her hair away from her face. "I can't seem to keep my thoughts lined up."

"You will. After you get some sleep." He shifted against the pillows to get comfortable. "Meanwhile your backup will stay awake." He nudged her into the crook of his arm then drew her head down onto his shoulder. "I'll do my best to keep the nightmares at bay."

"Okay." She relaxed against him. "I owe you, Mc-Call." Her voice was as rough as pine bark.

"You don't owe me a thing."

Easing back, he stared up at the ceiling. While her breathing evened and she slid into sleep, his restless thoughts drifted again to the divorce papers, still folded in his parka's pocket. He thought again about the fact he still didn't know if he would have signed them tonight.

Now, with the soft lines of her body pressed against his, he admitted to himself there was something else going on. He'd been trying to ignore it, work around it, deny it, but now there was no possibility of avoiding the reality. Something was buried inside him, deep inside, that had held him back from signing those papers. Was still holding him back.

She shifted, nuzzled against him. Breathed a quiet moan. He tightened his arms around her.

The last thing he wanted was to find something good about her almost getting murdered. But tonight's attack had brought them back together, at least for a time. So, while Heath was still on the run, Bran intended to keep her close. And he would use their time together to figure out what it was that had kept him hanging on.

He'd find out why he couldn't bring himself to let her go.

Chapter 5

Out of habit, Tory woke the next morning early and quickly. The instant jolt she felt wasn't from a sense of disorientation—she knew she was in the hospital and why.

Bran.

The punch that hit low in her belly and zipped up her spine came from the fact she was wrapped in a man.

Bran.

Mindful of her aching neck, she turned her head slightly while blinking against the January sunlight streaming in the window. She remembered the nightmare. The gripping terror. Could still feel the remnants of fear that had sent her burrowing into Bran's arms. Was aware that while he held her, she'd felt safe. And she vaguely recalled him assuring her he would stay awake and chase off her nightmares.

Yeah, right, she thought, watching him sleep.

She checked that thought when the word *dangerous* popped into her brain. Bran McCall didn't need to be awake to ward off all things evil. Not with the sun slashing

across the bed, transforming his face into razor-sharp
planes and angles. His rumpled dusty-blond hair and heavy
stubble of beard emphasized the tough warrior look. In
truth, the large, tawny-haired muscular male sleeping beside her was the most daunting sight she could imagine.

Daunting and *waaay* unsettling.

During the night their bodies had shifted; now they lay
on their sides, pressed together. She had one palm plas-
tered against his chest—thankfully she noted he was still
wearing his crimson sweater—and her right leg was
pitched over his slacks-clad ones. He'd tossed his left arm
across her hip. She was keenly aware that this was the
position they'd woken in every morning they'd shared a
bed. Mornings that had been preceded by nights of siz-
zling, mind-numbing sex.

During the months they'd been separated she'd worked
to convince herself she didn't miss the closeness, the fevered intimacy. The feel of the hard male body that fitted
perfectly—*so perfectly*—with hers.

But, Lord, she did.

She let out the breath she hadn't been aware she was
holding. When she drew in another, the scent of his musky
aftershave tightened her stomach. Beneath her palm she
felt rock-hard muscle and the strong beat of his heart.
Echoing in her mind was the memory of the crazed hammering of both their hearts when their bodies joined and
blood ruled.

Her eyes skimmed to his mouth. Heaven help her, she
wanted that mouth on hers. Wanted the dark, dangerous
taste of him humming through her system again. Waves
of mindless need swept over her, surging through her like
a storm, churning, quick and violent.

Defenses clicking in, she fisted her hand against his
chest. So, fine, the chemistry was still there—she'd figured

that out the previous day when they'd leaned beneath the hood of her car. But lava-hot chemistry didn't cancel out ice-cold reality. He needed a woman who would lean on him, willingly let him handle all of life's complications. That wasn't her, Tory thought, forcing back the vision of her weak, needy mother. That image slowly faded, only to be replaced with one of another woman.

Patience McCall. Having found several photo albums tucked in Bran's closet, Tory knew the petite brunette with dark, expressive eyes could have given Miss America a run for her money. A faint trail of envy curled inside Tory at the thought of how perfect Patience and Bran looked together—she encircled in the arms of the husband who'd towered over her. Even in photos he'd been openly shielding and protective.

Just as he'd been for *her* last night. She had needed his fierce protection. Had wanted his arms around her until she got her balance back. But she wasn't Patience, and being watched over like that on a daily basis would all but smother her.

Which was why she and Bran made a lousy match. *Irreconcilable differences*—the two words that figured prominently in the divorce papers said it all.

If only she had realized that the night Bran had nabbed Danny for gambling and hauled him home. If only she had bothered to get to know the man behind the cop before she'd jumped into bed and fallen head over heels in…:

Her breath hitched. She *had* loved Bran—she wouldn't have married him otherwise. But it hadn't taken long for problems to surface. The laughter stopped. Talking transformed into verbal showdowns. Even the physical intimacy they shared couldn't keep them together.

Suddenly desperate to put space between them, she eased into a sitting position.

"Tory?"

Needing a minute to close off her private pain, she turned her head toward the window.

Bran levered up, gripped her arm and nudged her around. Despite the fatigue in his face, his blue eyes examined her with razor sharpness. "You okay? Did you have another nightmare?"

More like a wet dream, she thought, swallowing the knot of emotion in her battered throat.

"I'm fine," she rasped. Her voice sounded as if it had been coated with a corrosive and her mouth was impossibly dry. "I could use some water."

"I'll get ice from the nurse."

"Thanks," she said, grateful for the prospect of a few moments alone to level out.

He brushed his knuckles across her cheek. Though the gesture was gentle, his eyes were hard. "You're here on my account. The last thing you need to do is thank me." He swung off the bed, snagged the plastic pitcher from the nightstand.

She watched him go, then shifted her gaze back to the window. While she stared out into the winter sunlight, regret for what might have been—and what could never be—filled the air around her like smoke.

Two hours later, Bran leaned against the windowsill and watched a tank-sized nurse in green scrubs check Tory's blood pressure.

"On the money," the nurse said. "How's your throat feel?"

"Like I drank acid."

"Sounds that way, too," the woman said. "Considering what happened to you last night, that's to be expected."

"When can I bust out of here?" Tory asked in a

scratchy whisper. "I need to call and tell my girlfriend when to pick me up."

Bran caught the look the nurse flicked at him. He had signed the admittance papers, so it was a matter of record that he and Tory were married. That she planned to leave with a girlfriend instead of her husband naturally raised eyebrows.

"You're our guest until the doctor releases you." The nurse checked her watch. "He'll be by in an hour or so."

"Thanks."

Bran crossed his arms over his chest. The friend Tory referred to was her P.I. pal, Sheila Sanford. His wife didn't know it yet, but she wasn't going anywhere with Sheila. Or anyone else other than him.

She was still pale. Her green eyes held a residual glint of pain. Despite her physical injuries, he knew she wouldn't allow herself to remain fragile much longer. Little by little she would summon the strength and will to stand apart from the need for his help. And from him. Tough, he thought. As long as Heath was loose, he was keeping his wife on a short leash.

After a few murmured instructions, the nurse headed out the door.

Pushing away from the window, Bran moved to the bed. "I talked to Nate while you were in the shower. He brought me up to speed on the investigation. Are you feeling steady enough to talk about that? Or do you want to get more rest right now?"

"Now's fine." She tugged on one sleeve of her pale-blue hospital gown before easing back on the pillows. "Speaking of rest, you look tired. Sorry I woke you with that flashback."

"It was a bad one." He could still hear her terrorized words that had rocketed him out of sleep and chilled his blood, still picture the fear in her eyes. "I hope my being here helped."

"It helped a lot," she said quietly. "I don't know what I'd have done if you hadn't been here."

Bran shifted his gaze to the window. It was ironic, he thought, how often he'd wished he could hear words like that from her.

"Bran?"

"Yeah?" He looked back, watched her gather her long hair in one hand, then clip it back.

"What did Nate say? Has Heath been nabbed yet?"

"No." He edged a hip onto the mattress. "Our guys are working the streets. If anyone knows where Heath is holed up, they aren't talking."

"What about the scum who attacked me? What's his name?"

"Easton Kerr."

"He's looking at an attempted murder charge. You think with some creative interrogation you guys can get him to give up Heath?"

Bran kept his eyes steady on hers. "Kerr won't be telling us anything."

"Why? He being a tough guy? Refusing to talk?"

"No." He waited a beat. "Kerr's dead."

"Dead? How?" Her eyes widened. "Did you...."

She didn't have to finish the question for him to read her thoughts. "Did I kill him for what he did to you?" he asked smoothly. "No, although I'd have been tempted. When Nate and I got to the library, Kerr was dead. In the back seat of your car."

He watched her go pale as realization dawned.

"I killed him?"

"Yes."

"I...couldn't see behind me." A line formed between

her brows. "I took a wild swing with my hammer. I knew I'd hit him because the chain went slack. I didn't hang around, just grabbed my Sig, dove out of the car and didn't look back." She shook her head. "I can't believe that one swing killed him."

"Consider it a lucky hit," he said pointedly. "The thing to do right now is ask yourself if you could have done anything differently."

"He wanted to kill me. He would have."

"Meaning, you had no choice. It was you or him."

She rubbed her forehead. "Yes."

"Even so, you're going to feel shaky over knowing you took a life. That's normal."

"Is that how you felt—" she asked, her gaze sliding to his right shoulder "—when you got ambushed and shot while you were a rookie?"

"Yeah." His insides still knotted when he thought about the night he'd killed the rapist who had pumped a 9mm slug into him. "If I hadn't managed to squeeze off a round I would be six feet under instead of him. Despite knowing it was a justified shoot, it took me time to level out."

He waited while Tory retrieved her water cup, took a sip. Then another. Her expression remained controlled but he saw the unease in her green eyes.

In an unconscious move, he rolled his shoulder against the ever-present ache that was a souvenir of the long-ago night he'd almost died. That ache had him thinking about the times Tory had straddled his back while her long, elegant fingers kneaded his shoulder. And always, always while her hands worked their magic his blood heated to a roiling boil. He would reach behind him and snag her waist, flip her onto her back and then....

"Bran?"

Pulling his thoughts from the past, he slowly relaxed his shoulders, his arms, his hands. "Sorry, what did you say?"

"I asked what else Nate said on the phone."

"A lot." He stabbed a hand through his hair. "It'd be best if I go back to last night and take you through things."

"All right."

"You, along with the spouses of two other cops involved in the credit-union shootout, were attacked within hours of each other. Only you survived."

"Oh, God." She pressed a shaking hand to her mouth. "God."

"Unsell is the fourth cop from the shootout. His wife works at an appliance store. She lost a filling at lunch and took off from work to go to the dentist. Less than an hour after that a man walked into the store and asked for her."

"Was it Heath?"

"The manager looked at a mug shot. He isn't sure."

"If Unsell's wife had been there, she'd be dead, too."

"No reason to think otherwise," Bran agreed. "The Unsells were scheduled to leave next week for a vacation in Hawaii. They're flying out today."

"How did Heath and Kerr find out the names of the cops' spouses and where they work?"

"The theory is they have some computer hacker pal who accessed the PD's personnel files. They contain emergency contact and insurance information. Spouses' places of employment are also listed. The department's forensic computer guy is looking at the system to see if it's been breached, but it'll take a little time to find out."

"Those files would also show the cops' home addresses. Why not just hit the spouses there?"

"Could be Heath and Kerr didn't want to chance lurking around and being spotted by neighbors. Or maybe risk having the cop who lives there come home unexpectedly. For whatever reason, we know for sure they conducted surveillance on their targets for a couple of days.''

''How do you know?''

''Kerr had pictures of you in his jacket. They were all taken from a distance. You've got different outfits on in each so we know they tracked you over a period of time.''

Bran reached into the back pocket of his slacks, pulled out an envelope and handed it to her. ''Nate made copies of these and dropped them by the nurses' station. Two were outside the library.''

He watched as she pulled out the pictures, shuffled through them.

''These were taken the first and second nights I worked the surveillance job there.'' She held up another photo. ''This was yesterday morning. I stopped at Pro Shooters to buy ammo for my Sig.''

''They did their homework, so you have to figure they knew you're a P.I.'' He scrubbed a hand across his face. ''They'd take it for granted you'd be armed. That could be why Kerr came at you from behind. You'd be too busy struggling against the chain to go for your weapon.''

''You have to give these guys an A for their research skills.''

''Among other things. We found notes at each murder scene.''

''Saying?''

''One of four. Two of four. If they'd hit Unsell's wife, you can bet there'd have been a note on her saying Three of four.''

Tory looked up from the pictures fanned on the bed. ''I take it you found *my* note on Kerr's body? Four of four?''

"It said more than that. Seems Heath wanted your murder to be special."

"Special, how?"

"The note said you were payback for my sending him to prison." Bran cocked a brow. "Guess nobody told the maggot that my busting him was merely an arrest and I didn't mean anything personal by it."

"The note tells you just how personally he took it."

"There's more," he said. "It wasn't just a length of chain Kerr used on you. It was a set of leg irons that had an ID number engraved on one cuff. We checked with the prison where Heath was incarcerated. The irons Kerr used were the ones Heath had on when the corrections cop transported him to the funeral home."

"Okay." She pressed her fingertips to her eyes. "That makes things really personal. Sort of an in-your-face to you for sending him to prison."

"That's how I see it."

She dropped her hand. "So, if it's *that* personal, why send Kerr to kill me? Why didn't Heath come himself?"

"Good questions. I plan to ask Heath after I lock him back in a cage."

"How did Kerr get in my car? It was locked. If he'd busted out a window I'd have noticed."

"We found a slim jim in the back seat," Bran said, referring to a narrow strip of spring steel used to bypass the cylinder and unlock vehicle doors. "Since they watched you, they knew you habitually lock your car doors. So Kerr brought the slim jim."

Bran paused, knowing she wasn't going to like the rest of what he had to say. "I don't know if you remember what we talked about last night. In case things are hazy, we agreed it's a pretty sure bet Heath will make another attempt on you."

''I remember. That's why I called Sheila after I got out of the shower. You were down the hall, talking to my nurse. I asked Sheila to put me up until he's caught.''

''If you've seen her in the past couple of days, they would have spotted her, too. Linked you to her.''

Tory fingered the fresh bandages the nurse had wrapped on her neck. ''I haven't seen Sheila since the night you came to the house and told me about Heath escaping.''

''Do you also remember I told you I'm not going to let him get near you?''

''If I'm at Sheila's—''

''And that you're not handling this on your own. Call Sheila. Tell her you'll be with me.''

She flicked her gaze from the phone on the nightstand to his face. ''Sheila's a P.I. She carries a gun, too. I'll be safe at her place.''

''I don't care if Sheila is a pit bull and packs an Uzi in her purse. You're staying with me.''

''Heath managed to dig up where all the spouses of the cops work,'' she rasped, her hands now fisted against the sheet that covered her to her waist. ''You think he won't find me at your apartment?''

''He might. But we don't need to worry about that. You and I are moving into a safe house.''

''No, we're not.''

''Until we know otherwise, we assume OCPD's files have been compromised,'' Bran continued, ignoring her heated objection. ''Meaning we can't use a place owned by the department. I talked to Mark Santini. He's arranged for us to use a house owned by the Bureau. Morgan, Carrie and Grace are going to the mall to buy some clothes for us—I don't want them going to your place or mine, just in case. They'll have delivered them to the safe house by the time we get there. Groceries, too. I'll borrow a car from the department's asset forfeiture inventory. That way, if anyone is watching, it can't be traced to me."

Tory stared at him. "Do you really expect me to agree to this? To move into an FBI safe house with you? Into any place for that matter?"

"You don't have to agree. You just have to do it. What concerns me is your safety." He leaned in. "You nearly died last night."

"My throat reminds me of that every time I swallow." She narrowed her eyes. "Sheila and I will move into the safe house."

"You want to invite her along, fine. There's only two bedrooms so she'll have to bunk with you."

"I'm not a fool, Bran. I won't do anything to put myself at risk. I also understand you think you need to protect me. You don't. I'll be fine with Sheila."

"You think I'm going to sit back after some worthless piece of crap put a chain around your neck and tried to kill you?" It took all of his control to keep his voice low and steady. "Not a chance. Things have shifted to a new playing field. I'll do whatever it takes to protect you. It's a shame if you've got a problem with that."

"What I have a problem with is you making all these arrangements without even checking with me. Without bothering to ask what I want. How I feel."

He didn't move a muscle while silence dropped around them. Her constant take-charge ways had left him battling feelings of impotence and hot fury. Those feelings had been fueled by the scrapes his ego had taken over her never coming to him for help with her brother's constant screw-ups. Or even to ask his advice.

"Shoe's on the other foot," he said evenly while the old hurts sliced at him. "It doesn't feel so good, does it?

To have someone jump in and make decisions that impact on you without asking your opinion?''

The instant the words were out, he felt a pull of regret through the haze of temper that had swept over him. Hadn't he told her last night what had happened between them in the past and what went on in their future didn't figure into how they dealt with the present situation?

He bit off a curse, thinking maybe his frustration over those damn erotic dreams he'd had of her over the past week had snapped the tight rein on the anger he'd kept in check for months. Anger that he'd loved a woman he couldn't make a life with, anger at her stubborn refusal to let him protect her even when her life was at risk, anger for reasons he couldn't right this minute put a name to.

"No, it doesn't feel good," she answered, emotion swirling in her green eyes. "It feels like we've never been further apart than we are at this moment."

She shoved back the sheet, eased off the bed and moved to the window. Keeping her back to him she said, "We've proven we can't live in harmony. So it would be idiotic for us to move in together when we know we'll wind up butting heads." Her voice was as chilled as the air outside the window. "Staying at the safe house with Sheila is a logical alternative to my moving in there with you."

"I agree." He rose, moved in, pausing inches behind her. "Problem is, logical alternatives don't mean a damn thing to me right now."

She turned to face him, her chin angled like a sword, her hands fisted against her hips. The light streaming in the window behind her silhouetted the model-perfect body beneath the thin hospital gown. "I'll move there with Sheila. Or your sisters. Or some other cop. But not you. You can't force this on me."

"You're a strong, tough woman, Victoria Lynn," he

said quietly. "And I'm a tough cop. Even so, I've got this sick feeling inside me over knowing how close you came to winding up at the morgue. For as long as I live, I'll see that chain garroting your neck. Hear you fighting to breathe. See you ripping at your throat. Because of me."

"No." She shook her head. "I don't blame you for this. You shouldn't blame yourself. It wasn't your fault." Her voice hitched. "You know that."

"Feels like it was." Regret roughened his voice. "The bottom line is, I'm just not tough enough to let you go off with someone else. I can't trust them to make sure Heath doesn't stumble over you."

"There's no way he'll find me at the safe house."

"Probably not. But I won't chance that happening while I'm not there with you. Dammit, Tory, I can't."

"Bran—"

"The bastard wants revenge." He took a step closer. "He wants you dead. *Four of four.* I'm going to protect you, no matter how much you dislike it or disapprove of it or fight it."

When he saw no easing of the stubborn determination in her eyes, he played another card.

"You don't want to go with me willingly, fine. I'll charge you with Material Witness to a Homicide."

Her mouth dropped open. "You'll what?"

"That'll put us before a judge. All I have to do is tell the truth: there's reason to believe Heath will make another run at you. That you need to be in my protective custody, even though you object to it. The judge will side with me, Tory. He'll put you under court order to stay with me."

A flush rose in her cheeks and she shot him a look that could have caught a bush on fire. "You wouldn't dare, McCall."

"Watch me. Your getting torqued doesn't make one hell of a difference to me. I'd rather have you mad than dead."

When she didn't respond, he swept his hand toward the nightstand.

"Call Sheila. Tell her you're staying with me for however long it takes to bring down Heath."

Chapter 6

"Santini told me there's a full rick of firewood stacked in the backyard," Bran commented as he followed Tory through the front door of the small brick house with the steep-pitched roof.

Beneath her heavy leather jacket, she gave an involuntary shiver. The air indoors held a definite winter chill and the safe house itself smelled musty from having been closed up for a period of time.

The living room in which she stood was about the size of two large pantries, but with the earth-toned love seat and padded armchair grouped in front of the brick fireplace the room looked cozy instead of cramped. The scarred coffee table and end table matched. A braided rug pooled bright color over the wood floor.

The deadbolt sounded a firm snick when Bran set the lock. "I'll get the heater going, then bring in wood and build a fire."

"Fine."

He strode past her toward the hallway that led toward the house's rear. With her eyes narrowed on his back, she yanked off the leather gloves he'd insisted on buying her from the hospital gift shop.

Just because the place looked welcoming didn't mean she had to like it, she thought, jamming the gloves in her jacket pockets. Any more than she liked the strong-arm tactics Bran had used to get her here.

It doesn't feel so good, does it? To have someone jump in and make decisions that impact on you without asking your opinion.

It felt like hell. Especially since she'd gone out of her way during the entire time they'd been married to take care of all "Danny" screw-ups and not dump them on her husband's shoulders. The actions she'd viewed as saving him major headaches had left Bran seething. Which circled back to the core problem of their both being too independent and take-charge to live together without wanting to throttle each other on a continual basis.

And now, thanks to a revenge-hungry killer, she and Bran were again living under the same roof. Not even in her wildest imaginings could she have come up with this scenario to cap off the end of their huge mistake of a marriage!

She lifted a hand to unzip her jacket. When her fingers brushed the bandages half concealed by her sweater's high neck, she felt her anger waiver.

Again, Bran's voice echoed at the back of her mind. *For as long as I live, I'll see that chain garroting your neck. Hear you fighting to breathe. See you ripping at your throat. Because of me.*

She pressed her eyes shut for a moment. Her aggravation over his playing hardball couldn't erase the memory of the raw regret those words had put in his eyes. Or the bleakness in his voice that had twisted something inside her. She understood it hadn't been the tough cop, but the man who'd tried to explain his need to put her in a protective bubble.

And it hadn't been the P.I., but the woman who had trembled upon hearing those words. Not because of Vic Heath—she trusted her own abilities and Bran's to survive that threat. But she was *very afraid* of the currents that had churned inside her when she woke this morning in his arms. Scared to death that the volatile physical pull she'd always felt toward him might be impossible to resist during their enforced closeness.

Which was why she'd been so insistent on staying here with any person on the planet except her soon-to-be ex.

Since her protests had gotten her nowhere, she resolved to keep tight rein on her control. She *would* resist the hot-blooded attraction she still felt. Their situation was already bad enough without tossing sex into the mix. Getting tangled up again physically would just rip scabs off wounds that were far from healed.

"I stuck my head in both bedrooms on my way to the back door," he said when he reappeared out of the hallway, his arms loaded with logs. "If you don't like the room my sisters stashed your suitcase in, we'll switch."

For the sake of harmony—and because sulking brought thoughts of her mother to mind—Tory bit back the comment that she wasn't liable to like much about the overly cozy house.

"Doesn't matter which bedroom I'm in," she said, shrugging off her jacket. Even that slight movement had her hissing out a breath. The muscles she'd wrenched during the attack seemed to get stiffer with each passing hour.

Suddenly weary, she rolled her shoulders while sending up a silent prayer that coffee was in her immediate future.

"Didn't you say your sisters were also bringing groceries?"

"Yeah." Bran dumped the logs into a wood box sitting on one side of the raised hearth. "Morgan left a note on the kitchen counter." He pulled off his black parka, tossed it on the love seat. "They put away the food that goes in the refrigerator and freezer. Left the rest of the groceries in sacks so we can stash things where we want them."

His mouth curved. "Morgan also left a couple of containers filled with her homemade cinnamon rolls."

"Really?" Knowing they had their own personal horde of feather-light pastries lightened Tory's mood. "Since I don't cook, I'll do the stowing as part of my kitchen duty."

He did a slow, intense study of her. "You look dead on your feet. Why don't you take a nap while I deal with the groceries?"

She flicked him a look before draping her jacket over the back of the love seat. "You just want to get Morgan's cinnamon rolls all to yourself."

"Can't slide anything by you." He tilted his head as if to gain a new perspective. "You over being mad at me for threatening to arrest you?"

"Fat chance, McCall."

"Had to ask. Look, if I swear I'll save you a few cinnamon rolls will you get some shut-eye?"

It would only add to the guilt he already felt to tell him that every time she closed her eyes she saw the chain drop past her face. It was a blood-chilling image she couldn't seem to shake loose.

"I want an even share of Morgan's rolls." She slid a hand beneath her ponytail and rubbed at the ache between her shoulders. "I'll put the groceries away."

''Your call. Do you need one of the pain meds the doc sent with us?''

''Stop right there. I want you to swear you're not going to turn into Florence Nightingale.''

He cocked one eyebrow. ''Okay, I'll back off the care-giver routine. Just agree that if you need something, you'll tell me.''

''Agreed.'' She glanced around the room. ''How about a phone? I need to call Danny. I want to let him know what happened before he hears it from someone else. And to tell him why he won't be able to find me at home.''

''He knows.'' Bran shagged a hand through his hair. ''About the attack, anyway. Sorry, with everything else going on I forgot to tell you.''

''Tell me what?''

''I called him on his cell phone last night while you were still in the ER.''

She didn't do a double-take, but almost. ''*You* called Danny?''

''The kid and I have our differences, but he's your brother. He came by the hospital after the sedative took you under. Said he would call today to check on you.''

While he spoke, she caught an almost imperceptible change in Bran's eyes, a slight tightening at the corners of his mouth. She had seen that look enough times to know what it meant.

''Okay, spill it. What did Danny do or say last night that didn't sit right?''

''He hit me up about borrowing your car until you got back on your feet.'' Bran flexed his hands against his thighs. ''For him to do that when you were lying in a hospital bed went all over me.''

Tory gritted her teeth. It had been barely a week since she'd warned her brother not even to think about driving her car again. As usual, Danny had chosen to overlook that small fact.

"I hope you didn't lend it to him."

"I didn't, for two reasons. First, your car is a crime scene until the lab guys get done processing it. Second, I didn't figure it was a decision you'd want me to make." He studied her now with the scrutiny of a cop. "Why wouldn't you want Danny to have your car? You used to loan it to him all the time. Has something changed?"

With a headache creeping up the back of her neck and her throat aching, she didn't feel up to discussing the topic that eternally magnified all the reasons she and Bran were so wrong for each other.

Instead, she summed things up by saying, "He put a dent in my car, so I banned him from driving it."

"I don't blame you." Bran pulled his cell phone off his belt, handed it to her. "To be fair, Danny was upset when he got to the hospital. He didn't calm down until he knew you'd be okay. Nate left this phone when he dropped off the photos at the nurses' station. It's a loaner from the FBI. Untraceable, in case Heath has a hacker working for him."

"Thanks." She stabbed in a number, listened. "His cell's turned off."

"He might be at home."

"He moved about a month ago." She frowned at the phone. "I don't have the new number memorized."

"Where's he living?"

"With a dancer named Jewell."

"Dancer? Like as in stripper?"

Tory handed the phone back. "She promotes herself as an 'exotic performer.'"

Bran rocked back on his heels. "Well, hell, I didn't know the kid had it in him."

She rolled her eyes. ''Whatever Jewell's talent, I don't know her last name so I can't get her number from information. It's on my cell phone's redial and in the day planner in my tote bag. Everything was in my car last night.''

The reminder of the attack took the lightness out of Bran's tone. ''Nate's bringing your phone and tote bag here. I expect him to show up any time. But I don't want you making calls or receiving them on your cell. That number's listed in my personnel file.''

''Good point.'' Easing onto one arm of the love seat, she rubbed the center of her forehead where the headache now throbbed. She knew she should go unpack, but just couldn't work up the energy.

So she stayed where she was while Bran shoved up the sleeves on his steel-gray sweater, then hunkered in front of the fireplace. He stacked logs on the grate with geometric precision. With each move his sweater shifted, revealing the outline of the Glock holstered at the small of his back.

''There's something else I forgot to mention,'' he said while he worked.

''About Danny?''

''No.'' He glanced across his shoulder. ''I asked Grace to buy an espresso machine while she and Morgan and Carrie were at the mall. I figured having one might make this place more bearable for you.''

''Uh-huh.'' Despite her resolve not to let his presence get to her, Tory's gaze had automatically journeyed downward. Why did the man's slacks have to snug so compellingly to his lean hips?

''In fact,'' he continued as he positioned another log on the grate, ''a couple of lattes sound like a good way to warm up. I'll do the honors after I get the fire started.''

''I'll make them,'' she said, knowing the husky rasp in

her voice wasn't totally due to bruised vocal cords. She curled her fingers into her palms. Dammit, the last thing she needed was a reminder that the man she planned to divorce had kick-ass buns.

Without comment she rose and headed down the hall-way in search of the kitchen.

"Big brother sent me back here while he finishes his manly duty of stoking the fire," Nate said when he strode into the kitchen a few minutes later. "Word is, some sweet talk might get my favorite sister-in-law to make me a latte."

Tory sent him a jaded look while the espresso machine hissed steam. "I'm your only sister-in-law, slick."

"Which makes you even more special." Grinning, he laid her tote bag and a manila envelope on the counter then pulled off his black overcoat.

As always, his suit looked tailored to his broad shoulders and tall, lean frame. Along with thick black hair, dark complexion and eyes, the middle McCall brother had a charmer's grin and dry wit. All made for a lethal combination that, according to his sisters, had drawn females like moths to a blowtorch since he was about five years old.

He glanced around the small kitchen. "So, how long did it take Bran to talk you into moving in here with him?"

"He threatened to arrest me if I didn't come peace-fully."

"Well, now." Nate gave his chin a thoughtful rub. "I'll have to try that next time a gorgeous woman balks when I try to get her alone."

"You have a lot of women balk, do you?"

He wiggled his eyebrows. "No."

"Didn't think so." She pulled an extra mug out of the cabinet and thought about the concern she'd glimpsed in his face last night. "You can hold the sweet talk, slick. I owe you a latte as thanks for backing up Bran in that parking lot."

Grin fading, Nate stepped around the counter and tugged her against him. "I'm damn glad you're alive and kicking, Tory McCall."

"Me, too."

Bran paused in the doorway of the tidy, nondescript kitchen, watching his brother comfort his wife. Since the moment they'd arrived at the safe house, *he'd* fought the urge to pull Tory into his arms. It hadn't seemed to matter that their marriage was all but dead. That only a piece of paper had kept them linked for the past months. All he knew was the more time they spent together, his need to hold her grew. That need, he admitted silently, was quickly extending beyond the parameters of comfort.

Feeling that urge take on a sharp edge, he squared his shoulders. "Hey, bro, you're holding up progress on those lattes."

"Taking care of personal business first," Nate commented. He skimmed his knuckles down Tory's cheek before releasing her.

"First?" she asked.

"There's a few things I need to update both of you on. And I've got some pictures I'd like you to look at. If you feel up to it."

"I'm fine," she said, then turned back to the espresso machine.

Hardly, Bran thought. He could see the headache in her eyes, had noted the care she used whenever she turned her head, saw her wince with almost every step she took. The snug ice-blue sweater that skimmed to the waistband of her jeans seemed to emphasize the paleness of her cheeks. The woman was tough as nails, but right now she was a picture of weakness and fatigue.

She turned, switched on the faucet to rinse out the small metal pitcher she'd used to steam milk. Outside, the day had turned a gloomy dense gray and he could see her reflection in the window over the sink.

She looked painfully fragile, as though a careless gesture could make her image disappear.

Forever.

It would be much the same, he realized, after he signed the divorce papers and a judge set their marriage aside. She would be gone from his life for good. A different kind of death than Patience's, but death all the same.

Even if he could have latched on to the emotion that twisted in his gut, he couldn't have put a name to it. All he knew was that for the first time since he'd walked out, he was far from certain he wanted their marriage to end.

He wasn't sure what he wanted.

Nate took a sip from a thick white mug. "You ready to talk business, bro?"

"Ready." Bran took a mental step back. Right now, concentrating on finding Heath was far preferable to trying to figure out what the hell was going on inside him.

Minutes later they'd gathered in the living room with their lattes.

Legs tucked under her, Tory curled into one corner of the love seat. Bran claimed the other end. Nate sat in the armchair on the opposite side of the small coffee table.

The love seat's compact size became intimately evident to Tory when Bran stretched an arm across its back and his fingers almost reached her shoulder. "I guess if there was anything new on Heath you'd have already said,'' he commented.

''Nothing on that front,'' Nate confirmed. ''We *have* made progress on figuring out if the PD's database got hacked.'' He shifted his gaze to Tory. ''Did Bran tell you that's the current theory of how Heath found out info on the spouses of the cops at the credit-union shootout?''

''Yes. Do you know for sure the system was breached?''

''Our forensic computer nerd is almost positive it was. He said the PD's files are encrypted with about seven layers of security. Considering how well the infiltrator covered his tracks, there's only one local guy we know about who Heath could get to pull that off.''

''Who?'' Bran asked.

''Carsen Irons. Word is, he's the golden boy of Oklahoma City's hacking community. People call him the Invisible Man.''

''Why?''

''Online he can go anywhere. See almost anything. And he leaves little trace. Irons has the rep that he'll sell info to anyone who can pay his asking price.''

''Like Heath.'' Bran leaned forward, his eyes narrowed. ''Nate, let's you and I go have a chat with Irons.''

Tory studied Bran over the rim of her mug. His face was set, his gaze hard and restless. A predator, she thought, with violence lurking in the depths of those razor-sharp blue eyes. The danger hovering around him sounded alarm bells and, Lord help her, sent a thrill racing up her spine.

''We can't talk to Irons,'' Nate said. ''He packed his servers and motherboards and disappeared. Law enforcement's looking for him, but don't hold your breath.

You've got to figure the Invisible Man knows how to stay that way.''

"So," Tory began, "it sounds like Heath bought the info on cops' spouses from Irons. Where'd Heath get the money?''

"He'd made tons selling meth before I popped him for distribution," Bran answered. "We never found any trace of his loot. That means he's had it squirreled away all this time. Could be he's had someone he trusts watching over the stash.''

"Maybe one of his pals from the Crows," Nate ventured.

"The motorcycle club?" Tory asked, then looked at Bran. "Didn't you say they'd disbanded?"

"That's what a couple of snitches told us.''

"They were right, technically," Nate explained. "Heath started up a new arm of the Crows in prison." He retrieved the manila envelope off the table. "I've got a picture of a tattoo I want Tory to look at.''

"Whose tattoo?" Bran asked.

"Easton Kerr's.''

The man I killed, she thought, cupping the mug between her hands. Despite the warmth against her palms, her fingers felt icy.

As if picking up on her disquiet, Bran eased sideways on the cushion. "You don't have to look at the picture if you don't feel up to it," he said, settling his hand on her shoulder.

"I'm okay." She set the mug on the coffee table.

"It's a tat of a small crow on Kerr's right hand," Nate added. "On the web between his thumb and index finger. As far as we know, all Crow members have an identical mark. When they move their thumb, the crow looks like it's in flight." Nate handed Tory two photos. "We know from the pictures we found on Kerr that they tracked you for a couple of days. We just aren't sure how many people Heath has helping him. I wanted to see if you noticed Kerr or anyone else with a similar tattoo. Some guy standing in the same checkout line with you? Or maybe gassing up his car or buying a latte the same time as you? Something like that, to test how close they could get to their target.''

She studied the inky-black bird silhouette against a man's ghostly gray hand. ''I don't remember seeing anyone with this tattoo.''

''Kerr's name wasn't on our list of known Crows,'' Bran said. ''Where'd he hook up with Heath?''

''In prison. Kerr was doing time for robbery and assault. Guards there say he and Heath got to be close buds. We're trying to find out who else joined up with Heath inside and has since been released. Might give us a lead on who's helping him.''

Leaning back, Bran rested an ankle over his knee. ''Speaking of Heath's associates, what's the status on Leah Quest?''

Tory looked up from the photos. ''Who?''

''The bastard's prostitute girlfriend,'' Bran answered. ''Quest and Heath became an item about two years before he got locked up. She visited him regularly in prison. We've had her under surveillance since Heath escaped.''

''*Had* being the operative word,'' Nate added while handing Tory another photo. ''That's Quest's latest mug shot.''

Bran swore under his breath. ''She slipped the surveillance?''

''Yesterday afternoon, right before the attacks. Quest went to a department store at Crossroads Mall. She picked out a couple of outfits then sashayed into a dressing room.

When she didn't come out, our guys went in. The outfits were there, still on hangers, but Quest was gone.''

Tory stared at the mug shot. Quest might be considered attractive except for the too-brassy red hair and eyes thickly lined in dark kohl.

"Quest pulled one of the easiest scams there is to lose a tail," Tory commented. "Tuck a different color wig into a big purse and wear two layers of clothes. Once you're in the dressing room you strip off the top layer, stuff everything into the purse and put on the wig. Poof, a minute later you walk out an entirely different-looking woman." She shrugged. "I've used the same routine a few times while tailing people."

Nate gave her a wry look. "We should have hired a smart P.I. like you to watch Quest. Maybe then she wouldn't have dropped off our radar screen."

"Just like Heath," Bran added. "And the Invisible Man."

"Just like," Nate agreed. "Right now, we've got nothing to lead us to any of them."

"Great," Tory muttered. "And until you do, we're stuck here."

"That's a fact." Bran met her eyes levelly. "For however long it takes."

Although he'd been in bed for hours, Bran's brain had never clicked into deep-sleep mode. So at 3:00 a.m. his eyes opened instantly when the faint noise drifted on the air.

Having left his bedroom door ajar, he lay motionless, listening and analyzing. This being his first night in the safe house, he knew the noise could have been the natural groans of the older, unfamiliar structure. Or merely the rush of icy wind against the windows. Maybe nothing.

For a moment, the house held the heavy hush of night. Then a faint thud sounded in the distance. *Living room.*

In one smooth move he slid his Glock from under the pillow and rose. Wearing only low-slung gray sweatpants, he crept through the darkness, the wood floor cold against his bare feet. He inched the door open wider, peered into the hallway where a night-light gave off a pale glow. Last night Tory had closed the door to her bedroom. It was now open. When he came abreast of the room he glanced in. It was too dark to tell if she was still in bed.

A dull thud whipped his head sideways. Adrenaline pumping, he tightened his hand on the Glock and turned a corner. When he stepped into the living room he blew out a breath at the sight of Tory kneeling in front of the fireplace. Another thud sounded when she added a log to those already burning on the grate.

"Can't sleep?" Although he'd kept his tone soft, he saw her jolt at the sound of his voice.

"No." The unnatural way she shifted to look across her shoulder at him evidenced her stiff muscles. "I decided to start a fire," she said, her voice a husky whisper. "Thought maybe I'd have more luck dozing on the love seat."

"Did you have another nightmare?"

"Sort of."

Guilt resurfacing, he moved across the room. "It's going to take time to work through what happened in that parking lot."

"I know." Placing a palm on the table, she levered herself up. "I'm still feeling kind of…off balance about it."

It was like a fist in the solar plexus, watching her turn to face him. Her tousled hair framed her face, then gushed to her shoulders in a waterfall of gold. Those shoulders—

and the rest of her—were draped in a long robe of milky white silk that snugged across her breasts and clung to her lean hips.

Having never known her to sleep in any attire other than thigh-skimming T-shirts, he about swallowed his tongue.

"Sorry I woke you."

"Not a problem," he managed when he found his voice. Scrubbing his free hand across his bare chest, he noted his heart now pounded for a far different reason.

Her gaze flicked to the Glock. "You planning on shooting someone, Lieutenant McCall?"

"If it hadn't been you in here, maybe." He laid the automatic on the table. And, because he'd seen the flicker of discomfort in her eyes when she stood, he moved to the fireplace. "I'll put more logs on."

"I can—"

He snagged her fingers, squeezed them. "I know you can." In the fire's buttery light her skin had a soft, fragile glow brought on by exhaustion. "You probably wrenched every muscle during the attack. So house rule number one is I do the heavy lifting around here. Got it?"

"We have house rules?" She raised her chin. "Guess you were too busy threatening to arrest me to mention them."

He saw the stark white bandage peeking out above the robe's high neck, and struggled to keep his voice light. "Getting you here whatever way I could took priority."

He pulled a couple of logs out of the wood box and added them to those flaming on the grate. That done, he made a circle motion with his index finger. "Turn."

Her eyes narrowed. "Why?"

"It'll be easier for me to massage your back if you're not facing me."

"This is a safe house, McCall, not a spa."

"That's one sharp observation from a crack P.I."

When she didn't budge he sidestepped her and slipped his hands beneath her hair. He could feel her nerves snap as he began to knead shoulder muscles that were taut as wire.

"Look, McCall—"

"House rule number two," he continued, increasing the pressure of his thumbs. "Back rubs are permitted for the walking wounded."

"I don't want…. Ahhhhh."

"Feel good?" With each pass of his hands across her shoulders, the white silk flowed like warm water.

"Like…heaven." The husky purr in her voice notched his internal furnace up a couple degrees.

When her head tilted back, the familiar weight and texture of all that glorious hair cascaded across his bare arms. An image popped into his brain of her lying beneath him, thick waves spilling gold across the pillow, her face flushed, her dark emerald eyes filled with desire for him. Only him.

Her muscles went pliant while his fingers moved along her spine in soothing strokes that, for him, were anything but soothing. The cool, clean scent of her was waltzing through his system, and needs long denied had the blood in his brain pounding like thunder. It didn't help that he knew every curve and slope of the body that had turned as soft as warm wax while his own muscles bunched tight.

"Think you can keep this up for about an hour?" she asked, her throaty voice misting over him like fog.

"I'm good for it." He wondered how long he could last before he took off to take a cold shower.

She arched her spine like a long, sleek cat, and he went rock-hard. Another minute or so of this and he'd be in the shower.

"So," she murmured. "Why hasn't the cop with the keen observation skills mentioned the robe I'm wearing?"

He stilled his fingers against her spine. "Because seeing you in it makes the cop think about the gorgeous, sexy body underneath that robe." Against his palms, he felt her heartbeat hitch, then quicken.

Greedy now, he slid his hands down her sides, settled them at the slope of her waist. "When we were together you slept in T-shirts or nothing. Never silk."

"The robe isn't really mine."

Because he couldn't help himself, he inched his mouth close to her ear. The soft sweep of her hair against his cheek had him closing his eyes. "If the robe doesn't belong to you, maybe you should take it off?"

Tugging away, she turned and met his gaze. He felt a dark, primal satisfaction when he saw the flush in her cheeks and unsteadiness in her eyes.

"I meant the robe isn't one I had before today. It's a get-well gift your sisters packed in my suitcase."

"Those girls are damn thoughtful."

"And not very subtle. They packed pushup bras and thong panties to take the place of my usual style of underwear."

His lungs clogged. "*Thong* panties?"

"In assorted colors. And styles. That had to have been Carrie's idea. I bet she spent an hour at Victoria's Secret." Tory raised a palm, dropped it. "I love your sisters, you know that. But they're wasting time and money. We need to make them understand that what was between us is over."

He wondered how the hell things could be over when the thought of the body under that robe clad in various-colored thongs had him fighting to get breath into his lungs.

"I'll talk to them," he said after a moment. "Tell them no more surprises. In your suitcase or mine."

"They left something in your suitcase, too?"

"A super-size box of condoms. In assorted colors."

"Well." He noted the hand she raked through her hair wasn't totally steady. "Goodness."

"Can't say I'm surprised," he commented. "Considering what they had waiting for us when we got home after we eloped. I had no idea there was a strip poker board game." Memories of erotic hours spent rolling dice, dealing cards and peeling off clothing spiked his pulse rate. "Then there was the paint-on body chocolate they left on the nightstand."

Tory shifted her gaze to the fire, then closed her eyes. "We should change the subject." Her voice didn't rise above a whisper.

Firelight shimmered in her hair; her scent churned in his blood. Before he could think, he'd lifted a hand and had taken a fistful of gold. Nudging her gaze back to meet his, he saw the change in her eyes, the faintest deepening of green that told him she was remembering, too. "That chocolate tasted good," he murmured. "But not as good as you."

"Bran, no." Her palms settled against his bare chest. "This isn't what I want."

"A cop who ignores the evidence is a bad cop. Your breathing's unsteady and your pulse is jumping."

"Because this…is crazy. We don't work." Her eyes shimmered like pools of heat as her fingers flexed against his flesh. "Can't work. Your sisters know that. *We* know that."

"You're right." His fingers fisted tighter in her hair. "Everybody knows."

Swamped by memory, filled with need, he settled his

free hand against her waist. Beneath his palm, he felt her tremble.

Inching her closer, he dipped his head. ''Let me,'' he murmured. ''Let me taste you again.''

Chapter 7

With her palms flat against Bran's broad, muscled chest, Tory felt the rapid pump of his heart. The heat.

One of his hands molded against her hip; she could feel the steel in his long, skilled fingers through the robe's slippery silk. His other hand was buried in her hair. The blue eyes gazing down at her simmered with desire. And that mouth—wide, generous and seductive—hovered above hers, ready to take.

A whip-quick pulsing excitement had her fighting the need to step fully into his arms. Press the entire length of her body against that heat. It was all so achingly familiar that she shuddered, responding to both the memory and the man.

She could see them tumbled in bed, rolling over crisp, white sheets. Could all but feel his hands slicking across her damp flesh that softened as needs sparked into flames as hot as those leaping in the fireplace a few feet away. She knew if she surrendered now the ride would be swift, hot and shattering. And the heart she'd spent months building walls around would be lost to him again.

When he buried his face in her hair and murmured her name, she realized those walls hadn't managed to free her from him at all. Otherwise, she wouldn't be struggling so desperately against the urge to stroke her hands over every magnificent inch of him.

Why did she have to want a man with whom it was impossible for her to share a life? A husband who had acknowledged that impossibility by walking out?

That cold, hard reality snapped her back.

"No," she whispered hoarsely, pushing from his hold. "You maybe want me now physically—"

"No maybes about it." His voice mirrored the raw emotion glinting in his eyes as he moved in on her.

She countered with another step in retreat, then another. Her calves collided with the love seat, blocking her escape. She all but heard her nerves fray. "Sex is the last thing we need right now."

He eased forward, stopping when they were eye-to-eye, mouth-to-mouth. "Speak for yourself," he said softly.

She could barely speak at all with his musky scent sliding around her, into her.

"A relationship built just on sex won't last," she finally managed. "You acknowledged that the day you walked out." The words burned her bruised throat and darkened his eyes.

"That day," he began, "I'd just found out from a patrol cop that you'd spent a couple of hours at the jail bailing out your brother. Dammit, Tory, that was the final straw. You're my wife and you didn't come to me for help. *The entire time we lived together you never came to me.* Refused to lean on me. For anything. Never gave one indication you needed me. You think that's easy for a husband to swallow?''

Her mind shot back to that awful day when she'd stood in the doorway of their bedroom, watching him shove clothes into a suitcase. The pain was still there, like a dull-edged knife through her heart.

''Rehashing this won't get us anywhere.'' She dug her nails into her palms, remembering there had been as much hurt in his eyes as she'd held inside her. ''I used to think we were too much alike. Now I wonder if we're too different.'' She shook her head. ''Everything's too jumbled in my brain to make sense of. All I know is we don't fit together like married people should.''

''Not when you think marriage is all about power and control.''

''I never said that.''

''You didn't have to.'' His brows drew together. ''Growing up, I watched my parents stand together as equal partners. That doesn't mean they didn't depend on each other for certain things. It's easy for me to see now how they worked in tandem when it came to raising six kids. If either mom or dad went into orbit over something one of us did, the other made a point of calming things down. They were, still are, a team. Equals. That doesn't make either of them weak. Or needy.''

''Needy's all I saw when I was little. I watched my father grow to despise my mother because she refused to stand on her own two feet. She was eight months pregnant with Danny when her constant clinging got too much for him to take. So he walked. And....'' Her breath had begun to hitch as age-old pain clogged the words in her throat.

''And your mother heaped all the responsibility she could on you,'' Bran said, cupping his palm against her cheek. ''Including Danny.''

She moistened her lips. His gaze followed the movement of her tongue. "Understanding where we both came from doesn't change things. We're the same people we always were. The fact we're stuck in this house because a scumbag wants to use me to get back at you doesn't make a difference. We don't fit."

He took her chin in his hand, fingers strong and firm. "Remember all the time we've spent at the police pistol range?"

She frowned, puzzled by the abrupt change in subject. "Yes. I also recall I usually scored higher than you. What does my being a better shot have to do with anything?"

"As *I* recall, we're about even when it comes to who bested whom while blasting at targets," he countered. "But that's not the point."

"There's a point?"

"Then there's all those hours we've spent at the gym, practicing self-defense moves. We both managed to hold our own while rolling around on a mat."

"To repeat myself, McCall, is there a point somewhere in all this?"

"Hearing you talk, we don't get along on any level. We've got nothing in common. Seems like those are a couple of areas where we do."

She batted his hand away before his touch dissolved what was left of her willpower. "You're turning this around. When we met we moved too fast. That was a mistake. You left because—"

"It was walk or throttle you." A muscle in his jaw ticked. "I've stayed mad the entire three months since then. Mad and hurt. I wouldn't let myself think about anything but the bad times we had. Seeing you again, spending time with you, reminds me there were good things mixed in."

"Not enough." She lifted her hands, let them fall. "We bickered over everything, not just how I dealt with Danny."

"True," he agreed quietly.

She blew out a breath. "I bet you and Patience never said a cross word to each other, did you? Then we got married, and you found yourself in the middle of a battlefield. That had to have been a shock."

"You've definitely given me a different perspective on marriage," he replied, his unwavering gaze locked with hers.

"I bet." She tossed her head. She needed to put distance between them but she was trapped between the love seat and a wall of hard, muscled male. "So, we agree our getting married was abject stupidity, fueled by mindless lust. One huge mistake."

"I'll agree with the mindless lust part. Jury's still out on the stupidity and mistake issues." He angled his chin. "I made a decision last night at the hospital. I intended on keeping it to myself while I thought things through. But now I think you should know."

His words might have been casual, but the determination in his tone had wariness sliding inside her like a band of smoke. "What decision?"

"I'm not ready to call things quits."

The comment came so clearly, so simply, she felt a slice of panic. When he'd walked away he'd left her shattered. She couldn't open herself up to him and risk that happening again. Never again.

"You…said you would sign the divorce papers." She was failing miserably at keeping emotion out of her voice. "That you'd bring them to the library last night."

"I did agree to bring them. I never said I would sign them."

Cold anger replaced her sense of panic. "Dammit, I'm trying to end our marriage with some measure of civility. I want to buy the condo, get on with my life. You should be looking out for your own future. Instead, you're standing here, playing word games."

"You think I'm playing games? Think again. Since that night I came by to tell you about Heath, I've dreamed about you. Hot, heavy dreams."

"You need to clamp a lid on all that testosterone."

"I need to do something about it," he agreed silkily. "Bottom line is, you're still inside me, churning my system. I'm not sure how much of what I feel for you is just an echo and how much is real. Until I know for sure, we're not calling this quits."

"What?" Her defenses sprang up to shield her. "The hell we're not. You're not the only one who decides—"

As if to prove his point, he framed her face with his hands and closed his mouth over hers. It was an easy kiss, almost friendly, if not for the heat rising from it.

And an easy, almost friendly kiss shouldn't have shot desire like a bullet through her and sent a line of fire searing up her spine.

His heated, lethal mouth didn't merely brush her lips— it absorbed them. Somehow, her hands wound up on his hips, and she realized she was clinging to him, that his body was hard, nearly naked and pressed close to hers. She dug in her fingers as much for balance as in response to the sudden, violent want pounding inside her.

With the walls she'd put up in shambles, her lips parted, inviting him in. The familiar dark, dangerous taste of him had visions of wild, raging sex spinning in her head. Even as a moan raced up her throat and a heady rush of anticipation turned her insides to molten glass he eased back.

"There's another area we're a good fit," he murmured.

She saw the desire in his eyes, heard the raw echo of it in her voice.

"I guess. Maybe." Consumed by a dazed kind of weakness, she dropped onto the love seat. She wasn't light-headed, she told herself. And her bones hadn't actually melted during the kiss. She just wasn't fully recovered from last night's attack and she'd been on her feet too long.

She eased back into the cushions while fighting to regain both her breath and sanity. Doing that would have been easier if the taste, the scent of him weren't humming in her blood. *You're in trouble.* The words flashed like neon in her brain. Huge, blinding neon.

He snagged his Glock off the table, then turned back to face her. He looked dangerous standing there half naked, the automatic clenched in one hand while flames in the hearth leapt behind him. Compelling, reckless. Lethal.

Heaven help her, she wanted to drag him down onto the love seat with her. Wanted his mouth streaking down her throat, his teeth raking her flesh. Wanted that hard, muscled body pressed against hers. *Inside hers.*

She clenched her fists against the desire that continued to scrape through her system. Her palms were damp, but she refused to sacrifice the dignity she was trying to rebuild by wiping them on her robe.

He studied her with his cool, assessing cop look that gave nothing away. "I'm going back to bed," he said finally. "Try to get some sleep."

"Right," she muttered. Despite her intention not to, she watched him stride toward the hallway. His low-slung sweatpants clung to his backside and muscular thighs like a second skin. Thinking of the body beneath the soft gray material sent another frisson of desire clawing through her with savage intensity.

He turned so suddenly she didn't have a chance to divert her gaze. When he saw she was watching him, his eyes darkened and the intimacy of the look he sent her went straight to her gut.

"Apparently," he said softly, "you're not done with me, either, Mrs. McCall."

When a knock sounded on the front door of the safe house two days later, Bran bypassed the peephole and looked out the window. Danny Dewitt stood on the porch, fingers jammed into the front pockets of his well-worn jeans, shoulders hunched beneath a faded denim jacket. Although the morning sun beamed sparkling clear, he stomped his scuffed boots against the cold while his breath made puffs of steam on the air.

Bran sliced his gaze to the driveway. The windows on the idling black sedan were too dark to see in, but he knew FBI Special Agent Mark Santini was behind the wheel.

Pulling the door open, Bran motioned his brother-in-law inside, then gave an acknowledging wave toward the sedan. The dark, sleek car reversed out of the drive and headed off.

He took an extra minute to check up and down the street of old, well-maintained houses. He saw nothing amiss.

"Thanks for setting it up for me to see Tor," Danny commented. "Having her tell me on the phone that she's okay helps, but I'll feel better when I see her."

"Understandable." Bran returned his Glock to the holster clipped inside the back waistband of his jeans. While his brother-in-law swept his gaze around the small, tidy living room, Bran studied him.

With thick, black hair worn in a short ponytail, a thin, lean face, lopsided grin and green eyes almost unnaturally vibrant, Bran supposed most women would term the kid "a hunk."

"Guess this isn't such a bad place to hide out," Danny observed while blowing on his bare hands.

"It meets our needs." Bran frowned. "Where's your coat and gloves?"

"In my pal's car. Rocco was supposed to drop them by my place last night. He never showed."

"I just put on a pot of coffee. Want a cup to help warm up?"

"That'd be good. So, where's Tor?" Danny asked trailing Bran down the short hallway.

"In the shower." Which, since their close encounter two nights ago, is where *he* had spent a good amount of time, standing under a stream of lukewarm water.

When they passed the bathroom he heard the shower's faint spray. He didn't have to imagine what her lean, fit body looked like with steamy water cascading over every inch of her flesh. Or what that yard of incredible golden hair looked like slicked back from her stubborn, sexy face. He knew. Which is one reason all the tepid showers he'd taken had done nothing to cool his blood. Heaped on top of everything else were the erotic dreams of her that continued to plague him, conjuring up memories of the past to mix with present needs. Needs that had coiled into a knot in his gut after that long, slow taste he'd had of her. During the three months they'd been separated he'd convinced himself he'd gotten her out of his system. The dreams and that kiss had proved him wrong. Now, he wasn't exactly sure what all he wanted from her, but it was more than just that one taste.

A hell of a lot more.

"I feel like some sort of undercover snitch," Danny commented when they stepped into the kitchen. "First, I get picked up by Alex Blade.'' He furrowed his forehead. ''Which one of your sisters is he marrying?''

''Morgan.''

''Then Blade handed me off to Linc Reilly. He's hooked up with Carrie, right?''

''Right.'' Bran pulled two mugs out of a cabinet. ''They called yesterday to let us know they're getting married the same day as Alex and Morgan. Double wedding.''

''Cool.'' Danny leaned against the counter. ''So, Reilly drove me around a while, then handed me off to the FBI dude, Grace's squeeze. Kind of a roundabout way of getting here.''

''A necessary one.'' Bran poured coffee into the mugs. ''We have no idea if Heath knows you exist, but in case he does we need to make sure he hasn't set up surveillance on you. You're Tory's only blood relative, it's logical she'd contact you to let you know where she is. Maybe even set up a meet. That'd be the only way he or one of his pals could get to her again.'' He had to clamp down on cold fury. ''I'm damn well not going to let that happen,'' he added, handing Danny a mug.

''I feel better knowing you're watching over Tor.'' Taking a sip, he frowned at Bran over the rim of the mug.

''Something on your mind?''

''I'm wondering if you and my sister are divorced yet.''

''We've got a few legal loose ends left to tie up.'' Emotional ones, too. ''Why?''

''Just asking. Knowing Tor, she put up a fight over coming here. She doesn't like anybody doing things for her. Guess you know that.''

''I figured that out about two minutes after we eloped,'' Bran said dryly, then shifted his gaze toward the hallway. He could hear the muted sound of a hair dryer. ''She ought to be out here in a few minutes.''

"I was hoping to talk to you alone."

"About?"

"A car."

Bran's fingers tightened on the mug's handle. "Before you get started, you need to know I told Tory you hit me up at the hospital about borrowing her car."

"I know. She chewed me out on the phone—about took off a piece of my hide. Says she's got this new 'Danny policy' about forcing me to stand on my own two feet."

"What brought that on?"

"She said I turned eighteen and it's time she cut the cord."

"She's doing you a favor, even if you don't see it that way." He set his mug aside. "Since you're bringing up the subject of cars again, it sounds like you didn't take her policy to heart."

"It's not that." Danny stared somberly down into his coffee. "Some stuff has happened over the past couple of weeks."

Bran furrowed his brow. He'd never seen the kid so serious. "What stuff?"

Danny glanced across his shoulder to check the hallway. "My girlfriend, Jewell, said if I don't get my act together, she won't see me again. Can't let that happen." He took a deep breath. "We're gettin' married."

"You and the strip…" He caught himself. "The exotic performer?"

Danny slid onto one of the long-legged bar stools at the counter. "Doesn't bother me if you call her a stripper. Jewell's a sweet girl who got tossed out of the house by her stepfather. She needed money to live, so it was dance or do tricks." His mouth curved. "Lucky for me she chose dancing."

The dreamy look that accompanied the kid's smile had Bran hooking a brow. "Sounds like true love."

"It just hit me between the eyes."

"Yeah." He had felt the same way when he'd met Tory. And look where marrying in haste had gotten them. "I take it your sister doesn't know yet?"

"Thought it'd be best to tell her in person." Danny leaned forward on the stool. "Thing is, Jewell's pregnant."

Bran whistled. "Your whole life is about to change, pal."

"It already has. Jewell knows this guy who owns a hamburger joint and he hired me. Jewell's not dancing anymore, she's tending bar instead. My shift overlaps with hers, so I can't use her car to get to work. That's why I wanted to use Tor's, just until I save enough to buy my own."

Bran studied the kid through narrowed eyes. Every cop instinct he'd developed over fifteen years on the job told him Dewitt was being sincere. "Why didn't you tell me this at the hospital?"

"Get real." Danny met his gaze head-on. "You weren't open to listening to anything *I* had to say after I asked about borrowing Tor's car. When you jumped me, my pride got scratched. Figured I'd show you I didn't need your help."

"I was preoccupied, having just seen your sister almost get murdered on my account." He raised a hand, dropped it. "That's no excuse. I was wrong to take my anger out on you. I should have let you have your say."

"Yeah, well, that night I was still thinking I could depend on Rocco to drive me to and from work. Last night he forgot about me. I had to call a cab, which made me late. That pissed off my boss, big time."

"Sounds like a rough night." Bran glanced toward the hallway. He could no longer hear the hair dryer. "You still haven't explained why you want to talk to me alone about your sister's car."

"Not about her car, *a* car. I need to know if you'll loan me the down payment for one. I swear I'll pay you back at any interest rate you set."

"Why hit me up instead of Tory?"

"I was thinkin' about doing that, but Jewell won't let me. She says Tor's got big problems of her own right now. Hell, I know Jewell's right. There's some bastard trying to kill my sister." Danny pursed his mouth. "That's bad enough, but then she had to move back in with you."

Bran barked a laugh. "Can't decide which is worse, can you?"

"I bet Tor knows." Danny rested his forearms on the counter. "Look, I'm asking for your help, man-to-man. I'd appreciate it if we could keep this between us."

Bran retrieved the coffeepot, topped off their mugs. Until—or if—a judge pounded a gavel to mark the end of his and Tory's marriage, Danny Dewitt was family. Despite the fact the kid was mostly being forced to accept responsibility for his actions, he seemed sincere. And Jewell-the-stripper sounded like one hell of a smart woman.

"Agreed, we'll keep this between us," he said. "And I'll help you get a car."

"Man, thanks."

"Listen up, Dewitt, if you think I'm going to hand you cash and send you off to a car lot, think again. What I'll do is cosign a loan." Bran dipped his head. "You miss *one* payment, start looking for me across your shoulder. I'll have the car towed back to the dealer. Then I'll take a bigger piece out of your hide than Tory or Jewell ever thought about taking. Understand?"

"Got it." A look of immense relief spread over the kid's face. "Thanks."

"Don't mention it."

"Don't mention what?" Tory asked as she stepped through the door.

"How much better my coffee tastes than yours," Bran said smoothly while Danny whipped his head in her direction.

As if on automatic pilot, Bran's gaze slid downward while she moved to the counter and dropped a kiss on her brother's cheek. Her jeans were intriguingly taut, worn with a short red sweater. It wasn't her outerwear, though, that gripped his attention. Lately, he couldn't see her without thinking about the damn thong panties his sisters had packed in her suitcase, and wondering which assorted color was currently snugged against the most intimate part of her body.

"*My* coffee's best," she said, keeping her gaze focused on her brother's face.

For the past two days, she'd sensed Bran's gaze drop to her rear every time she walked by him. Although a few choice comments had popped into her head, she'd kept quiet. She couldn't exactly hammer him for leering when she'd spent so much time thinking about those condoms his sisters had smuggled into his suitcase. *In assorted colors.*

Danny grinned. "I'm not gettin' in the middle of a coffee war." Using a finger, he nudged back one side of her hair and checked her throat. "At the hospital your neck was wrapped in gauze."

"No more bandages," she said, forcing her voice to remain light. She still had occasional flashes—almost vision-like in their clarity—of the first link of chain dropping before her eyes. Then the second. "Just a few scrapes left to heal,'' she added, even as her stomach tightened against the memory of the attack.

''Good, that's good.''

Sensing the nerves behind her brother's smile, she took a step back and examined his face. ''What's going on?'' She looked at Bran. ''And don't feed me the line about coffee.''

Bran crossed his arms over his chest. ''Danny has some news.''

Since Bran's expression told her nothing, she turned back to her brother. Whenever he showed up with ''news'' it was always bad. ''You're here because you've gotten yourself into another bind, right? Did you get more tickets? Wreck a car? Danny, you're out of luck if you expect either Bran or me to deal—''

''I came here to make sure you were okay,'' he snapped.

She didn't know Bran had stepped around the counter behind her until his hands settled on her shoulders. ''Have a seat while I pour you some of my award-winning coffee.''

''I don't want to sit.''

''Yes, you do.'' She had little choice but to settle onto the stool beside Danny's when Bran increased the pressure on her shoulders. ''Just listen to what your brother has to say.''

The mildness in Bran's voice had her remembering what he'd said about his parents. *If one went into orbit over something one of us did, the other made a point of calming things down.*

''Fine.'' Her spine as stiff as wire, she shifted closer to the counter and began straightening the stack of folders filled with the information on Heath that Nate had compiled. All the while, she reminded herself of her new

Danny policy. Tough love. No more enabling. Force him to stand on his own. *Be calm.*

"There's a lot of stuff going on," he began.

Wasn't there always? She threaded her fingers together hard enough to snap bone, then settled them on top of the file folders. "What stuff?"

"I'm gettin' married."

"You're what?"

"To Jewell. You're gonna love havin' her for a sister-in-law."

Bran sat a mug of steaming coffee beside the folders, then put an index finger beneath her chin. "Your mouth is open," he murmured.

She snapped her jaw shut. "Jewell. You're going to marry Jewell, the—"

"Exotic performer," Bran added before shifting sideways to lean a hip against the counter. "Might as well tell your sister the rest of your news, Danny."

She blinked. "There's more?"

"We're havin' a baby." Danny grinned. "You guys are gonna be Aunt Tor and Uncle Bran. Well, until your divorce goes through."

"A baby." She pressed her fingers to the thudding in her left temple. Why hadn't she had the good sense to haul her little brother to a vet and have him neutered?

Stay calm, she reminded herself and forced a smile. "Congratulations. I told you I'm buying a place of my own, right? A *one-bedroom* condo." Although the folders were already aligned, she began tapping their sides against the counter. "You'll have a wife and a baby to support—"

"I'm not asking if we can move in with you, Tor. I got a job."

She bobbled the folders, spilling papers and photos onto the counter. "*You* have a job?"

"Jewell laid down the law, said she wouldn't see me if I didn't shape up. Get an income that comes from somewhere other than gambling. She means a lot to me. I can't lose her, Tor. I just can't."

She stared at her brother, while tears threatened to sneak through her defenses. With his dark hair pulled back, his face looked sharpened, honed. The mossy green eyes that so often held a no-care-in-the-world look stared back at her with an intensity she had never seen. This, then, was the man beginning to emerge from the boy she'd raised.

"It...sounds like Jewell is special."

"She is. Bran says it's true love."

Tory slanted her estranged husband a look. "Are you suddenly an expert on affairs of the heart?"

"Always have been. After all, it doesn't take a rocket scientist to figure out everything depends on chemistry." His gaze lowered to her mouth. "I know a lot about chemistry. So do you."

While her stomach fluttered, she began shuffling reports and photos into a stack. Since the night they'd kissed, the chemistry between them had kept the air in the safe house so electrified she was surprised the place hadn't imploded. Now, all he had to do was look at her mouth and she felt the pull. Dammit, they weren't meant to be! The last thing she wanted was to get involved again and open herself up to even more hurt. So why was she consumed with red-hot, soul-searing need that peeled her resistance away one thin strip at a time?

"Hey, the crow!" Danny pointed a finger at one of the photos she'd yet to shove into a folder.

Although they weren't touching, Tory sensed Bran's spine going as stiff as hers.

"What about it?" they asked in unison.

Danny looked up. "What are you guys doing with a picture of the professor's tattoo?"

Chapter 8

In the space of a heartbeat, Tory watched Bran's demeanor transform from casual to steel-eyed cop as he snagged the photo off the kitchen counter.

"Dewitt, are you saying you know a guy with this identical tattoo?"

"Yeah. Well, no, I don't *know* him." Danny scowled. "Tor, remember that morning I brought your car back with the little ding?"

"The big dent. What about it?"

"I told you Rocco and I had been out all night, playing poker, right? A guy sitting in on the game had the same tattoo as in that picture." Danny pointed to the web between his thumb and index finger on his right hand. "Here. When the professor moved his thumb, it looked like the crow was flying."

"The professor." Bran stepped closer to the long-legged stool on which Danny sat. "What's his real name?"

"Beats me. All anybody called him was 'Professor'. I did hear the guy who set up the game call him 'prof.'"

Tory watched Bran shuffle through the other photos that had spilled across the counter, coming up with the mug shot of Easton Kerr. "Is this the man with the tattoo? Is he the professor?"

Danny shook his head. "Doesn't look anything like the dude."

Bran laid the photo aside. "Who sets up the games? And where are they held?"

"A guy named Jazz runs them. The one I went to was in one of the hotels on Meridian. Rocco was the one who knew about it, so I rode there with him. Didn't pay much attention to which hotel we wound up in."

"Where's Rocco now?"

"That's always a good question," Danny said. "I can try to get him on his cell. Thing is, he told me the games Jazz sets up are never in the same hotel twice in a row. And never on any type of schedule."

Tory shoved the remainder of the reports she'd spilled back into a folder. "That's a good way to make it hard for the cops to track an illegal game."

"One of the best," Bran agreed. "Danny, tell me about Jazz."

"He's a big black dude. He goes by Jazz because he likes that type of music."

"What's the game?"

"Five card draw."

"And the set-up?"

"First thing, nobody gets in the door without a referral. I only got in 'cause Rocco knows Jazz. Once you're in, buying into the game costs one hundred dollars up front. And Jazz pulls ten percent from each winning pot."

"How many tables?"

"We were in a suite, so there were three set up."

"How many players at each?"

"Seven."

"That's about the maximum number who can play that game using one deck of cards," Tory said. "So, on a good night Jazz has twenty-one people paying him one hundred dollars each just to play. Then he rakes in ten percent from each winning pot. Not bad when the only overhead he probably has is the hotel suite."

"It is," Danny confirmed. "You want to drink or eat anything, you have to bring it with you."

"Is that the only time you've played in one of Jazz's games?"

"One and only. I'm not planning to go back since Jewell put her foot down over me gambling."

"You may have to go back," Bran said. "When Santini picks you up from here he'll drop you off with Alex Blade. I'll call and have Nate take you off Blade's hands. He can show you pictures of all of Heath's associates we know about. If the professor is one of them and we find out his name, your work is done. If not, I'll disguise my appearance and you'll be getting me into one of those poker games."

"*Us,*" Tory said. "He'll need to get both of us into a game."

Bran shot her a look. "Heath and his pals want you dead. You think I'm going to let you get anywhere near the professor, think again."

"I *am* thinking. I worked a case where a woman hired me to follow her poker-playing husband because she suspected he was having an affair with a woman dealer. For a couple of nights I played at the same table as the two-timing creep. That means I learned a lot about how these games work." She looked at her brother. "Jazz sets up three tables, and tells the players where to sit, right? In case people who know each other have some sort of system to cheat worked out.''

''Yeah. Jazz put Rocco and me about as far away from each other as possible.'' Danny's eyes widened. ''Wait a minute, the professor brought a chick with him. She was playing at the same table with Rocco, so I never talked to her.''

Again, Tory watched Bran dig through the files, this time retrieving a photo of Leah Quest. ''This is Heath's girlfriend. Was she the woman with the professor?''

''Nope,'' Danny said. ''The woman playing poker had blond hair, not red. And her face was rounder. I saw Rocco talking to her during a break, so he maybe caught her name.''

Tory met Bran's gaze. ''It's going to take three people to cover the tables. If the professor is there, one of us will play in the game he does. Same goes for the blonde. If we're lucky, we might pick up information about where they both live. Work. Hang out. That could lead us to Heath.''

Bran folded his arms over his chest. ''Three people need to go in,'' he agreed. ''You're not one of them. Don't forget they surveilled you. Took photos. The professor and his girlfriend might have been in on that.''

''Do you think Heath's girlfriend is the only female who knows how to put on a wig and change an outfit to disguise herself? You've seen me when I had to tail people while I worked cases. More than once you said my disguises would have fooled even you.''

''Forget it. I'll get some other cop to go in with Danny and me.''

She narrowed her eyes. ''Name one cop who plays poker with the same skill I do.''

"She's got you there, Bran," Danny piped in. "Tor's the poker queen. She taught me everything I know."

"That's right." Her mouth took on a smug curve when she saw Bran frown. "You thinking about all the times I beat the pants off you playing poker? Literally."

Sliding off the stool, she started to turn toward the coffeepot. His hand whipped out and locked on her arm.

"Hey—"

"Do you know what happens this afternoon?" His voice was low, and as hard as his fingers that pressed down to the bone.

All thought of jerking from his grasp died when her gaze rose. His eyes held the same look of danger she'd seen the night she was attacked.

"No," she said carefully. "What happens this afternoon?"

"Funerals. Two of the cops who were at the credit-union shootout are burying their spouses. I talked to both cops on the phone. Listening to them, it's like they've had their souls cut out. When I think about how close you came to winding up in a box...."

With a vicious oath, he let her go, turned and gripped the edge of the counter. "Dammit, Tory, I can't stand the thought of you getting hurt again. Maybe worse. I put one wife in the ground. I won't risk putting you there, too. Period."

She let out a shaky breath as everything inside her softened. "I'm not a danger junkie," she reminded him quietly. "I don't have a death wish. I'm not going to do anything that will get me hurt. But I *have* to do something."

"How about stay alive?" he asked as he rounded on her.

"That's my plan." The way he looked at her, his eyes

so cold and fierce, his face so set, had the breath backing up in her lungs. Violence trembled around him. "Bran, listen to me. Just listen."

Wanting to make him understand, she chose her words carefully. "In my car, when Kerr attacked me, I had a split second to think about how I didn't want the world to go away. I thought of how my life was just going to wink out, like a soap bubble. Of how desperately I wanted to live." She forced a swallow past the knot in her throat. "I was so scared."

"I'm sorry." He snagged her hand, rubbed his thumb over her knuckles. In the space of a heartbeat, his eyes had transformed into blue smoke and the emotions that swirled in them were painful to watch. "I can tell you a hundred times how sorry I am. How I'll regret for the rest of my life they came after you instead of me."

"It's not your fault." She fought the urge to curl her fingers around his. "I'm telling you how I felt because I need you to understand why I want to have a part in getting Heath. Why I *need* to be involved."

She closed her eyes, saw the chain drop, felt the cold links cinch against her throat, tasted the fear. When an involuntary shudder swept through her, it was Bran who tightened his hand on hers. His fingers were warm and steady, and she very badly wanted to step into the comfort of his arms.

Her heart aching, she reminded herself that whether or not he was right about their not being done with each other, there was no way they could permanently close the abyss that existed between them. And even if they managed somehow to narrow it, she would never again trust that he would stay for the long haul. She had barely survived his leaving the first time.

The cold reality was that their marriage existed only on

paper. They were together again temporarily. When Heath
was no longer a threat, she and Bran would go back to
their separate corners in the separate worlds they'd begun
to create after they split up. And that would be the end of
Mr. and Mrs. Bran McCall.

She slid her hand from his, curled her fingers into her
palms. "I don't know if it's revenge or justice I'm after,"
she said quietly. "Maybe both. Heath scared me. He made
me feel like a victim. I *hate* that. I want to have a part in
making him pay."

When Bran remained silent, she angled her chin.

"One reason I'm a P.I. is that I can't stand sitting at a
desk, waiting for things to happen. That's what we're doing right now. We've barely been here three days and I'm
going slowly nuts doing nothing."

"Doing nothing is keeping you alive."

"I know how to keep myself that way," she countered.
"Otherwise, I wouldn't have walked away from that car
the other night. You know that. You *know* I can handle
myself."

He raked a hand through his sandy hair. "That's not
the point."

"I need to work. Take some action. I've never asked
you for anything, Bran. That's a point you've made, loud
and clear. So, I'm asking now. If you have to go into that
poker game, take me with you. Give me a part in finding
Heath."

"Dammit, woman." He put a hand on either side of her
face, tilted her chin up. His eyes, burning blue, stared into
hers. "You finally come to me for something and it's the
one thing I don't want to give you."

She felt a hitch under her ribs while she studied the
lines and hollows of his face. *If only,* she thought. "This

just proves how off the timing between us always was.'' She attempted a smile, but it wouldn't gel. ''Still is.''

His expression closed up and he dropped his hands. ''Everything,'' he said, his voice cold and controlled. ''If we do wind up at one of those games, you'll agree to do *everything* I say. Follow orders. Otherwise, you'll stay here.''

''Agreed.''

He shifted his gaze to Danny. ''If we go into that game, I want your pal, Rocco, to get Tory in.''

''That'd be four of us,'' Danny commented. ''There's only three tables.''

''Exactly,'' Bran said. ''You said Jazz won't seat people who know each other at the same table. That means he'll separate you and me. Jazz knows that you and Rocco are pals, so chances are good he'll put Rocco at a different table from both of us. We'll have all three tables covered in case the professor shows up to play.''

''And since I go in with Rocco,'' Tory began, ''Jazz will put me at a different table from him.''

''Right.'' Bran's eyes were sharp and intense and not entirely comfortable to look into when he was in cop mode. ''You'll wind up sitting with either Danny or me. And if the professor and his girlfriend show, you might wind up sitting next to a friend of Heath's.''

''I can handle it.''

''I'm not sure I can.'' Bran hooked his finger under her chin, tugged it up. ''The disguise you wear had better be good.''

She thought about the chain, felt a faint, uncomfortable tug of panic. ''It will be.''

''Uh, Jewell says I've got a lot to learn about relationships,'' Danny said. ''I know she's right. Even so, I gotta ask this one question.''

Tory turned. "What?"

"Taking into account the way you guys look at each other sometimes, are you sure you ought to be getting divorced?"

Late that afternoon, Nate called Bran to let him know that Danny Dewitt had viewed photos of all of Heath's associates. None of the pictures matched the man calling himself the professor. Nate also advised that the PD had no record of anyone using that alias.

That left a poker game as the sole lead to the nameless man with the crow tattoo matching Heath's.

Bran consulted with Danny's pal, Rocco, then orchestrated a plan to gain his and Tory's entry into the next game run by the small-time gambling promoter named Jazz.

The game was scheduled for that same night.

Per Bran's plan, Danny vouched for him in order to gain admittance into the hotel suite. The fake beard and mustache Bran wore was slam-dunk assurance no one would peg him as the cop involved in the credit-union shootout.

Ten minutes after Bran and Danny arrived at the suite, Rocco ushered Tory through the doorway.

Standing amid a grouping of the players assigned to his table, Bran sipped Scotch. He schooled his expression to one of idle interest while he watched Tory smile up at Jazz, a coffee-skinned hulking giant who looked as though he could snap tree trunks in his hands.

As he studied her, Bran's gaze narrowed over the rim of his glass. He'd left the safe house while his sister Carrie was still helping Tory don her disguise, so he hadn't seen the finished product.

He had to admit that if she hadn't walked in with Rocco, he wouldn't have recognized her right off. Not with her double-take-gorgeous face framed by raven-black hair cut in a chin-length swing. He saw nothing to hint she was wearing a wig. Or contacts that turned her green eyes to a rich, whiskey brown. And no way in hell would he have guessed the little mole right at the corner of her full, red-glossed mouth wasn't a gift from the gene gods.

"There's one sexy broad." The comment came from a tall, wide-shouldered car salesman named George with a heavily lined face and dark hair. After several of the men in their group voiced their agreement, George added, "Let's hope to hell Jazz points her to our table."

Seconds later George's hope was fulfilled. Glancing their way, Tory skimmed her heavily made-up eyes across Bran without any sign of recognition. She looked back and nodded to Jazz while unbuttoning her long black coat.

"I always enjoy these games a lot more when there's some scenery," George said.

The husband in Bran snuffed out his irritation and let the cop take over. "You play in Jazz's games a lot?"

"Every time I get a chance," George responded. "The one-hundred dollar cover fee isn't too rich for my blood. And I figure Jazz earns the ten percent from each winning pot just by making sure no scam artists or worse get through the door."

"You can't be too careful these days." Bran wondered what George would say if he found out he would be playing cards tonight with a cop and a P.I.

Thoughtful, Bran took another sip of his drink. He had covertly checked the right hands of all the players in the room and hadn't spotted a crow tattoo. If the professor didn't show tonight, the salesman might at least be a source of information.

Bran edged back his suit coat and slipped a hand into the pocket of his slacks. The small gold pin in his lapel secreted a camera lens the size of a pinhead. As he shifted, the wireless camera beamed images of everyone in the suite to a remote receiver. "Are most of the regulars here tonight?"

"Some." George's gaze swept over their fellow players. "A few first-timers like you. And the broad." He shifted back toward the door. "Oh, man, get a load of that dress!"

Bran's hand froze with the glass of Scotch two inches from his mouth. His initial thought was that his sister must have painted the form-fitting, cleavage-baring glitter of flame over Tory's trim, lean body. His gaze slid downward to the shimmery, smoky black hose caressing mile-long legs that could turn a man to stone. The hand in his pocket fisted when she strolled in his direction on spiky heels the same hot-sex color as the dress. Judging from the way the dress clung to her hips, he doubted there was room for even a pair of thong panties between material and flesh.

"Sweet mother of Finn," George muttered. "I'd die a happy man if I could spend a couple of hours of sizzle and burn with that gorgeous number."

Bran set his jaw. The lech might draw his last breath tonight, but he would *not* die happy.

No one had to tell him that every man's gaze was *on his wife.* Or what they were thinking as she sauntered across the suite, since the same hot thoughts were presently scorching his own brain. But, unlike every other male in the suite, *he* didn't have to imagine what it would be like to tumble her naked into bed. Consume her in slow, blood-stirring swallows. Feel those sleek, endless legs wrapped around him. Dammit, he knew. Knew, too, that on the day he'd walked out, he'd thrown away his right ever to claim her again.

And a hell of a lot of other rights, too. Rights he'd been thinking a lot about lately.

"Gentlemen, I'm Tracy," she said as she stepped into their midst. The little mole at the edge of her mouth did a sexy upward slide when she smiled. "Jazz said I'm playing at your table."

"I'm Brian," Bran said, trying to ignore the come-and-get-me fragrance that pumped off her skin into his lungs. "Welcome to the game."

Rings glittered on her fingers as she waved a greeting to each man who introduced himself. She cocked her chin. "Jazz told me he would leave it to some of you veterans to give me the specifics on what type of poker we're playing tonight."

Bran knew she wasn't so much interested in learning they were playing three raise, ten-dollar limit, jacks or better to open as she was in identifying the regulars who might have played previously with the professor.

Beaming a smile, George offered his arm. "Why don't you sit by me, Tracy? If you've got questions about the rules, I'll be right there to give you answers."

"Well, you're really a sweetheart." She slid her hand into the crook of his arm. "It's a comfort to have a strong man looking out for me. Oh, and Jazz said he's expecting one more gentleman to join our table, but that we should go ahead and get started."

Her gaze flicked to Bran before she stepped to the table with George. He settled into the chair across from hers, knowing they were both wondering if the professor was the expected gentleman.

Two hours later, the chair beside Bran was still empty. And the pile of chips in front of Tory looked like a miniature mountain.

No one had to tell him she played poker with a combination of impulse and skill. Still, the men gathered around the table weren't slouches, so he had to figure a small measure of her success was due to that attention-diverting red dress. And all that creamy skin. Then there was that little mole that relentlessly pulled his gaze to her red-glossed mouth.

George shuffled the deck, then plunked it in front of her. "Okay, Tracy my love, cut 'em thin so I can win."

Her laugh was low and carelessly sexy. "You sure have a way with words, George."

The salesman's response to her comment was a smooth chuckle that ran along Bran's nerve endings like a dull razor.

"I've got a lot of words for you, sweetheart," George said as he dealt the cards.

"And I bet they're all equally clever."

Bran gathered up his cards. And tried not to mangle them while a possessiveness coiled deep within him, a fierce, primitive thing that shocked him with its strength.

Mine, he thought. Dammit, she's *mine*.

At least she had been until he walked out. Broken his vow to stay through better or worse.

Tossing his cards onto the bone pile, he reminded himself his main concern right now was keeping her safe. Alive. He rolled his right shoulder against the ache from the bullet that had nearly ended his own life years ago. He couldn't afford to divert his attention by examining the feelings he'd walled inside him the day he'd left her. Or those that had begun avalanching down on him after he and Tory had moved into the safe house.

"How about we take a break?" the short, rotund man to Bran's right suggested after the hand played out.

Raking in the pot, Tory nodded. "A break sure sounds good."

Although several of the men rose and wandered off, Bran made no move to do the same. Not as long as George seemed so entranced with the way Tory's breasts strained against the dress's glittery red material.

She took her compact out of her small beaded purse and checked her makeup. Bran knew that while she powdered her nose, she surreptitiously snapped the shutter of the camera hidden in the compact, taking several up-close photos of George.

Dipping one hand into her purse, she retrieved a lipstick tube. "I guess whoever Jazz is holding that empty chair for isn't going to show tonight."

"Bet it was the professor," George said.

"I don't know him." With an expert swipe, Tory applied another coat of gloss that made her mouth look pouty and moist.

Although his system was on the brink of going haywire over the memory of those sensational, relentless lips driving him close to madness, Bran shored up his willpower and forced his attention to George. "This professor," he said evenly. "Where does he teach?"

"He's no teacher—I'm not sure why he's called that. I get the impression he mostly hangs at this yuppie club in Bricktown where his girlfriend waits tables. The place features good music and strong whiskey." George craned his head and checked the players at the other two tables. "Kandy didn't make it tonight, either, so she must be working."

Tory snapped the compact closed. "George, didn't I tell y'all when we sat down that I'm new in town? I've been looking for a nice club where I can have some fun, and here you are talking about one. The...." She furrowed her brow. "I don't guess you said the name of the place where this Kandy works."

"Chappell's." Easing closer, George lowered his voice. "I guarantee you'll have lots of fun if I'm there with you." He slicked a finger across her knuckles while studying the rings of glittery stones and twists of gold. "Before we get anything started, I guess I should make sure none of these is a wedding ring."

"You're in the clear," she said without missing a beat. "I sure don't have a reason to wear one of those."

Chapter 9

While Tory and Bran played poker in a well-lit hotel suite, a pudgy man with pale skin and narrow-set eyes sat in a dim, dank basement on the outskirts of Oklahoma City. He shivered from a combination of cold and fear.

"You told me you were going to scare those people." Trying to force his voice to remain steady, Carsen Irons stared down at the four names circled in blood-red ink on the printout he'd hacked a week ago from the police department's database. "Not kill them."

Vic Heath leaned an elbow on the computer monitor that sat on the card table before Irons. Heath was a tall man with heavy shoulders and deep-set black eyes, shaggy brown hair and a beard over hollowed cheeks. Although it was late January, the prison escapee and murderer wore a muscle shirt that displayed the full-sleeve tattoos that covered both arms. At the end of those arms were hands with fingers as thick and tough as hickory sticks.

"Well now, Mr. Invisible Man, I pride myself on always keepin' my word.'' The makeshift cast on Heath's left wrist looked eerily white in the monitor's glow. ''So I guarantee you those folks got *real* scared right before they died.''

Irons felt a shiver whisper down his spine. What had started out as a typical job for him—hacking into some heavily secured database and selling the information for a tidy sum—had turned into a horrendous nightmare. He, and a good amount of his high-end computer equipment, had been snatched from his house, tossed into this dank, cobweb-shrouded basement and chained to an iron spike in the floor. Beneath the card table that rocked on one shortened leg, he shifted his right foot. The shackle that the man he knew only as the professor had clamped around his ankle was a constant reminder of his imprisonment.

''Yeah, you've got to figure the husband and wife of those cops got scared when they realized their time was up,'' Irons agreed, then cleared his throat. No way could those victims have been more frightened than he was himself. After all, *they'd* experienced quick, relatively painless deaths. Heath had been terrorizing him for days. Threatening him. Threats that had turned vicious after the fiasco with the McCall woman when she'd somehow lucked out and killed Easton Kerr instead of winding up dead herself.

Irons gripped the edges of the keyboard in front of him so hard that his knuckles turned bone-white. He could still see the stone-cold violence in Heath's dark eyes when he'd forced him to hack into the M.E.'s database and pull up the coroner's report on Kerr's death that gave all the details on the guy's demise.

Including that Victoria McCall had killed him with one blow to the head.

Over the past days, Irons had heard enough to figure

out McCall's husband had made the arrest that initially sent Heath to prison three years ago. The same cop's involvement in the credit-union shootout where Heath's brother and cousin had gotten gunned down was some twisted hook of fate. An unfortunate one for the cop.

Not to mention the cop's wife.

As an in-your-face payback to McCall, Heath had wanted the cop's wife strangled with the shackles he'd worn when he'd murdered the prison guard. Heath's plan to kill her personally had been sidetracked when he'd fallen during his escape and broken his wrist. Without the use of both hands, he couldn't cinch the chain that connected the manacles tight enough around the throat of what would no doubt be a fighting, struggling woman who made her living as a private investigator. So Kerr had volunteered to do the murder. And had died instead.

Thinking about his own situation had the fast-food hamburger Irons had eaten for dinner threatening to come back for a return visit.

Even if Heath kept his promise to release him when he "got good and ready," Irons knew there was no way he could go to the cops. Providing Heath the contact information on police spouses made him an accessory to murder. Two murders, and one attempted murder...*so far*. If he survived this ordeal, he could never go home. Never use his real name again. He truly would have to become invisible for the remainder of his life. Lucky for him he'd already established several fake identities.

Irons's gaze drifted through the murky dimness, past the sagging couch he'd slept on for countless days to the set of wooden stairs on the far side of the basement. The stairs shot up to a heavy door, its coffee-colored paint peeling in strips. If he could only figure out a way to get free to use those identities....

"You got the bugs worked out of that software you wrote?"

Irons looked up. If his software worked—and he knew it would—the police would probably have cause to add another murder count against him.

"Yes, the voice-emulating program's ready."

"About damn time." Heath pulled a cell phone off the waistband of his jeans, slapped it on top of the printout. "Do what you have to do so I can make the call."

Irons's fingers trembled as he plugged the cord already connected to his computer into the phone. He typed a few commands, waited for the program to load, then nodded to Heath. "Ready."

Heath dug a piece of paper out of the back pocket of his jeans, glanced at it, then looked at Irons with eyes devoid of both conscience and soul. "Your software screws up, you and I are gonna have big-time problems, Mr. Invisible Man."

Irons felt the fast-food burger rise a couple of inches. "The software's gold. I loaded the captain's voice off the tape of the press conference he gave after the two killings. I guarantee you'll sound just like him. The thing I can't control is what you say and how you say it. Bottom line is, you have to talk like a cop. I've got no control over that."

Sneering, Heath picked up the phone. "I've been dealing with cops most of my life. You think I don't know how the hell they talk?"

Cool sweat slipped clammily down Irons's back while Heath punched in the number. He could almost hear the snap of equipment when the long-distance connection clicked in, imagined beams relaying to a satellite somewhere in space, locking onto a bank of switches, then a phone in a hotel in Honolulu ringing.

"Room forty-twenty-nine," Heath said. "Yeah, Unsell, this is Captain Everett. What are you doing in your room instead of out on the beach?" While he spoke, Heath pinned Irons with a cold, merciless stare. "That much of a time difference, huh? Look, I'm calling to let you know we popped Heath. We're keeping word of his arrest under wraps from the media because there's one more of his guys still on the street. But Heath is locked in a cage. Yeah, we're all relieved. Figured you'd want to know the coast is clear so you can bring your wife home when you're ready."

Panic pounding like an anvil at the base of his skull, Irons glanced down at the printout. Drew Unsell, wife of Sergeant Fulton Unsell, was one of the four names circled. The woman had lucked out and lost a filling an hour before Heath strode into the store where she worked, intending to put a bullet in her head. If her husband brought her back to Oklahoma, Irons didn't think she'd be as lucky a second time.

And he had no reason to believe Heath would let him go after the killer carried out his vendetta against the cops. Irons nibbled at a thumbnail, ripped off a piece of nail, spat it out, tasted blood. Somehow, *some way,* he had to get himself out of this mess.

Heath ended the call, jerked the cord off the phone and clipped it back on his belt. "Unsell bought it. Thought he was talking to his boss. Now, you just gotta watch the airlines to see if they book a flight."

"Right." Irons fiddled with the neckline of his heavy sweater. "Uh, are you sure you want to do this? It's only going to take another day or so for me to finish building your new identity, then get the fake IDs from my contacts. You lay low until then, the cops'll wind up chasing their tails. You and Ms. Quest could be in Mexico this time next week.'' And maybe by then *he'd* figure out a way to get himself out of the basement. Alive.

"I'll lay low after my work here's done." Heath stabbed a finger at the printout. "I could live without gettin' the Unsell woman." His finger moved up the list. "This Victoria Lynn McCall's another matter. It was her old man put me in the joint. Now she's killed Kerr. Getting her's like a mission for me." Heath's eyes narrowed. "One I can't complete until *you* find her."

"I've been trying, you know that." The acid in Irons's stomach churned faster. "The last time she used her cell phone was the night of the attack. She hasn't used a credit card since. Same goes for her husband. Utilities on their house don't show spikes like someone turning lights, appliances and TVs on and off. The newspaper's been stopped with no start-up date given. No one's there. You have to figure the cop's got his wife off somewhere. Only they didn't fly because I'd have found them in the search of the airline databases when I got a hit on the Unsells. The McCalls are just gone."

"So you've said." Heath clamped his good hand on Iron's shoulder. "You're gonna find them for me, right?"

Despite the chill of the basement, Irons's skin turned hot. "The minute one of them uses their phone, a credit card, something that I can track, I'll find them. Until then…"

"You're staying right where you are," Heath finished and settled his right hand on the printout.

Irons stared down at the black crow tattooed on the web between Heath's thumb and index finger. It was easy to imagine those thick fingers clenched around his own throat. Sitting there, sheer black panic almost overwhelmed him.

He'd spent desperate days searching databases for the

McCalls. Surely one of them would surface soon. Good God, one of them had to surface!

"The McCall bitch dies first," Heath said. "Slow. That's what she gets for killin' Kerr. Once that's done, I'm gonna make sure her old man knows how she died. Eat his heart out. Eye-for-an-eye, for his killing Andy and Kyle."

Irons nodded. He figured Heath's brother and cousin were scumbags, just like Vic. "So, after you kill the McCall woman, it'll be over?"

"Hell, no. It won't be over until I put a bullet through Bran McCall's brain."

One hour after he left the poker game, Bran was back at the safe house, the sleeves on his dress shirt rolled up, his hands jammed in the pockets of his slacks as he prowled the living room. Though he'd left the hotel after Tory, the intricate switch-off he'd set up with his soon-to-be brothers-in-law had timed his own arrival here before hers.

Which was good, since he needed time to get a handle on himself. On the situation. On what he would say when she walked through the door wearing that glittery red excuse for a dress and the catch-me-do-me heels. On the anger that layered over the frustration when he thought about their in-shambles relationship.

For months he'd done a good job of blocking thoughts of their marriage, of their separation, *of her.*

His eyes narrowed. When Patience had died, he had wanted to share the grave with her, had missed her as much as a man would miss breathing. Three years later he'd met Tory and she'd rocked him back on his heels. And when he'd left her, he hadn't let himself miss her. He'd intentionally kept himself too busy with the job because he'd been too mad, too frustrated, too…a lot of other things he couldn't put his finger on to allow himself to think about her.

Now, after having spent several days with her in the close confines of the small safe house—and nights lying awake, picturing her in the bed in the next room while her maddening scent filled his lungs—thoughts of her threatened to swallow him.

As did the realization that his abrasive, contrary, I-don't-need-you, sexy wife was quickly slipping through his fingers.

And maybe, *just maybe,* that was the last thing he wanted to happen.

I sure don't have a reason to wear one of those. The cop in him knew her comment about a wedding ring had been a smart one, meant to try to coax George-the-salesman into revealing more information that might lead them to the professor.

The man in Bran wanted to kill the slimy lech just for touching her—for no longer allowing him to ignore the fact that if their divorce went through, she would be free to let any number of men put their hands on her. Take her to bed.

Swearing, he jerked the knot on his tie loose. His emotions were so jumbled he wasn't sure what he wanted the future to hold. But he was damn sure *that* wasn't on his wish list.

When he heard the purr of an engine in the driveway, he pulled his Glock from the holster against his spine, strode to the front door and eased back the curtain's edge. In the buttery glow of the porch light he saw Tory slide out of the passenger seat of Alex Blade's sedan. Clad in the black wig, coat, sheer smoky hose and spiky heels, she had the look of a thoroughbred: dark, lean, fit and sultry.

His fingers tightened on the Glock. Right this minute, he didn't want to think about why he'd left her. Didn't want to ponder their questionable future. God help him, all he wanted to do was get her naked, sink his teeth into her and brand her his.

Shivering beneath the wool coat, Tory scaled the porch steps, thinking that in the dead of winter, only idiots wore half dresses like the one Carrie had shoehorned her into. Then there were the four-inch stilettos that had her arches screaming.

She had a gloved hand on the knob when Bran swung the door open.

"Welcome home," he said. He waited for her to move inside, then he stepped out onto the porch, holding the Glock against his thigh.

Across her shoulder, Tory saw him nod in the direction of Blade's car, already reversing out of the driveway.

She pulled off her gloves, slanting Bran a look while he closed the door and set the deadbolt. He seemed almost lost in his thoughts, his profile hard, unyielding...and gorgeous, as always. She wasn't sure how long he'd been there, but he'd had time to strip off his suit coat, unknot his tie and roll the sleeves on his dress shirt up his forearms. Gone was his fake beard and mustache; his sandy hair was mussed, as if he'd shoved his fingers through it numerous times.

"Even though the professor was a no-show, I'd say the poker game was a success." She smiled while he re-holstered the Glock. "We found out he has a girlfriend, Kandy, who works at Chappell's. And that he hangs out there."

"*You* got that information, Tory. All on your own."

The edge in his voice had her looking up from unbuttoning her coat. He had moved from the door and now stood only inches away. She was used to the way he watched her, but this was different. Deeper and intense. Much the same way he'd gazed at her while he sat across the poker table from her.

She slid off her coat, folded it over one arm. "I guess our next order of business is a visit to Chappell's. I'll go change clothes and we can start working on a plan."

As she turned, he shifted, blocking her. "That's second on the agenda."

The softening of his tone had her hesitating. "Even though the club is the only lead we've got to finding Heath?"

"Even though," he said, stepping closer.

The scent of his intensely masculine aftershave had whispers of awareness stirring her senses. "I can't imagine what would be more important than that."

He settled his hands on her shoulders. "I wanted to tell you what I think about that dress."

Just like that, the flame that had never been quite extinguished between them flared. Standing motionless, she felt her heart hitch while his gaze skimmed down to her toes, then up.

"Bran—"

"I've had my hands on every inch of you," he murmured. "Still, I'm not sure I knew you were built like that."

She saw the desire in his intense blue eyes, felt the raw echo of it sound through her.

"Uh…Carrie and I decided a man-eater dress would help coax more information out of the male poker players than a flannel shirt and baggy jeans."

"Man-eater." He lifted a hand to stroke the dark wig. "It worked. You got a response from every male in the

room. Including me. This," he traced a finger over the
little fake mole beside her mouth, "has been driving me
crazy all night."

Her pulse stuttered, began to race. "It's not real. You
know that."

"Doesn't seem to matter." He ran his knuckles down
her cheek. "Nothing seems to matter but my getting my
hands on you."

How easily his voice took on an intimate tone, she
thought, feeling her blood pound as need sprang free inside her, primal and raw. She knew she should move.
Should shrug off his touch. But she didn't. Couldn't, not
while the brush of his hands sent waves of anticipation
straight to her core.

"Every man in that suite was thinking about taking you
to bed. About what he'd do to you after he got you there.
About how it would feel to have you move beneath him
in the dark. To make love to you." He lowered his mouth
toward hers, inch by inch. "I didn't have to imagine." His
breath feathered across her skin. "I know."

"That's...in the past."

He traced his lips over her jaw, knowing just where to
make her tremble. "The future, too."

A deep, depthless yearning slashed its way into her
heart despite the locks she'd placed there. The coat slid
off her arm to the floor. "This isn't a good idea," she
said, even as her hands gripped his shoulders for balance.
The feel of his lips skimming across her flesh sent everything inside her into a mindless rush—her heart, her blood,
her head. "It's not smart."

"I don't give a damn about smart." His mouth seared
a heated path down her neck to her shoulder. "Do you?"

Her throat had gone dry and she couldn't seem to order

herself to breathe. "I...don't know...what I give a damn about. I can't think. I need time to think."

"Feel." He dragged her closer, pressing his arousal against her belly. "Just feel."

When his mouth closed over hers, heat speared upward, spreading like wildfire as teeth scraped, tongues touched. Digging her fingers into his shoulders, she arched against him, reveling in the feel of his lean, athletic body, straining center to center, core to core with hers.

It seemed that everything around her went dim, colors blurred and the world went out of focus. Like some fatal drug, his taste had her pulse pounding, her blood churning fast and her mind spinning away from the last vestiges of sanity.

His hands streaked up her ribs, the heels pressing the sides of her breasts until she wanted to scream for his full possession.

He feasted on her mouth, her throat while he tugged at the low, snug bodice.

The glittery red material slithered off one shoulder and down her arm. Desire clawed at her as his fingers slid beneath the low, silky black bra to knead, torment her already aching nipple.

His mouth returned to hers, coaxing, enticing and relentless.

She couldn't breathe for wanting this. For wanting *him*.

That wanting surrounded her like a thick fog, closing in on her. Trapping her. In the next heartbeat she realized she had no control over the raging need. The incinerating desire. No control over anything.

The sliver of panic jabbing through her belly had her tearing her mouth from his. She fought for air, for some remnant of sanity. For a way to protect her heart that yearned, yet found it impossible to fully blank out the past hurt. So much hurt.

"If...we do this...it's just sex," she managed. Hearing the breathy weakness in her voice, she fought to strengthen it. "Nothing more."

He went still, lifted his head. "It would be more," he said, his eyes glinting down at her with heat, hunger and need. "A hell of a lot more. You know that."

"I don't want it to be more," she countered, even as her body strained and vibrated against his like a plucked string. "You left. Walked away."

"I walked," he agreed. "And for three months I thought that was what I wanted. To give you up. Put an end to things." He slid his hand from her breast, wrapped his arm around her waist. "That kiss the other night told me I was wrong. *Tonight* only confirms that." His other hand cupped the side of her throat, and she knew he felt her pulse pounding against his palm. "What's between us isn't over. You know that. You *feel* it."

She stiffened her spine and met his gaze head-on while she struggled to cling to the fine edge of reason. "How I feel doesn't matter."

"The hell it doesn't."

Pushing out of his embrace she stepped back, giving herself time to take a steadying breath. Then another. "Being with you can't be anything more for me than just sex. I won't let it be more. It'll just be two people scratching a particular itch."

His eyes darkened and she could almost feel the fury, the hurt, her words sparked inside him. "There's a hell of a lot more between us than just scratching itches."

"A lot of hurt and pain, at least for me," she said, feeling more control now that he was no longer touching her. "Right now, while your blood's running hot, you don't want to think about the problems that drove you away. It's easier to remember what we do to each other in bed.''

"I'm remembering a hell of a lot more than that.''

"Not the arguments. Or our differences of opinion that had us debating almost every subject. Try thinking back to all that.''

"Dammit, I'm remembering how it sliced me apart to leave. How it felt when you almost got killed and I realized how close I'd come to losing you forever.''

She felt tears welling up in her eyes. She couldn't let herself lower her defenses. It would hurt too much if he decided to walk away again. She wasn't willing to risk her heart twice.

"You have lost me, Bran.''

His mouth thinned as he took a step toward her. "That's hardly the message I just got from you.''

"What you got was all physical. Lust and heat. You touch me, and my mind goes blank. I can't think. Can barely breathe. It's always been that way for me.'' She flexed her fingers, curled them into her palms. She felt like a jumble of nerve ends and sparks. "I'm not sure I'll ever stop wanting you in that way.''

"But only in bed? That's all the feelings you have for me now?''

She slicked her tongue over her swollen lips and tasted him all over again. Her emotions, worn thin over the past months, were now reeling. In truth, she had no idea how she felt. All she knew was she had to protect her heart.

"We're not living in this house together because of how we feel about each other,'' she said, evading his question. "The facts are, I trust you to find Heath and take him down. Until then, I'll trust you with my safety. But nowhere else. I watched you walk away once. That was enough pain to last a lifetime. I won't ever trust you enough not to do that again.''

''I was hurting too, Tory. I wanted a wife who would turn to me. *Need* me.''

''You wanted another Patience. That's not me. I handle on my own whatever comes along. That's what I do. I have to handle things because—''

''—you don't want to be like your mother,'' he finished.

''I *can't* be like her. Ever.'' She stared into his eyes that had darkened to the hue of a stormy sea and felt regret knot in the pit of her stomach. And because that regret reached up to her heart, she cupped her palm against his cheek. ''This just goes to prove what a lousy match we make.''

Muttering a curse, he strode to the window, shoved back the curtain and stared into the night. The rigid set of his shoulders bespoke the tension inside him, like a live wire dancing with dangerous electricity.

With an unsteady hand, she retrieved her coat from the floor. When she straightened, he turned, his face now as calm as carved stone.

''Speaking from experience, if we'd had sex tonight, I'm sure it would have been great.'' He raised a shoulder. ''But you made your point, sweetheart. And I'm suddenly out of the mood to scratch that itch.''

She winced inwardly at his words, but said nothing. After all, he was just tossing back what she'd said to him.

He slid his hands into the pockets of his slacks. ''Turns out you were right.''

''About?''

''The first thing on our agenda should have been planning a trip to Chappell's.'' His voice held the brusque precision of a cop reporting an official incident. ''How about you go put on something a little…warmer, then meet me in the kitchen? We'll talk there.''

''Fine.'' *All business,* she thought as she turned. Her fingers clenched on the coat. It was harder, much harder than she ever had thought possible to fight the need for him.

Still, she forced herself to walk away on trembling legs. Because they had such diverse basic needs—and no future together—it would be best for both of them, and far less painful, to keep things all business.

From the way she had responded to his touch, his kiss, she wasn't sure how long she could do that.

Chapter 10

The following night Bran swung open the door of Chappell's and followed Tory inside. The club was dimly lit with a sharp wash of blue light illuminating a small stage where several musicians were in the process of setting up. Round wood-topped tables rimmed the edge of a crescent-shaped dance floor. Thickly upholstered booths lined the walls.

An island bar dominated the middle of the room; the illuminated, mirrored column that stabbed through its center looked like a glistening icicle. Around the bar sat long-legged stools, most occupied. Bran noted that the customers' dress ran the gamut from work shirts and jeans to dark suits and ties. Chappell's clearly drew a cultural mix, from blue-collar workers to businessmen to yuppie-looking couples in date-mode.

With any luck, one of tonight's customers was a man known as the professor. Considering the club's dim, hazy light, he figured they'd have to get close in order to spot the crow tattooed on the web of the man's right hand.

He purposely stayed a few steps behind Tory while they edged their way past tables, booths and milling customers. Several waitresses were in view, but none matched the description Danny had given of the professor's girlfriend, Kandy. Bran's discreet check of the club's employees had pegged her real name as Kandace Krutchfield.

When he came abreast of the booth where Nate sat, flirting with a slim-faced woman whose blond mane spilled over her shoulders, he kept his expression unreadable. Nate's ''date'' was C.O. Jones, a sergeant assigned to the department's Intel Unit. If they did spot the professor tonight, Nate and C.O. planned to tail the man when he left the club.

Although Bran would prefer pulling the professor in for questioning, he knew now wasn't the right time. Just because the guy and Heath had identical tattoos didn't *prove* they knew each other. If the cops questioned the professor and had no charge to hold him on, chances were he'd go underground, and their one possible lead to Heath would drop off the radar screen, just as the bastard's girlfriend, Leah Quest, had done after she strolled out of that department-store dressing room in disguise.

A few steps ahead of him, Tory continued threading her way toward the bar while slipping off her cropped fox jacket. The sensuality in her movements had him thinking of full moons and sultry sex. At the edge of his vision he saw several men look her way. As she had the previous night at the poker game, she wore a disguise. A different one.

Tonight's wig was once more black, but short and spiky, making her eyes seem huge and her cheekbones sculpted. Her miniskirt was the color of India ink with a slit that soared up one endless thigh. Chandelier earrings dusted the shoulders of a tight scoop-neck black tank top that outlined the trim curve of her breasts and showed enough cleavage to get a man's blood stirring. Her wide, full mouth was painted blood-lust red.

After hanging her jacket on the back of one of the long-legged bar stools, she slid onto its padded seat. The black skirt hitched up her thighs. One more inch, he thought dourly, and he could haul her in on an indecent exposure charge.

While she snagged her compact out of the jacket's pocket, he pulled off his coat, settled on the stool beside hers and ordered drinks from a harried bartender. Snagging a pretzel from a bowl, he shifted his gaze to the lighted mirrored column in the bar's center and did a double-take at his own reflection. He doubted he would ever get used to seeing himself in the fake beard and mustache that made his face seem thinner. Almost hollow.

The mirror beamed back the images of several male patrons sitting behind him who still had their eyes glued to Tory. *He* was determined to keep his mind and his eyes on the people around them. Hoped to spot a certain blond waitress and her boyfriend.

Bran figured keeping his attention on the case ensured he would avoid a replay of last night when his blood had burned for the woman perched on the stool beside his. Burned so hotly that he'd *had* to get his hands on her.

And when he did, what a kick in the ego that had been. To have his wife tell him she wanted him only for bouts of hot-blooded sex. That she didn't trust him. Would never again trust him.

He wished he could blame Tory for twisting the knife so expertly, but she'd been right. He had solemnly vowed to take her for better, for worse. Instead, when the going got rocky he'd walked. Now she had no reason to believe in him. Would never trust him with her heart again. Without that, their marriage didn't have a snowball's chance in hell. And that, he thought, was that.

After her pronouncement he had managed to block the need for her that had boiled inside him while they sat in the kitchen and planned this visit to Chappell's. But later that need had surfaced when he'd heard the muted sounds of her getting ready for bed in the room adjoining his. And again in the middle of the night when he'd awakened to the safe house's deep silence, thinking of her, imagining her beside him. *Wanting* her.

And over time that wanting had heated his temper to a white-hot fury. Dammit, if Tory's claim was on-target that they'd based everything between them on sex, why was he so seriously ticked off? At her. At himself. At their entire damn situation.

The bartender delivered the two Scotches Bran had ordered.

He dug a bill out of the pocket of his slacks, tossed it on the bar, then waved the guy a signal to keep the change.

Tory checked her reflection in the compact's mirror, then snapped it shut. "Light's too dim near the bar to get a good picture," she said under her breath.

"Just our luck."

She raised her glass, angled it toward him. "How about a toast?"

"Sure." Picking up his glass, he shifted on his stool to face her. His gaze moved to the edge of her mouth where she'd again affixed the sassy little fake mole. His fingers tightened on his glass. Had she included the beauty mark in tonight's ensemble because he'd told her it had driven him crazy?

Well, he had news. He wasn't going to let the fake mole

get to him again. He wasn't going to let *her* get to him.
From now on he would do his damnedest to keep his emotions in check. Shove his feelings—whatever the hell they
were—for his estranged wife to some remote corner inside
him. He would get his personal life sorted out after they
took down Heath.

He touched his glass to hers. "Here's to quick endings," he said, just as the musicians began a sound check.
The shadow that passed over her eyes registered in his
brain at the same instant a blond waitress appeared out of
a door beside the stage.

His gaze flicked to the tall, dark-haired man behind her.
Mentally, he ran through the description Danny had given
of the professor, and decided they had a match.

With adrenaline charging his system, he glanced at
Tory. The edge that had settled in her eyes told him she'd
also spotted the couple.

Leaning in, he helped himself to another pretzel.
"That's got to be Kandy," he murmured against Tory's
ear. Damning the straight-up-sexy-scent of her that in-
vaded his lungs, he added, "The guy behind her fits
Danny's description of the professor."

Tory gave him a slow smile as if he'd whispered something suggestive. "To a T."

He shifted his gaze to the mirror. From behind the rim
of his beer mug, Nate gave a subtle nod to indicate he and
C.O. had spotted the couple.

On stage, one of the musicians coaxed a low, sexy throb
from a sax; another's voice slid into an earthy, mellow
tune. The waitress trailed a finger down her companion's
cheek. Even as she turned and headed toward the bar, the
man snagged the hand of a short brunette standing nearby
and tugged her onto the dance floor.

"Fickle guy," Tory commented.

"Yeah," Bran agreed, rising off his stool. "Let's get a good look at him."

"I was about to suggest the same thing."

Tory felt the bite of Bran's fingers against her upper arm as he escorted her through the fringes of couples moving on the dance floor where the light was a warm, smoky blue. She knew if that same hand were against her bare flesh she would feel the ridge of callus running under the fingers and along the tips.

After last night, she doubted she would ever feel his hands on her again.

Despite the Scotch she'd sipped, her mouth was dry when they shifted into dance position. His hand settled firmly against her waist, she felt the slope of muscle in his shoulder where she rested her palm. *Here's to quick endings.* Unsure whether Bran's toast referred to the case or to their relationship, or to both, she lifted her gaze to his. The sandy beard that covered his cheeks and jaw made his face seem leaner. Shadowed. More broodingly handsome.

Brooding certainly described his mood. Which, she conceded, was her doing. In an attempt to protect her heart, she had hurt him with her comment that she no longer trusted him. She had heard it in his voice, seen it in his eyes, in his cool demeanor while they'd sat in the kitchen of the safe house, formulating their plan for tonight. That coolness had continued throughout the day. It was as if he had slammed down a wall to shut her out.

While a tenor sax wailed, she unconsciously curled her hand into a fist against his shoulder. She hadn't realized how much she preferred Bran's heated emotion over his calculated disinterest.

And if there was nothing left between them, why had she lain awake all last night, feeling the ache that his indifference had punched into her stomach? And why was that ache even now reaching up to rip at her heart?

She shoved the maddening questions aside when his smooth steps brought them near the man who'd appeared out of the back room. Peering over Bran's shoulder, she studied him through the dim light.

He was tall, with shaggy black hair, designer stubble, long legs, narrow hips. He wore a black T-shirt tucked into tight black jeans. When he smiled at something his partner said, Tory decided he had the face of a poet, lean, high-boned with dark, intense eyes.

With his right hand curled around the brunette's left, Tory couldn't see if he had a tattoo. As if sensing her thoughts, Bran executed several quick steps, bringing them on the couple's opposite side.

She felt Bran's shoulders stiffen, and knew he'd also spotted the crow tattoo on the web between the man's thumb and index finger. There was no doubt in her mind this was the professor who had played poker with Danny a few weeks ago. So, here she was, inches away from a man who had a tattoo identical to that of the man who wanted her dead.

The next instant a deep, intuitive disquiet swept through Tory and she realized the professor's gaze had shifted her way. Her throat tightening against an unsettling flutter of fear, she reminded herself she was in disguise. That even if he'd been the one who had snapped pictures of her over the days before the attack, there was no way he would recognize her. No reason for him to think that blond P.I. Tory McCall who habitually dressed in jeans and T-shirts was the brunette dancing beside him, wearing a snug tank top and a skirt the size of an oven mitt.

She let her gaze slowly rise past Bran's shoulder. When

her eyes locked on to the professor's, his mouth curved. He winked.

She knew it was crazy, but for a mindless instant she was back in her car, struggling against the cold links of chain garroting her neck. Fear skittered through her, snatching her breath away, making her tremble.

Settling his palm at the small of her back, Bran drew her closer. "Steady," he murmured. As the music pumped over them, the professor and his partner disappeared amid the sea of other dancers.

"Do we need to keep them in view?" Tory asked, while their bodies swayed in synch.

"Not right now." Easing his head back, he met her gaze. "Nate and C.O. are on that side of the dance floor. They'll watch him." His eyes narrowed. "Are you okay?"

"He winked at me."

Beneath her clammy palm, Bran's shoulder went as taut as high-tension wire. "The professor?"

"Yes. Made my skin crawl."

"Heath and his pals can't get to you again." His voice was a lethal whisper, his mouth hard and unsmiling. "I'll make sure of that."

She could feel his heart beating against hers, quick now, and not too steady. Although logic told her it was due to having a man who might possibly lead them to Heath nearby, that didn't stop her from acknowledging how well their bodies fit together, as if their molds had been made to match. Of how right it felt to have his arm locked around her waist and his fingers entwined with hers.

"I trust you not to let Heath...," Her voice trailed off. After last night, the word *trust* wasn't exactly the smartest one to use.

"You trust me with your safety, but in no other way. I got that message loud and clear."

The hot-wired edginess inside her turned her belly into a minefield. Without thinking, she slid her hand over his shoulder so her fingers brushed the back of his neck. "Bran, I—"

He halted his steps at the same instant the music died. For a moment they stood unmoving, he staring at her with eyes that sliced at her heart. It was just as well their dance had ended, since she had no idea what she'd been about to say.

His fingers untangled from hers as he took a half step back. "How about we sit the next one out?"

They now knew what the professor looked like. They could watch him from a distance. Watch him, without continuing to touch each other.

"Good idea." Turning, she moved back toward the bar, waging a marathon-struggle against a longing too deep for words. Too wide for tears.

Two hours later, Bran clicked off the untraceable cell phone the FBI had loaned him. Disgusted, he tossed it on the dash of the SUV he'd checked out of the department's asset forfeiture lot.

"Dammit to hell," he muttered, giving serious thought to snapping the steering wheel in two with his bare hands.

"What did Nate say?" Tory asked from the passenger seat.

He looked her way. When they'd left Chappell's a few minutes earlier, he had moved the SUV to the far reaches of the club's lot. With the idling vehicle parked in heavy shadow beyond the last of the sodium-vapor arcs, her face was a canvas of gray light and shadows.

"He and C.O. lost the professor."

Tory groaned. "How?"

"A cement truck blasted through the red light at an

intersection. Nate had to do some fancy steering to avoid getting rammed broadside. When he finally got back on the road, the professor was gone.''

Bran was aware that Tory had tailed numerous people in her career as a P.I. So she knew that, contrary to its representation in film and on television, vehicular surveillance had a small success rate. Even with a team of three or four vehicles tailing one, too many things were left to chance. And more often than not, something went wrong. Like Nate's too-close encounter with the cement truck.

''What was the professor driving?''

''A motorcycle. Harley.'' Shifting forward, Bran turned up the heater's fan. ''Nate said there were plenty of curving side streets he could have turned off on. Another reason the professor disappeared from view so fast.''

''Does Nate think he snapped to the fact he'd picked up a tail?''

''No. The guy wasn't weaving in and out of traffic or taking any other sort of evasive action that made Nate think he knew he was being followed.''

''Has Nate had a chance to run the Harley's tag?''

''Yeah, it checks to a Harry Smith. Nate ran the name through the department's database. He got no information back on the name.''

''What about the address on the motorcycle's registration?''

''It's an empty lot on the city's southeast side. There was a house there until about six months ago when the city condemned, then demolished it.''

''So, this Harry Smith could have lived there, and never bothered to get his address changed on his license?''

''It's possible.'' Bran bounced a fist against the steering wheel. ''We have to wait until the Department of Motor Vehicles opens in the morning to get a look at the picture of the guy they've got on file to see if it matches the professor. Nate'll also run the name through the utility companies to find out if they've got this guy as a customer.''

''Harry Smith,'' she said, then frowned at him through the shadows.

''What?''

''He doesn't look like a Harry.''

Bran arched a brow. ''What the hell does a guy named Harry look like?''

''Not like the professor. When I saw him up close, my first impression was that he looked like a poet. Not like a guy named Harry.''

It was Bran's turn to frown. ''Did you form that opinion before or after he winked at you?''

''Before.''

When she'd first told him about the wink, the thought of the bastard flirting with her had lodged in his brain like a tumor. It'd been all he could do not to smash his fist into the guy's face. That reaction, he knew, had nothing to do with his being a cop, and everything to do with his being her husband.

For the time being, anyway.

He scrubbed his hand over his jaw. Christ, why did all of his thoughts have to circle back to their screwed-up marriage?

''So,'' she began, ''want to bet that Harry Smith isn't the professor's real name?''

''No.'' He set his jaw. ''And my gut tells me his having the same tattoo as Heath is no coincidence. They're pals. If the professor doesn't have Heath hidden away somewhere, he probably knows where he is.''

Tory's gaze slid to Chappell's front door. ''Too bad we can't just walk back into the club and ask Kandy.''

''We ask her anything about the professor, she'd close down like a trunk lid, then tip him off.'' Bran pursed his mouth, his mind working. ''So, tomorrow night we come back. Keep our fingers crossed the professor shows up again. We put more undercover couples on the street, and hope to hell when he leaves that someone manages to follow him to wherever he goes.''

She nodded thoughtfully. ''After the professor walked out of that back room with Kandy, he danced with about ten different women. If you hadn't been around, he would have probably hit me up for a dance.''

''So?''

''That wink he sent me was a blatant invitation. What if I follow up on it tomorrow night and ask him to dance? Chat him up. Shmooze with him. Maybe find out something about him.''

''Forget it.'' Just the thought of the guy putting his hands on her knotted his gut.

''Forget it, and do what?'' she countered. ''Hope the cops don't lose him tomorrow night when they tail him? What if someone manages to stay on him, and he winds up at Kandy's apartment? We already know about his connection with her, so that won't get us any closer to finding Heath.''

''The idea of having someone dance with the guy is good. But not you. A couple of female cops can waltz him around. Get friendly with him.''

''I doubt any female cops have played in one of Jazz's poker games. I have.''

Leaning forward, she settled a gloved hand on his thigh. ''Think about it, Bran. I ask the guy to dance. The instant he tells me people call him the professor, I light up like a runway. Tell him I heard his name at Jazz's poker game. That gives us an instant connection. A reason to talk more.'' She tilted her head. "If he decides to excuse himself and call Jazz, maybe describe me to him to check to see if my story pans out, it will.''

Bran looked down at the gloved hand she'd placed on his thigh. He could almost feel the energy inside her, feel her thought processes revving, hear her mind racing, see her body bracing for action. Although he'd glimpsed the P.I. side of her before, it hadn't intrigued him as it did at this moment. Hadn't pulled at him. Hadn't made him burn from a combination of need and hot-blooded admiration, of aching desire and frustrated lust.

Hadn't made him want to latch his mouth on hers and claim her for reasons he couldn't begin to explain it. All he knew for sure was that she was his. *His.*

Since he had no idea what the hell to do about that, he let his frustration bleed onto the topic at hand.

"Dammit, you think I didn't feel you tremble when we got close to that guy? How are you going to hold up if he's got his hands on you?''

"I admit he gave me the creeps. I got a little shaky.'' As she spoke, she lifted a gloved hand to her throat. "It wasn't because he recognized me, I didn't see anything like that in his eyes. The wink got to me because just for a minute it was like Heath was there. I think until he's locked up, I'll keep having these Twilight Zone moments when I turn and see him standing right behind me when he's not.''

She shifted her gaze out the windshield. When she spoke again, her voice was like smoke. "It helped me to be here tonight. To do something that might lead us to him. Doing that makes me feel less like a victim. I've *got* to keep working with you on this.''

"You're a civilian. Cops should handle this from now on.''

"I'm a licensed private investigator. I carry a gun, just like any cop. I know how to handle it and myself." She gave him a pointed look. "You know it, too. My instincts tell me the professor is our link to Heath. Yours have to be telling you that same thing. I'm going to dance with him, Bran. Talk to him. One dance, one conversation might give us the break we've been waiting for."

"It's not a question of you being able to handle yourself. I just don't like the idea of you getting any closer to that guy than you did tonight."

"I know." In the shadowy light, her eyes looked huge, her mouth glossed and tempting. "Sitting at the bar, you made a toast to quick endings. I don't know if you were talking about just the investigation or us, too."

He made no attempt to clarify. How could he when he wasn't sure himself?

"All I know is nothing will be over," she continued, "or resolved, until after Heath is back in a cell. If my dancing with the professor makes that happen sooner, it'll be worth it. In every way."

He knew she was right. Logically, he knew. But whatever his mind told him, his gut wanted to keep her on the outskirts of the investigation. And, dammit, his heart just wanted her. Their marriage was as good as over. The longer they interacted the more they hurt each other, and still he wanted her.

He gripped his hands on the steering wheel and burned for her.

Chapter 11

"**W**hat's up with Bran?" Morgan McCall asked the following afternoon. "He's sitting out there, looking like he's got a burr under his butt. He about took my head off when I asked him what his problem was."

Standing in a dressing room near a worktable piled with bolts of fabric, Tory slid into the slinky tube of blue silk that was her bridesmaid's dress. "Out there" was Morgan's reference to the living room of the cozy cottage-like house owned by the seamstress who'd designed and sewn first the youngest McCall daughter's wedding dress and now Carrie's.

"It's the tension," Tory replied. "Over Heath. Over having our lives—everything—put on hold." *Over having to live in the safe house's close quarters with an estranged spouse.* "Bran and I are past ready for Heath to get caught."

"All of us are ready for that." Roma McCall sent Tory a concerned look while she helped her youngest daughter step out of yards of snowy silk and lace. "Are there any new leads on him?"

"Maybe," Tory said, thinking of the professor. "We've got a line on a guy named Harry Smith. Bran and I both think he's an associate of Heath's."

Tory ended the statement with a frown on her face. Even though Nate's visit to the Department of Motor Vehicles had verified the picture on Harry Smith's driver's license matched the professor, she still couldn't reconcile the name with the poetic face. "Anyway, we're going back to the club he hangs at tonight, hoping to find out more about the guy."

"I'm praying Heath and everyone he knows gets caught soon," Roma said, draping the dress across the worktable. "Morgan's and Carrie's wedding is two weeks away. I can't imagine the security precautions we'll need to take if Heath is still on the run."

"You'll have four cops at the altar saying 'I do' and the majority of the police department sitting in the pews." Morgan tugged on jeans and a black sweater, then smoothed her long blond ponytail. "Even the president doesn't have such security."

"I'm sure you're right," Roma said, then turned and took a good look at Tory. Her mouth curved. "Dear, you look gorgeous."

Holding a pair of spiky heels in one hand and hitching the long skirt with the other, Tory padded barefoot across the room. She paused in front of a full-length mirror, gave herself the once-over, then nodded.

"I have to hand it to you, Morgan, people will see this dress and think 'snazzy.'" She angled to see the back where blue silk dipped to her waist. The sleek skirt turned seductive when the movement parted a long side slit, revealing an ample length of leg.

"Snazzy sexy," Morgan amended, crossing to her. "Bran won't know what hit him when he sees you in this."

Tory said nothing. After two days of Bran's polite remoteness, she doubted the slinky blue dress—or anything else she wore—would have any effect on him. It was as if he had finally accepted the fact their marriage was over.

That the thought was like a dart to her heart had her blinking against a sudden ache. What was wrong with her? Hadn't it been that acceptance that had compelled her to contact a lawyer? To have Bran served with divorce papers? Although he hadn't said, she sensed he would soon sign them without further prodding from her. Why did the prospect of that suddenly make her heart feel as if it had started bleeding?

"Good grief, look at the time," Morgan said. "If I don't leave now I'll be late for line-up." She pecked Tory on the cheek, then her mother.

"Dear, on your way out tell Mrs. Jacobson that Tory's ready to have her hem pinned as soon as she's done with her other customer."

"Ten-four." Morgan grabbed her coat and purse, then dashed out the door.

Roma gave a light laugh, her dark eyes sparkling. Today her honey-brown hair was scooped into a neat twist and she wore a tidy jacket and trousers in rich chestnut flannel. "What Morgan means is she might not be half an hour *early* for line-up. That child has never been late for anything in her life."

Pulling in a steadying breath, Tory returned her mother-in-law's smile. "You and Mr. M raised six great kids."

"Yes, we did." Stepping forward, Roma met Tory's gaze in the mirror. "The one sitting out in the living room right now strikes me as very unhappy. As do you. I worry about you both.''

"I'm sorry." Tory turned, taking care not to step on the dress's raw hem. "The last thing Bran and I want is to worry you.''

"It's my job to worry about my children," Roma said quietly, cupping her palm against Tory's cheek. "All of them.''

The tears stinging her eyes caught Tory off guard. What would it have been like to have a wise, compassionate, giving mother like Roma McCall? she wondered. "Bran says while he was growing up, there was no slipping anything past you.''

"With six headstrong children, I couldn't afford to let much get past me." Roma shifted her hand, smoothed it over Tory's long blond hair. "Would it help to talk about it?''

"Yes. No." The thought of discussing her marital problems with Bran's mother had Tory's palms going damp. "I don't know what to say, Mrs. M. When Bran left, I was stunned and hurt. So hurt. The other night I said some things that hurt him." A frown tightened her brow. "And now I'm not even sure that what I said is how I really feel." She shook her head. "I have no idea if that even matters. I guess the bottom line is Bran and I just turned out to be a bad match.''

"How so?" No matter how mild they were, Roma's eyes were sharp and searching.

"Do you remember what I told you about how it was for me growing up?''

"Of course. Your mother shirked her responsibility, leaving you to fend for yourself, for the household. You had to raise your brother.''

"I watched her neediness drive my father away. In the

end, he couldn't stand to be around her. He left her, *us,* before Danny was even born.''

''Which is something you had no control over.'' Roma's eyes softened with compassion. ''And now you don't want to lean. On anybody.''

''I'm not sure I can bring myself to do that.''

''Do you think that's what Brandon needs? A woman who leans on him?''

''I don't just think it, I know it.'' Tory dipped her head. ''To be honest, Mrs. M, your son needs another Patience.''

''I can tell you my personal observations if you'd like to hear them,'' Roma began quietly. ''I don't know if they will help, but they might.''

''You and Mr. M have been married nearly forty years. All of your kids turned out super. I have to figure you have a very good handle on people.''

''Believe me, a lot of things were hit and miss for me when it came to marriage and raising a family,'' Roma said. ''But when Brandon was born, I knew nothing about raising children. I relaxed after Nathan and Joshua came along. Then the girls. A lot of my being able to relax had to do with Brandon's stepping naturally into big-brother mode. He was always a fierce protector, especially of the girls. With me getting my landscaping business off the ground and Ian working his shift at the department, the girls got into the habit of turning to Brandon when toys needed to be fixed and knees got scraped.'' Roma's mouth twitched. ''Or some boy got overly friendly. Always, Brandon took control, dealt with whatever came along and generally made things better. When he met Patience, she was happy to have him do that for her, too.''

''And *he* was happy doing that.'' Tory raised a shoulder, shifting a thin, blue-silk strap against her flesh. ''Then she died and I came along—''

"And I'm thankful you did."

"Even though your eldest son is sitting out there on the couch right now, brooding?"

"Even though. Tory, I loved Patience with all my heart, and I grieved when she died. It was a terrible time for all of us. But in my heart I always wished she had been a little more strong-willed. Like you. You're a much better match for Brandon."

Tory wouldn't have been more surprised if her mother-in-law had picked up a bolt of fabric and hit her over the head. "I'm...excuse me?"

"Brandon and Patience started dating when they were in junior high. With her, he didn't have to change from big-brother role, he just continued in control, dealing with whatever came along. It was Patience's nature to shy away from confrontation and she deferred to Brandon without what I'm sure was conscious thought. I don't believe they ever even argued. For myself, I can't begin to imagine being married to a hardheaded Scotsman and not finding anything to argue about." Roma shook her head. "At times I've been so angry with Ian that I've been tempted to order him outside to spend a few nights with the dog."

Tory's mouth twitched at the image of her tall, strapping father-in-law huddled in the doghouse with the McCalls' German Shepherd, Fiona. "Arguing is one thing Bran and I seem to excel at."

"Because you're so much alike," Roma said simply.

"Too much. That's the problem."

"Not the way I see things, Tory. In my mind, equals make the best marriage. You're equals, yet you have different strengths, which complement your different weaknesses. What you're not good at, Brandon is. What he's not good at, you are."

"If we're such a good match, how come we want to

brain each other with the handiest blunt object most of the time?''

''I can't give you a definitive answer,'' Roma said gently. ''All I can say is that marriage is a school of learning all to itself. You learn about compromise, not only about where your spouse is willing to bend, but yourself as well.''

''What if neither is willing to bend? Or can't bend?''

''In that case, I'd say the love necessary to hold a marriage together just isn't there.''

The memory of how good things had been between her and Bran when they'd first met rose inside Tory, taking her breath. ''I...wouldn't have married your son if I hadn't loved him. I think the same goes for Bran where I'm concerned.''

''I saw how the two of you were together before the problems started crowding in. It was obvious how much you loved each other.''

''And now?''

Sighing, Roma pressed a kiss to her cheek. ''I don't think either of you would be so unhappy if your feelings for each other had changed.''

''Bro, you have to keep in mind Tory knows what she's doing,'' Nate McCall said that night when he edged in beside Bran's barstool. Clad in gray wool slacks and a crisp white shirt, its sleeves rolled up two careful turns, Nate looked more like a mid-level executive than a homicide cop.

He caught a bartender's attention, ordered a bottled beer. ''She's a pro,'' Nate added, his voice low enough to negate any remote possibility of being heard over the band's steady beat.

"If I didn't think she could handle herself, she wouldn't be where she is right now."

Keeping his eyes on Tory's reflection in the mirrored pillar in the center of the island bar, Bran felt adrenaline bolt into his bloodstream while he watched her tug the professor onto the dance floor. The greasy pool of emotion that churned in his gut had him tightening his fingers on the glass of Scotch he'd yet to drink from.

As she had last night, she wore the dark, spiky wig and brown contact lenses. Instead of the miniskirt, she'd opted for a pair of skinny black slacks that missed covering her navel by a good inch. The hem of her red sweater stopped short of her waist. The tiny silver bar in her belly button glinted when the light was just right.

Against his drink glass, Bran's fingers itched to touch that small piece of silver.

Nate raised a brow. "So, that's my point. Since you know she can handle herself, you ought to relax."

"I *am* relaxed."

"Is that why you look like you've got a metal rod for a spine?"

Biting back a curse, Bran forced himself to loosen up, muscle by muscle.

"Nothing's going to happen to her," Nate said. "We've got undercover cops outside. There are three cop couples mixed in with the other dancers on the floor. I'm here. You're here. Tory's safe."

"Yeah." The band's melodic, druggy rhythm seeped into his brain. "I don't like the fact he's got his hands on her."

Nate paid for the long neck the bartender delivered, then shot Bran a smug smile. "Because we're pretty sure Harry Smith's connected to Heath, or because she's your wife? Or maybe a little of both?"

Bran slicked a cool, killing look his brother's way. "Back off, Dr. Phil."

Nate sipped his beer. "Guess that answers my question."

"I wish to hell other answers were as easy to dig up."

"Like what?"

"Earlier today, I took Tory over to that seamstress's house. The one who's sewing all the wedding dresses? Anyway, it's obvious she and Mom had a talk."

Nate glanced at the dance floor, then caught Bran's gaze. "What about?"

"My gut tells me you're looking at him."

"What got said?"

"Who the hell knows? But it was something that made Tory get real quiet the rest of the day. A couple of times I caught her watching me. Giving me this unreadable look."

"Maybe she was admiring your great physique."

"Yeah, you got to figure she and Mom talked about what a stud I am," Bran drawled.

Keeping his gaze locked on the dance floor's mirrored reflection, he raised his hand to scrub across his jaw, and stopped short at the feel of the fake beard. Dammit, he didn't think he'd ever get used to wearing the disguise.

"The looks Tory gave me were more in the line of thoughtful. Deep and thoughtful."

"Those generally mean trouble for the male species," Nate advised.

"This observation from a guy who doesn't have relationships, just encounters."

"You got it. I get more than one deep, thoughtful look from the same woman, I have to figure she's decided our 'encounter' ought to shift gears. Develop strings. That's when I know it's time to move on."

In the mirror, Bran watched Tory smile at something the professor said.

You have lost me, Bran.

Her comment had been eating at his gut like acid since the instant she'd made it. Now, sitting there watching her dance with another man, he felt an imperceptible shift inside him, and he knew without a doubt his walking out on their marriage had been the biggest mistake of his life.

His life, which down the corridor of the next fifty or so years suddenly looked desolate.

No more Tory, turning over in the middle of the night and reaching for him. No Tory to share quiet Sundays with. No Tory to debate him, to stand toe-to-toe with him and take him to the wall when she disagreed with his views.

He set his jaw. It had taken him so long to come to his senses. Too long to realize his mistake that now there was nothing he could do about changing her mind.

No way he could see to gain her trust again.

No Tory.

"Song's over," Nate murmured. "Let's hope she found out something we can use about Harry Smith, aka the professor. I'm ready to get Heath and all his pals in a cell and wrap up this case."

"Yeah," Bran said. "The sooner everything's over, the better."

"Where you going, dollface?"

Tory glanced at the couples moving off the dance floor, then looked back at her partner. He was again clad all in black, his T-shirt and jeans showing off his well-disciplined physique.

"The band's taking a break," she said while attempting to untangle her fingers from his.

"That doesn't mean I want a break from you." Keeping his hand firmly linked with hers, he inclined his head toward the bar. "That guy over there you were dancing with last night?"

Tory flicked a look at Bran. Although he hunkered on a barstool with his back to the dance floor, she knew he was watching them in the mirrored pillar. Nate stood beside him, grinning while he chatted up a petite undercover cop.

"What about him?"

"He going to slam a fist in my face if you and I have a drink?"

"Well, I *did* come here with him." She adjusted the strap of the small leather purse that hung off one shoulder. "But he and I met just the other night so we've got no claim on each other."

"A woman with no strings is my favorite kind." His gaze traveled down, all the way to the sharp heels of her black ankle boots, then back up again. "Especially a tall, lean one with legs up to her ears. Let's you and I go over to my booth and have that drink."

"Sorry, sugar, I just don't drink with a man who hasn't properly introduced himself."

When he grinned, his poet's face took on an edge of charm. Tory had to admit that all that shaggy black hair, piercing eyes and dark stubble went a long way to drawing a woman's gaze.

"I told you to call me Lucky."

"You said that's because I asked you to dance."

"Yeah." In one smooth move he released her fingers and wrapped an arm around her waist. When his palm settled on the bare flesh between her sweater and slacks, she held back a shiver. She gave thought to the small black crow tattooed on the web of that hand, and suppressed shiver number two.

"I'll make you a deal," he said.

"What sort of deal?"

"You let me buy you a drink and I'll tell you all about myself."

She squelched the nerves she felt creeping in. She would let her system jitter later. "Well, I never could resist a handsome man."

"I doubt there's a man alive who could resist you," he said as he prodded her across the now-empty dance floor.

She slid into one side of the booth, remaining close enough to the end of the seat that he couldn't slide in beside her. Shrugging, he settled across from her.

"You shy, dollface?"

"Just like to keep my distance."

It took the blond waitress about five seconds to move in with her order pad. Kandy Krutchfield's expression was as cold as winter. "Get you something?"

Seemingly amused, he grinned at her. "Now, Kandy, don't get upset. Tracy and I are just going to sit here and chat."

"Better be all you're going to do, *lover.*"

Tory arched a brow. The professor's girlfriend was sending a clear message she'd already staked a claim.

After ordering tonic water with a slice of lime, Tory slid a hand into her purse. While the professor ordered for himself, she pulled out her compact with the small camera embedded inside, then a tube of lipstick.

"I get the idea you're not a single man," she said after Kandy stalked off.

"Kandy and I are sort of like you and the guy at the bar. We've got no claim on each other."

"Doesn't sound to me like she knows that."

He shrugged. "She'll get over being mad."

"Hmm." Tory gave him a slow smile. "So?"

His brow furrowed. "So, what?"

"You promised to tell me all about yourself. Let's start with your name."

"My friends call me the professor."

Her eyes widened. "You're kidding, right? I was around a guy the other night who was talking about you." She opened the compact, then pulled off the cap on the lipstick and swivelled up the hot-red tube. "Well, or some other guy who goes by that same name. I suppose there could be more than one man calling himself the professor."

Over the top of her compact, she saw the caution kick into his dark eyes. "Just who was doing the talking?"

"A salesman named George." She snapped two close-ups of the professor while she applied an arc of red to her lips. "We were playing poker at the same table. At a game run by a big man named Jazz. You know him?"

"Jazz." He visibly relaxed. "I've played in a couple of his games since I've been back."

"Back from where?" She laid the compact and lipstick tube on the table between them.

"Houston."

Kandy appeared and served their order. After spearing them both with a warning look, she moved off.

"Houston's a nice place," Tory observed. "What business are you in?"

"Oil-field work." He sipped the whiskey he'd ordered, then raised a brow when she left her tonic untouched. "Have you changed your mind about what you want to drink, dollface? I'll be happy to buy you something that's got more kick than tonic water."

"You'd just be wasting your money. Like I said, I don't drink with a man who won't tell me his name."

"I told you, all my friends call me the professor."

"You and I aren't friends."

He settled his hand over hers. "We will be. So we might as well start out on a friendly basis."

Clearly, he wasn't going to be more forthcoming on the subject. Since she didn't want to spook him with additional questions, she shrugged.

"I think there's just one small problem with our becoming friends." Sliding her hand from under his, she picked up her glass.

"What's that?"

"Kandy won't like the idea."

"Let me worry about her. You concentrate on me."

"Okay." She took a sip of tonic. "So, *professor,* in addition to doing oil-field work, do you teach?"

"You bet." He fingered the compact while his eyes stayed on hers. "You want to sign up for one of my classes?" The low, seductive drop in his voice sent a loud-and-clear message about the subject of the lesson.

"Maybe." Just the thought of him putting his hands all over her brought on the rusty edge of revulsion. "Maybe not."

"It's too bad I've got plans later or we could start your lessons now. You going to be here tomorrow night?"

"I've got a busy schedule, sugar. I'll have to check my calendar."

Chuckling, he bounced the compact in one hand, as if weighing it. The crow tattoo looked like it was in flight.

"You want to play hard to get, dollface, that's okay with me. I'm a man who savors a challenge. Something tells me you and I are going to get along really well. Become intimate friends."

"We'll just have to see." She tilted her head. "I'm a

cautious girl. I like to take things nice and slow while I'm getting to know a man."

"I do slow really well." When he laid the compact in her palm, he let his fingertips linger against her wrist. "All-night-long slow. By the time I'm done with you, dollface, you'll be melting like ice cream in August."

"Oh my." The nerves she'd held back began to drum. She'd never wanted to escape so badly in her life. And under the thunder of her heart she realized it was Bran she wanted to escape to.

With the thought too unsettling on too many levels, she forced it away.

Careful not to touch the fingerprints the professor had left on the compact's surface, she tilted her palm and let it drop into her purse. "Sugar, you sure know how to get a woman's attention."

He leaned in. "I know a lot of things, dollface. That's one reason they call me the professor."

Chapter 12

Bleary-eyed, Bran sat up in bed the following morning, sheet and blankets rumpled around his waist. Mood surly, he stabbed a hand through his hair, sure in the knowledge that no human being could toss and turn more than he had throughout the night.

His brain had simply refused to shut down.

One reason was the hit they'd gotten on the prints off Tory's compact. Wynn Yale, aka Harry Smith, aka the professor. Bran figured the latter alias evolved because the guy had the same last name as the Connecticut university. Go figure.

On Nate's to-do list was finding out how Yale had managed to get a legitimate Oklahoma driver's license in the name of Harry Smith.

Of more importance was the background check on Yale that turned up a ten-year-old arrest for assault when a disagreement in a Houston, Texas, bar got out of hand. Yale had been arrested with a pal—Vic Heath.

That decade-old arrest was the first firm link the cops had between the two men, other than the crow tattoo.

Unfortunately, Yale had not led them to the escaped killer last night after he left Chappell's. The undercover teams that tailed his Harley from the club had reported Yale drove directly to the apartment of the blond waitress, Kandy Krutchfield. To ensure that Heath wasn't holed up inside, an Intel Unit cop affixed listening gear to one wall of Krutchfield's apartment. The only voices heard had been Yale and Krutchfield's.

Aware of the distant hum of the furnace as it kicked on, Bran glanced at his cell phone on the nightstand. Since he hadn't gotten a follow-up call from Nate, he figured nothing else of note had gone down.

Propping his back against the headboard, he scrubbed a hand over his stubbled jaw. The dreary rays of weak winter light seeping around the curtain matched his mood. To himself he would admit it wasn't just Yale's link to Heath that had interfered with his sleep. It was the realization that had closed in on him while he sat at Chappell's: he'd lost control over a very big segment of his personal life. Even if he wanted to fight for his slinky, sexy P.I. wife, she had pronounced their relationship dead. Tory was lost to him.

Totally.

He felt the hurt, the anger, the bone-searing frustration starting to brew in his belly.

Had she felt like this when he walked out, he wondered? Was this what he'd done to her? Had he left her feeling hollow? Helpless? Lost?

Muttering an expletive, he shoved off the sheet and blankets and rose. At that same instant the scent of bacon drifted in through the heater's vent.

He clipped the cell phone to the waist of his gray sweatpants, then pulled on a sweatshirt. Since the only other occupant of the safe house didn't cook, he stalked out of his bedroom and headed down the hallway to check things out.

Pausing in the doorway to the small, tidy kitchen, he felt the emotion already brewing in his gut begin to churn when he spotted Tory. Having coerced one of his sisters to replace the silk nightgown and robe for more "practical" clothing, she wore a sleek black sweater and sexy black leggings that made her legs look eternally long. A clip anchored her blond hair into a ponytail that wove its way down her spine.

Her back to the door, she stood at the stove, muttering to herself while she used a dinner fork to prod strips of bacon around a skillet.

Burning bacon.

Striding barefoot across cold linoleum, he reached around her, flipped off the burner.

She yelped as if he'd scalded her.

"Fire's too high."

With a hot pad clutched in one hand, she aimed the fork at him like a weapon at the ready. "Good grief, don't sneak up on me like that."

"Just trying to prevent a grease fire."

She looked down at the skillet, then huffed out a breath. "One minute the bacon's fine, the next it's cremated."

"Like I said, you had the fire too high. What the hell are you doing trying to cook anyway?"

"Temporary insanity." She stabbed a strip with the fork, slapped it onto a plate covered with a paper towel. "I thought you might want breakfast."

He narrowed his eyes. "Why?"

"It's the healthiest meal of the day."

"So I've been told." He wondered dourly if the talk

she'd had with his mother the previous day encompassed some sort of scheme to get him to eat more healthily.

Tory glanced across her shoulder while she continued shifting charred bacon from skillet to plate. "I could scramble some eggs. *Try* to anyway."

He moved to the opposite counter and poured himself a mug of coffee. "Pass."

"There's cereal. Even I can manage that."

He studied her over the rim of his mug. Even when they were first married she'd never tried to cook. What the hell was going on? "If I want something, I'll fix it myself."

"Fine." She slammed the fork on the counter, then spun to face him. "So, is this how it's going to be, McCall? For the remainder of the time we're trapped in this house together?"

"Is this how what's going to be?"

"You sulking. Giving me the cold shoulder."

She took a step toward him, temper and nerves rushing across her face. For the first time he noted the smudges of weariness under her eyes. She didn't just look tired. She looked worn. He wanted to touch her so much that his fingers ached from it.

"Acting surly," she continued. "You've been this way for days."

"Excuse the hell out of me for my bad manners. You told me our marriage was over, that the only interest you have in me is to use me for sex. That you no longer *trust* me. You think that's easy for me to deal with? Think again. I'm as fed up as you apparently are with this entire situation. Problem is, this is the best I can do until we get out of here and end things."

Her fingers clenched on the hot pad she still held. "So, you're going to sign the divorce papers?"

"You keep hammering it into my head how wrong we

are for each other. So, maybe I've come around to your way of thinking. Yeah, I'll sign the damn papers and be done with it.'' He had to keep a grip on his emotions or his heart was going to crack right there. ''You can go buy that condo. Purchase furniture that suits you. Hook up with someone who makes you happy.'' Just the thought of her spending the rest of her life with another man made him want to tear steel with his teeth.

Standing stock-still, she stared at him, her green eyes dark with emotion.

''Why are you looking at me like I just slugged you?'' Frustration had him biting out the words. ''That's what you've wanted all along. For me to sign those papers.''

''It was.'' She lobbed the hot pad onto the counter. ''Then Heath decided to screw with our lives and here you and I are together.''

''There's not a lot I can do about that.''

''And *I* can't seem to do a lot about the fact I don't know what I want anymore.'' She jerked the clip out of her hair, sending a cascade of blond waves over her shoulders. ''I've been up all night, pacing. Around dawn I decided if I could find something to *do* that maybe some answers would come to me. Since I've cleaned my gun about ten times since we've been here, I couldn't bring myself to do it again. The only other activity option around this place is cooking, so that's what I did. *I cooked!* That ought to tell you I don't have a clue what I'm doing.'' She sent him a scalding look. ''Are you happy now, McCall?''

For an instant, fugitive hope reared its head, but he beat it back. Just because the woman was confused didn't mean anything. *You have lost me, Bran.* She had sounded pretty damn sure of herself the other night. Absolutely confident, in fact.

If pride was all that was left to him, then he would protect it fiercely.

"I assure you, I won't be happy until this entire mess is settled." He set his mug on the counter with a snap. "You got quiet yesterday after we left the seamstress's house. I caught you a couple of times giving me some sort of look. Does your sudden…confusion have something to do with what you and my mother talked about?"

She flexed her fingers then curled them into her palms. "Roma said some things that started me thinking. That made me look at things in a way I hadn't before. She made me realize I'm not sure how I feel."

"About?"

"Us."

His eyes stayed steady on hers. "What about us?"

"I don't know. What I think. What I feel. It's all just knotted inside me."

Because his hands had gone unsteady, he crossed his arms over his chest. With Patience, he'd never felt like he was in over his head. That's how he'd felt from day one with the woman who stood watching him with turbulent eyes. And he was pretty sure he was never going to surface again.

"All right," he said after a moment. "All right, here's the message I'm getting. You aren't sure how you feel about us. No longer certain you want me to sign the divorce papers. Am I right?"

"Yes." She shoved her hair behind her shoulders. "I think so."

He felt the first tingle of relief loosen the fist around his heart. Still, he frowned. He had never seen her so unsure of herself. *He* had never felt so unsure of himself. "Where do you suggest we go from here?"

She turned a little so she was no longer facing him. "What if I decide I want…"

There was something in her voice that put a hitch under his ribs. "That you want what?" he asked, forcing his voice and his expression to remain neutral.

She only shook her head. When she shifted her gaze back to his, he saw wariness, touched with heat, flicker in her eyes. "I'm not playing games, Bran. Or trying to drive you crazy. I'm just not sure if what we once had is salvageable."

He said nothing for a moment, his eyes on hers. "Do you want it to be?"

"What I want is for us to stop hurting each other. The other night when I told you if we slept together it wouldn't mean anything to me, that wasn't true. I knew that, but I still said it. I saw in your eyes how it hurt you. And I'm sorry." She wrapped her arms around her waist. "It was just a way to protect myself. Because if I do sleep with you again, it will mean so much more."

"For me, too."

"I just don't know if I'm brave enough to take that risk."

"Tory—" He was just about to reach for her when his cell phone chimed. Which he figured was perfect timing since he wasn't at all sure that touching her right this minute was the best thing to do.

While Bran answered the call, Tory turned, moved to the sink and stared out the slatted blind at the gray winter morning. The throb that had stayed in her head throughout the night had settled down to a weary drumbeat.

Had she actually been going to tell him she wanted to make a try at staying married? she thought with a quick flutter of panic. Had she been going to say the words before they had fully registered in her mind? Before she was *sure* that was what she truly wanted? Before she knew if it was possible for her ever to trust him again to stay when times got bad?

She drew in a shuddering breath. She'd been so sure a divorce was what she wanted. So positive it was the best— *only*—way to go that she'd felt no doubt when she'd told her lawyer to draw up the papers.

Then she'd talked to Roma yesterday.

And spent the entire night awake with her mother-in-law's comments running through her head while she tried to analyze her confusing emotions. The cold light of dawn had brought with it the realization that she couldn't say for sure her only motive for serving him with the papers had been to get Bran out of her life. Maybe, just maybe she'd done it to break the three months of silence that had existed between them after he'd left. Perhaps she wanted to get his attention. End their stalemate.

Her heart thumped while Roma's words tape-looped in her brain. *I saw how the two of you were together before the problems started crowding in. It was obvious how much you loved each other.*

What if, despite everything else, they *still* loved each other? Love wouldn't change who they were—two headstrong people who'd been unable to make a go of their marriage the first time around. There were no guarantees about a rematch. She already knew what it was like to be without Bran. She had survived his leaving once, and she in no way wanted to subject her battered heart to that kind of pain again.

"They came back? Why the hell did they come back?"

The hard edge in his voice as he spoke into the phone broke through her thoughts. She swivelled, her eyes widening when she took him in. His shoulders were stiff, his free hand fisted against his thigh. His face was a pale contrast to the dark murder in his eyes.

"Yeah." His mouth thinned while he listened to the caller. "Get back to me," he said a few moments later.

She stepped to him when he clicked off the phone. "What happened? What's wrong?"

"Drew Unsell, the wife of one of the cops from the credit-union shootout. Remember she lost a filling and left work right before Heath showed up there?"

Tory nodded. "You said she and her husband went to Hawaii."

"They flew back." She saw the unsteadiness in the hand Bran shoved through his hair. "This morning."

"Why? Why did they come back before Heath got caught?"

"Because they thought he *had* been caught. Unsell swears Captain Everett called and told him we had Heath. That the coast was clear."

"What happened?"

"They got off the plane here and Drew stopped at a rest room. Nate said it was packed at the time, a line of women waiting. Drew made it into a stall. That's where they found her, with a stab wound to one kidney."

A solid wall of emotion slammed through Tory. "Is she...."

"They had her in surgery. She died on the table." He swore viciously. Then again, quietly. "No one saw anything. Nate thinks whoever stabbed her tailed close behind her to the stall, stabbed her right as she was going in, then shut the door. You had the noise of toilets flushing, water running, women talking. A couple of women who came in on the same flight remember that some baby getting its diaper changed was throwing a tantrum while they were in the rest room. If Drew screamed, no one heard her."

Tory tried to force away her shock. Tried to think. "The killer had to have been a woman. Or a man in one hell of a good disguise."

"Yeah."

"How did the killer get the knife through security screening?"

"Nate doesn't know. I once arrested a guy who was carrying around a knife he'd honed from the snout of a marlin. The thing was about four inches long and as sharp as any metal blade. It's like bone, so a metal detector wouldn't get a hit off it. Something like that could have been used to kill Unsell."

"So, who made the call to her husband?" Tory asked. "Who knew where they were in Hawaii? Who could have sounded like the captain enough to fool one of the cops who works for him? Who would have been able to find out when they were coming back?"

"All good questions. All unanswered as of now."

"What about Wynn Yale? The professor?" She didn't even want to think about the possibility that the man who'd had his hands on her last night had stabbed a woman only hours later.

Bran shook his head. "The cop sitting on the apartment said he and Kandy stayed there all night. They're still there."

"There's one woman associated with Heath who's unaccounted for," Tory pointed out. "His girlfriend."

"Leah Quest. Nate's got a uniform showing pictures of her at the airport to see if anyone remembers seeing her there this morning. So far, nothing."

"She changed into a disguise in that department-store dressing room to lose the cops. If she did the murder this morning, she was probably in disguise again."

"Yeah." Bran fisted his hands and looked into her eyes.

"You might as well hear the rest. The killer left a note on Drew Unsell's body. It said 'Three of four.'"

Awareness rose inside Tory like a floodtide, lapping at the back of her throat.

She was the only one left.

The only spouse of the cops still alive. Four of four.

She imagined the weight of the chain looping her throat. Her breath instantly hitched; fear settled over her like an icy vapor, rippling against her spine.

Suddenly, the personal problems she and Bran faced receded into the background. Right now she needed to be held. Needed *him* to hold her.

"Bran." Stepping to him, she wrapped her arms around his waist.

His arms enfolded her. "I'm here."

She closed her eyes, felt the steady beat of his heart. "I'm not a coward," she said against his chest. "Not a wimp." A chill ran through her. "I just...."

"I know." He stroked her hair. "Heath's not going to get to you," he said quietly. "You have my word. I'll die before that happens."

With Wynn Yale their sole link to Vic Heath, the cops tightened the net around the professor.

That night at Chappell's, Morgan's fiancé Alex Blade paused in the parking lot beside Yale's Harley. Using a silent drill, it took the undercover cop ten seconds to surreptitiously bore a minute hole in the motorcycle's tail-light.

Hours later when Yale drove the Harley out of the parking lot, a team of cops followed. Using a leapfrogging technique, that team tailed the professor only one mile before passing him off to another. After several more hand-offs, Bran executed a smooth lane change on the busy interstate and had the Harley in sight.

"That's a pretty sneaky tactic, McCall," Tory commented from the passenger seat. "Cool, but sneaky."

"Yeah, Alex said some Fed gave him the tip about drilling taillights."

Bran kept his gaze focused on the brilliant spike of white light emitting from the red taillight ahead of their sedan. The white light was laser-like in quality and at night could be seen clearly at a distance of several blocks.

"We're on the other side of the city from where Kandy lives," Tory commented. "So we know he's not heading to her apartment. At least not right now."

"If Yale keeps moving, we'll have to hand him off to another team." Bran glanced toward the passenger seat. With the bill of her baseball cap pulled low, he could barely make out Tory's features in the dim glow from the lights on the dash. Still, he didn't need to see her face to know her eyes were shadowed with concern. That morning's news about Drew Unsell's murder had shaken them both.

Leaning forward, she flipped a lever, taking the heater's fan down a notch. "I just hope wherever he's going, Yale winds up leading us to Heath. Tonight."

"Tonight would be good." More than anything, Bran wanted Heath in a cage. And not just because he was a murdering bastard who no doubt still had Tory on his kill list. Bran knew he and his wife didn't stand a chance of fully dealing with their problems until the maggot was behind bars.

Roma said some things that started me thinking. That made me look at things in a way I hadn't before. She made me realize I'm not sure how I feel.

He flexed his fingers on the steering wheel. Since their

talk this morning, he had begun to hold out a simple and steady hope that he'd been wrong to think she was lost to him. That somehow, some way, he could get her to trust him again.

Just then, the right-turn signal on the Harley flashed.

''What's the status on the bike?'' Nate's voice asked from the car radio's speaker.

Bran depressed a separate foot pedal and spoke into the overhead mike clipped to the windshield visor. ''Subject vehicle is presently taking the Riker Road exit.'' The foot pedal and mike enabled the driver to avoid having to raise a microphone to his mouth, thus possibly being noticed and identified as law enforcement.

''Ten-four,'' Nate responded. Bran knew the other unmarked cars monitoring the radio transmission would head that way to take over the tail if necessary.

Noting that Yale powered down the Harley to the exit ramp's posted speed, Bran did the same. Clearly the professor wanted to avoid getting pulled over on some traffic violation.

Bran hung far enough back to keep Yale from suspecting he'd picked up a tail. For added insurance, earlier in the day Bran had switched the SUV he'd driven to Chappell's the previous two nights with a different make and model SUV from the department's asset forfeiture inventory.

The Harley went only a block before the turn signal flashed again. The motel Yale pulled into was three-story, built with all units connected in a U-shape around the parking lot. A neon sign blinked on and off, announcing there was still a vacancy. On one side of the hotel, a truck stop teemed with business. Several eighteen-wheelers were pulled up to a concrete fuel pad with a double line of gas pumps. A sign on the building behind the pad advertised that breakfast was served twenty-four hours a day.

Bran turned the SUV into the parking lot of a convenience store located on the opposite side of the street from the motel. He pulled to a stop, then depressed the radio pedal. "Yale's at the Sundowner Motel."

"He going to a room?" Nate asked.

"The office," Bran answered while his gaze tracked the man clad in black leather. Lucky for them, the office was lined with windows with no discernable curtains or shades. From where Bran had parked the SUV, the hotel's small office was a fishbowl.

Tory dug into her leather tote at her feet and pulled out a pair of binoculars that were three sizes bigger than her hands. Nudging up the bill on her ball cap, she peered through the powerful lenses.

"The clerk's a woman," she said. "Yale looks like he's in Mr. Charm mode, acting all friendly and relaxed. He's got one elbow on the counter, leaning in toward her. Smiling. He's flirting with her, big-time." She slid Bran a look. "Guess he isn't too broken up about my being a no-show tonight at Chappell's."

"Maybe he's just trying to salve his wounds. Doesn't look like he's in a hurry to do whatever he came here to do."

She peered back through the binoculars. "Unless it's to put moves on the hotel chick."

"Good point."

"Okay, now he's checking in," she said after a few minutes passed. "He just pulled a wad of bills out of his pocket. She's got him filling out a card."

Bran relayed the information to Nate, then added, "Yale just walked out of the office. Doesn't seem to be in a rush. Hasn't checked over his shoulder to see if anyone's watching him. He's taking the stairs to the second level. Opening a door to a room with no light shining on the other side of the curtain. First thing he does is switch on the room's light, so it doesn't look like there's anybody already inside waiting for him.''

Tory lowered the binoculars. ''He might be waiting for Heath to show.''

''Possible,'' Bran said. ''Or he could be meeting some chick at a place Kandy won't think to look. Because of that arrest in Houston, we can place the professor with Heath ten years ago. That's their last contact we know about. And since this morning, Nate's found out that Yale has a grandmother who lives here.''

''You thinking now that his being in Oklahoma City about the same time Heath escaped from prison is a coincidence?''

''Hell, no. I'm just looking at all the possibilities.'' He sent a smug smile her way. ''That's why they pay me the big bucks.''

''At taxpayers' expense,'' she commented, then looked back at the motel. ''I've got a listening device in my tote. Both rooms on each side of Yale's are dark, so maybe one or both are vacant. If we were in one of those rooms, we could listen through the wall, find out for sure if he's alone in there. And if he does get company, we'd be able to monitor their conversation.''

''You're reading my mind,'' Bran said. ''Even if he is meeting some woman for a session of burn-up-the-sheets, we need to hear what they say. Sex has been known to loosen lips. Lead to interesting pillow talk. We might find out something that turns this case in our favor.''

''We can definitely use a break.'' She slid the binoculars into her tote. ''Depending on what Yale does, we might be in a room more than a couple of hours.'' While she spoke, she kept her gaze directed out the windshield. "Maybe overnight."

Aware of the edge of caution that had settled in her voice, Bran studied her profile, both angular and soft. Just looking at her had the ache he'd been carrying around surging back to life.

He'd been feeling that ache since she'd told him she was no longer positive she wanted him to sign the divorce papers. Was unsure whether what they'd once had was salvageable.

Suddenly, sitting there beside her while the scent of her—cool soap and skin—stirred every hunger he'd ever known, he admitted to himself that *he* was sure about a few things. Things he had fully realized that morning when she stepped into his arms in need of comfort. *His comfort.*

It was then he'd totally lost the battle to keep his head above his heart. Holding her had been like suddenly having back a crucial part of himself he had spent months refusing to acknowledge was missing. He was in love with this sexy, take-charge, independent, hardheaded woman. Had never stopped loving her.

So, since he would rather die warring with her than living in peace with anyone else, he was going to have to come up with a way to get her back. Figure out how to erase the wariness he saw in her eyes when she looked at him. Manage to convince her she could trust him again, and that he'd been a fool to turn his back on the one good thing that had happened to him in years.

Letting instinct rule, he decided now was the time to start. He just hoped to hell he wasn't too late.

"Tory." Reaching across the seat, he snagged her hand. "There's something I want to say. Something *I* need to say before we drive across the street and get caught back up in this case.''

"I'm listening." In the glow of the dash lights, her green eyes looked huge beneath the bill of her cap.

The ingrained need to protect his heart had him hesitating. Truth, he reminded himself. No matter how much it exposed him, she would never begin to trust him unless he told her his true feelings.

"You were right the other night when you said I wanted another Patience. When we got married, I expected you to be the kind of wife she was. I *wanted* you to be. And I spent months trying to force you into the same mold. That's not you. It'll never be you."

"I'm not sorry for being who I am."

"You didn't let me finish. I *like* the woman you are, Tory. Soft yet tough. Strong but feminine. Until now, I hadn't seen both sides of you. Wouldn't let myself see." He shook his head. "I was wrong to walk away from you. I know that now. I should have fought back my temper, stayed and tried to work things out. Fought for our marriage."

Her hand trembled against his palm, and he could swear he felt her nerves sizzle. "If you're asking for a commitment or promises—"

"I'm not," he said, even though he was ready to make them to her. But he knew doing so would be too much. Too much, too soon. "You don't know how you feel, you made that clear this morning. There's a lot of baggage between us that we need to sort through. Compromises we both need to make. All I'm asking is that you give our marriage a second chance. Give *me* another chance."

"I...need time, Bran. Time to think about it."

"I figured that." He squeezed her hand before loosening his hold. "Take as much as you need."

When he reached to shift the SUV into gear, she settled her palm on his arm.

"Just so you'll know," she said quietly, "I doubt I'll think about much else."

Chapter 13

Tory drifted awake the next morning on a lumpy mattress that sagged in the center. It took her a few hazy minutes to remember she was in a motel. And that a pal of Vic Heath's had checked into the room on the other side of the wall painted an eye-popping sugar-pink. At least Wynn Yale, aka the professor, had been there last night when she'd closed her eyes and sunk into oblivion.

The weak winter sun seeping in around the curtain told her it was past dawn.

Smelling coffee, she turned her head on the pillow.

Bran sat in profile to her in one of the chairs at the round table they'd shoved directly beneath the painting of a clipper ship hanging on the pink wall. A green light glowed on the front of her audio surveillance device they'd set up last night, indicating the unit was monitoring the room next door. Another small light told her no listening devices had been activated in the general vicinity to eavesdrop on her and Bran's conversation.

Hearing nothing going on next door, she let her gaze drift back to Bran.

Dressed in jeans and an ice-blue sweater that matched his eyes, he looked lean, spare and tough. His sandy hair was mussed from obvious finger-combings; day-old stubble shadowed his jaw. He had his sock-clad feet propped up in another chair while he sipped coffee from a foam cup. Her gaze shifted to the hand he rested on his jeaned thigh. His fingers were long, as strong and competent as they had been the first time they had touched her.

Now, just watching him put a quick tingle in her belly, followed by a helpless little thud just under her ribs. She curled her own fingers into her palms.

All in all, the man looked deliciously inviting.

Closing her eyes, she summoned back the words he'd spoken last night. *All I'm asking is that you give our marriage a second chance. Give* me *another chance.*

She'd been right when she'd told him she would think of little else. And after she'd fallen asleep, she'd dreamt of him. Of them.

Even as hot, liquid temptation rose inside her she reminded herself that she'd had good reason when she'd asked him to give her time to think things through. She needed to be smart. Cautious. For both their sakes.

Her resolve strengthened, she propped up on one elbow. "Bran?"

He turned his head, his mouth curving. "Morning."

"Morning."

She thought about all the mornings they'd woken up wrapped in each other's arms, and felt her heart hitch.

"I take it nothing's going on next door?" she asked, determined to keep her thoughts safely on the reason they were where they were.

"Not since Yale turned off his TV around 2:00 a.m."

She glanced at her watch. "We agreed you would wake me at three so I could take the second shift. That was nearly four hours ago."

"You were sleeping like a rock." He tapped his fingers on the tabletop. "From the peek I got at Yale's registration card when I checked in, we know he paid for his room for three days. He's holed up here, waiting for someone or something. If that something is a phone call, the equipment we're using will only let us hear his side of the conversation. I need to call Nate, have him hunt down some spy-ware that'll let us eavesdrop on what both parties say."

"I can save Nate the hunt. Last month I bought a piece of state-of-the-art snoop equipment that can monitor both sides of Yale's conversation on his cell and the motel phone."

Bran arched a brow. "I forgot for a minute what a hotshot P.I. you are, McCall. So, why wasn't that new toy in your tote bag instead of this one?"

"Because it's bigger and heavier, that's why. As to its present location, my pal, Sheila, borrowed it for a surveillance job. Since you and I are stuck baby-sitting Yale, we can have Nate pick up the equipment from her. He can figure out some way to get it to us without putting a blip on Yale's radar screen."

"Sounds like a plan."

Shoving the sheet and bright red comforter aside, she shifted her pillow and propped her back against the headboard. She'd fallen asleep fully clothed and on top of the comforter. Although she still wore her jeans and snug jade sweater, her black leather ankle boots were now on the floor beside the bed.

"Thanks for taking off my boots and tucking me in,"

she said, making a futile attempt to finger-comb the tangles out of her long hair.

"I wanted you to be comfortable."

"I was. And you've got to be exhausted. Do you want to try to get some sleep now?"

"Later. I fired up the coffeemaker in the bathroom about an hour ago. Made it double-strength. I've had too much caffeine to get any shut-eye for a while."

She sent him an amused look while continuing to work on the tangles. "That's your typical M.O., McCall. Loading up on the high-test stuff right before your shift ends. Then you get home and can't sleep."

"I'm a glutton for punishment." He pulled his cell phone off his waistband. "Speaking of caffeine," he said while punching buttons, "after I talk to Nate I plan to pour myself a refill. You want some?"

"Sounds good. I'm tough enough to survive one cup of high-test."

"I don't know if you're *that* tough." Glancing up, his gaze met hers for one fast, hot beat before his mouth curved. "This stuff'll put hair on your chest."

His grin clicked her throat shut. It was the same one she'd fallen in love with before they'd even exchanged one word.

Her palms went damp. Her pulse skittered. Oh, boy. "I'll get our coffee."

She slid out of bed, snagged her leather tote from beside the nightstand, and headed to the bathroom.

Working long hours on surveillance jobs had gotten her in the habit of carrying around certain essentials. Digging a toothbrush and toothpaste out of her tote, she put them to good use, hoping the simple, mundane task of brushing her teeth might get her system to level.

It didn't.

She dashed cold water on her face, the pulse-points on her wrists, then attacked the tangles with her hairbrush, all the while keeping her gaze locked on her reflection in the mirror over the sink.

"Okay, who are you trying to kid?" she whispered. "You need time to think, but not about *everything*."

She wanted the man. Period.

Certainly lust had something to do with that, but so did her heart. And right now it was beaming the message that all the thinking on her part wouldn't put her and Bran on the road to reclaiming the closeness they once shared. Which, once accomplished, might help her figure out if their marriage stood a chance of survival.

"One step at a time," she lectured her reflection. "That's the smart way to handle this."

Feeling more in control now that she'd put her foot on the first rung of the ladder, she filled a foam cup with coffee that had the consistency of river silt. A stream of steam rose from the cup as she moved into the adjoining room.

He was sitting on the edge of the bed, his cell phone clamped between his shoulder and cheek while he jotted a phone number on the small pad of paper on the nightstand.

"Got it," he said. "Thanks. We'll see you in a couple of hours." After ending the call, he glanced up. "Nate gave me the number for the cops in the surveillance van across the street. He'll call Sheila, then get back to me after he figures out the best way to get your equipment here."

"Good." She paused inches from the bed, the scent of coffee and warm, musky male drifting into her lungs.

He ripped the page off the pad. "Last night the clerk

mentioned the restaurant at the truck stop next door makes deliveries to the rooms here.''

"Glad to know we won't starve.''

"Yeah.'' He rose. "I'll call and order breakfast. You want the usual?''

"The usual is my favorite.'' She offered him the cup. "I brought you coffee.''

He glanced down. "I thought you wanted some, too.''

"I changed my mind.'' She stepped closer until only a whisper of space separated them. "I want something else.''

His eyes narrowed on her face. "Really?''

"Really.''

He curled his fingers around hers, but didn't take the cup.

The feel of his hand on hers started an instantaneous chain reaction. Her nerve endings sizzled. Heat jumped along her veins, notching up her inner thermostat several degrees. Her body shuddered.

The heat, hunger and need in his eyes confirmed he'd felt her response. "You going to tell me exactly what that something else is you decided you want?''

She swept him a look under her lashes. "Do I really need to?''

"No.'' He slid the cup from her fingers and placed it on the nightstand. "But I'd like to hear *why* you made that decision. Why now, Tory?''

She moistened her lips. "I've been thinking about what we both said last night. You want a second chance. I need time to work through certain issues.''

His eyes stayed steady on hers. "Go on.''

"It dawned on me a few minutes ago that some things need less thinking about than others.''

"For instance?''

"At the safe house you pointed out certain activities we enjoy doing together. Like shooting at the police pistol range. Practicing self-defense moves at the gym. We should start out doing those kind of things again. Sort of a test to see how we get along. Take things one step at a time."

He settled his hands on her shoulders. "We can't exactly take off right now for the pistol range or the gym."

"Agreed." She looked at the bed then back at him. "You mentioned one other activity."

"And I'm all for engaging in it." He slid his hands up to cup the sides of her throat. "We've made some progress in the past twenty-four hours. I don't want to screw that up. Last night you told me you need time to think things through. Are you sure you're ready for this?"

"I think...." She blew out a breath. "I'm *tired* of thinking. Tired of trying to figure out if it will be good or bad for us to wind up back in bed." She raised her hands, curled her fingers around his wrists. "I don't know the answer to that. Don't have a clue if we'll figure out how to live together again. That'll take time. Dammit, all I know for sure is that I want you."

"That's putting it plain."

"You want plain, McCall, here it is. If you don't seriously put your hands on me right this minute, I'm going to implode."

He let out a laugh that was low and rippling and flowed across her skin. "Well, I sure as hell can't let that happen."

"Glad to hear it."

Her hands streaked up into his hair; the sound in her throat as his lips crushed to hers was one of triumph. The familiar taste of him shot to her head like hot, potent whiskey.

In a fever to mate they stripped off sweaters and jeans within the space of a minute. Driven by greed, her hands skimmed over his hard, solid chest. He fought off his briefs and socks, then tumbled her backward onto the mattress.

A wave of pleasure rippled through her when she heard him groan.

A part of her brain knew the image she made, sprawled across the bed, clad only in swatches of silk, her skin already flushed, her legs parted in surrender while the man she wanted loomed over her.

His eyes heated to blue fire as his fingertips skimmed the edge of the stringy thong that barely covered her. "These from my sisters?"

Nodding, she felt the soft, wet pulse between her legs began to pound. "The rhinestone-snowflakes-on-black-silk model," she said in a hoarse whisper.

"Bless 'em."

His hand slid upward; with a quick and expert flick of fingers, he opened the front hook on her black silk bra, tugged the straps down her arms and tossed it aside. He leaned down, his eyes filling her vision with a glittering steel-blue as he took the tip of her breast into his mouth.

And feasted.

The sharp nip of his teeth had her body arching. A whimper caught in her throat. His fingers skimmed down her ribs, her belly, plunged beneath the thong. When they entered her, that whimper became a moan.

Murmuring mindlessly, she dug her nails into the hard ridge of his shoulders and felt wild, reckless energy burst inside her. She wanted more. Wanted all. Wanted *him.*

His mouth moved to her other breast, suckling while his fingers reached deep inside her. She could no longer think, just feel. Fever kindled in her blood; she writhed beneath his touch and saw hundreds of lights dance behind her eyes. It seemed a lifetime had passed since she'd felt the tension and heat of his body.

Anticipation wound like a spring inside her, tighter and tighter, pounding for release.

The frantic hunger clawing viciously in her belly had her straining against him, panting, shuddering. Bombarded by sensation after sensation, she slid a trembling hand down and closed her fingers around him. He was rock-hard, and she could have sworn she felt fire burst in his blood.

She heard his ragged groan the instant before his mouth came back to hers, fast and fevered, strong and seductive. Their kiss turned quickly desperate, quickly ravenous. Insatiable. Savage.

The scrap of black silk that shielded her ripped jaggedly against one jerk of his hand.

When he drove himself hard and deep inside her, she arched once more and felt her muscles clench around him. Her vision grayed. She matched him for speed, for fury, their bodies moving in familiar synch, fueled by the same urgent, relentless need.

He sent her soaring up like a rocket, taking her higher, faster, forcing her toward the border between reason and insanity. Her senses battered, she went wild, nails scraping against his damp skin, heat pumping.

A weak cry of stunned release ripped up her throat. Still, he gave her no respite. She clutched at the tangled sheet while he continued moving, pummeling her system. His taste, his scent flooded her senses. The world narrowed until nothing else existed but the confines of the bed and the man who gave as ruthlessly as he took.

She crested again, her moan of dark pleasure echoing through the still air seconds before his own.

* * *

They lay in silence, morning sun seeping through the curtain on the room's lone window. The surveillance equipment on the table emitted no sound, silent verification that the man in the room next door had yet to stir. No roar of traffic drifted in from the nearby road. With his face buried in the curve of Tory's throat, Bran heard only the beat of his own heart. Felt hers beat against his.

He had the taste of her in his mouth and the long, firm length of her beneath him. His mind slowly cleared, bringing with it the realization that his weight was probably interfering with her breathing.

Propping up on his elbows, he gazed down at her. Her long hair was a wild mass of gold over the sheet, her eyes were closed, her cheeks flushed, her lips barely parted. "Can you breathe?"

Her eyes fluttered open. Her mouth curved. "Ask me later. My entire body's numb."

"Just in case...." He rolled onto his back, pulling her with him so that she lay sprawled across him. "Better?"

"Hmm. I have to say that everything's better."

"Are you including us in that statement?"

She lifted her head, her eyes pools of smoky jade. "We're better than we have been in a long time."

He smoothed her hair across the slope of one bare shoulder. "But not all the way better," he said.

She glided her palm over his chest. "We made such a mess of our marriage. If we do ever get to the all-the-way-better level it's going to take time."

"Yeah." He wrapped his fingers around her wrist. "I made a mistake walking away from you."

"You said that last night."

"I'm saying it again." Shifting her hand from his chest,

he pressed his mouth against her palm. "It was the biggest mistake of my life. One I won't make again."

A hundred emotions, all unreadable, crossed her face. "Our problems are still the same. We're the same." She shook her head. "We can't stop being who we are."

"You're right. So, we need to make changes. Work out our problems so we can both live with who each other is." He nipped her chin, then trailed his mouth down to nuzzle her throat. "I figure we got a start on working out things this morning."

"It was a good first step to take."

"Like you said, one at a time."

"Hmm."

Lying there, warm and sated with her sprawled over him, he decided to take the second step.

He curled his fingers in her hair, tugged her head back. "You told me yesterday you don't know how you feel. About me. About us. I get that." Even now, the prospect that he might not come out on the winning end of those feelings put knots in his gut. "But *I* do know how I feel. I love you, Tory. I always have."

She cupped her palm against his cheek. "You love me, but you left."

"I didn't say I was a genius. Patience and I were married a long time, so maybe I thought I knew how all marriages were supposed to work. I was wrong."

"I wish I knew the best thing to do, for both of us. But I just don't have any answers right now. Only a lot of questions." She shook her head. "Everything is still so mixed up inside me."

He pressed a kiss to her temple. "I'll be here, no matter how long it takes for you to figure things out."

"Even if it takes awhile?"

"I've got all the time in the world. And while you're

doing all that thinking, I vote we just keep taking certain small steps."

She lifted a brow. "Instead of the one we just took?"

"Hell, no. In addition to."

She nipped his chin. "Repeating small steps can be a good thing."

Because he could settle, at present, with having her back at least physically, he lightened the mood.

"So, Mrs. McCall, what do you want for breakfast?"

She tilted her head. "The usual still sounds good."

His hands streaked down her back to give her bottom a friendly squeeze. "I'd like to have a little more time to regain my strength, but if you insist, I'll give 'the usual' my best shot."

Her mouth twitching, she slapped a palm against his chest and levered up. "The usual *breakfast*, McCall. Hot food, and lots of it. I get dibs on the shower while you call the restaurant."

She rose off the bed, blond hair cascading past her shoulders, looking like a tall, golden goddess emerging out of the sea.

Just watching her, he felt himself stir. It was too damn bad one of them had to monitor the surveillance equipment to listen for sounds in Yale's room. And stay near the window to watch to see if he got a visitor. Otherwise, she wouldn't be showering solo.

"I seem to have a problem," she said, sending a pointed look at the ripped thong lying on one corner of the bed. "I have a few toiletries in my tote bag, but no extra underwear."

He grinned. "How is that a problem?"

"Apparently it isn't for you."

"Nope." Snatching up the torn piece of silk, he let it dangle between his thumb and index finger. "Okay, so I owe you a new thong. You want the same rhinestone-snowflakes-on-black-silk model, or something different?''

"Surprise me. In the meantime, you might want to call Nate back. Ask him to get a change of clothes for both of us from the safe house.''

"Consider it done,'' he said, watching her disappear into the bathroom.

When the door closed behind her, his grin faded.

Their relationship was on an entirely different plane now. One much improved over even last night. Still, he had no idea where that left them. No idea of the best direction to take for them to reach the "all the way better'' level. The only thing he knew for sure was that he intended to keep her in his life—for the *rest* of his life.

In order to do that, he was going to have to figure out a way to regain his wife's trust.

Chapter 14

"So, Yale hasn't left his room since he checked in last night?" Nate McCall asked the question several hours later as he settled into one of the chairs at the round table.

"No, he did the same thing we did," Bran said. "Ordered breakfast from the truck stop restaurant and had it delivered. Then he turned on the TV."

Sitting cross-legged on the bed, Tory did a visual check of her primo snoop-ware Nate had picked up from Sheila. The black instrument on the table between the two men might have been mistaken for some high-tech radio. The audio of the war movie on Yale's TV was a low hum on the air. A glowing green light confirmed that no other surveillance device was in operation nearby to monitor their conversation.

Nate glanced up and scowled at the painting of the clipper ship hanging on the bright pink wall. "This place isn't exactly the Ritz. How's the truck stop food?"

"Better than anything I can cook," Tory answered,

studying his grimy tan coveralls and scuffed workboots. He wore a red Oklahoma Sooners hat backward, the plastic strap across his forehead. A pair of geeky horn-rimmed glasses rode low on his nose. "Speaking of class acts, scruffy hotel maintenance man is a good look for you, Nate."

"I think so, too." Grinning, he rested a boot on the battered toolbox in which he'd carried in the surveillance equipment and a change of clothing for her and Bran. "All I need to do is strap on a tool belt and chicks will swarm around me."

She exchanged an eye-rolling look with Bran. Women already swarmed around the middle McCall brother.

Bran leaned forward in his chair. "Not that your love life isn't a mesmerizing topic, but I'd rather talk about the professor. He's got that ten-year-old arrest when he and Heath were nabbed in the Houston bar brawl, but no criminal history before or after. So, all of a sudden he needs a fake identity and somehow scams a legitimate Oklahoma driver's license. And it's an almost certainty he's helping his escaped killer pal. Yale could even have murdered one of the first two of the cops' spouses. Why? What's Heath got on him?"

"After we found out that Wynn Yale is his real name, we did some discreet checking," Nate said, his expression now as serious as his voice. "He and Heath went to the same school here until their freshman year in high school. That's when Yale's family moved to Houston. One of our guys talked to the principal at the junior high Heath and Yale attended. During one summer break, Yale, his kid brother and Heath went swimming in a farm pond. Yale's brother got the cramps, and went under. He would have drowned if it hadn't been for Heath."

Bran nodded. "So, Yale owed Heath for saving the kid."

"Right. The principal said it wasn't long after that they all showed up at school with the crow tattoos. Fast forward to the present. Heath's younger brother and cousin die during the credit-union robbery. Yale maybe figured his way of paying back Vic was to help him get revenge against cops."

Outside, a car door slammed. Since Tory was closest to the window she slid off the mattress and inched the curtain back.

Her eyes narrowed when she saw the tall, slim woman with red hair on the brassy side. With one hip cocked, she leaned into the passenger window of a cab to hand the driver a folded bill. She wore a white turtleneck sweater beneath a fluffy cropped fake fur jacket and jeans that looked as if they'd been painted on. A purse and an oversized tote bag hung over one shoulder.

Tory thought back to the mug shot of Heath's girlfriend that Nate had shown her the day she and Bran moved into the safe house. "Leah Quest just showed up," she said quietly.

Bran and Nate both moved to the window, taking turns at a covert look outside.

"That's her," Bran concurred, then turned back to the window.

"Yeah." Nate's mouth settled in a grim line. "We've checked the airport surveillance tapes. If Quest murdered Drew Unsell in the women's rest room, she was in a good enough disguise that we can't spot her on tape."

"She's taking the stairs this way." Bran's voice was ice-cold. "It'll be interesting to hear what she and the professor have to say."

Bran sat on the bed while Tory took his chair at the

table. She did a quick check of the equipment's settings, then adjusted the volume control. When Quest knocked on the door to the adjoining room, the sound came clearly through the speaker.

As did the conversation between her and Wynn Yale.

"How you doing, handsome?"

"Now that you've made it here safe, great."

"Guess you'll be taking off now?"

"That's the plan. I left the room key on the nightstand. Room's paid up for three days."

"I'm hoping I won't be here that long."

"Tell the man to stay safe."

"Will do, handsome. Just as soon as I see him."

The door to the room opened, then clicked shut.

Bran moved back to the window. "Yale's heading down the stairs," he said quietly. "Making a beeline across the parking lot to the Harley."

While Bran spoke, Nate dug a small handheld radio from one of the pockets of his coveralls. Keeping his voice low, he radioed the two cops in the surveillance van parked across the street at the convenience store.

Tory heard the Harley's engine roar to life, then the motorcycle drove away in a blast of noise.

After signing off, Nate set the radio on the table. "I'll leave this in case you need to contact the surveillance team in a hurry."

"Don't you need the radio?" Tory asked.

"I've got a spare with me. We have two unmarked cars nearby to tail the Harley. I'll catch up and stay close in case they need me to leapfrog and help keep tabs on Yale."

He picked up the toolbox, dropped a kiss on the top of Tory's head. "If Heath is 'the man' Yale and Quest were talking about—and I'm betting he is—we at least know she's in contact with him. Which means he might show up next door.''

''I'm hoping he does.'' Bran stepped to the door, his eyes narrowed, glinting.

Nate gripped his brother's upper arm. ''Look, I know you've got a personal score to settle with the bastard.'' Nate glanced at Tory. ''We all do. But no heroics, bro. If Heath shows, call in the troops. They're right across the street.''

''Yeah.''

Just then, the volume of the television set next door jacked up. The audio from what was obviously some shopping channel show blasted out of Tory's equipment.

Grimacing, she adjusted the volume. ''Let's hope we don't have to listen to that for long.''

''Better you than me.'' Nate shoved his horn-rims higher on the bridge of his nose, then slipped out the door.

Bran bolted it behind his brother, then turned. ''So, we wait.''

''Looks like it.'' She took in the lines that fanned from the corners of his eyes, the fatigue in his face. ''You were up all night. Why don't you get some sleep while I listen to the shopping channel? Who knows, I might hear about a bargain I can't resist.''

''Hitting the bed sounds good.'' He cupped his hand against her cheek. ''You want to join me?''

Her pulse scrambled at his touch. ''I doubt you'd get much sleep if I did.''

''I wasn't thinking about sleep.''

''I know.'' Smiling, she batted his hand away. ''Cool your jets, Lieutenant, and get some rest.''

''I'll save you a spot in case you change your mind.'' He pressed a kiss against her temple before moving toward the bed.

Tory diverted her gaze to her equipment. But her

thoughts stayed on the gorgeous, sexy man settling on the mattress a few feet away.

Her husband.

For months she'd allowed herself to think of him only as a loose end she needed to tie up. Now they were back to having spectacular sex. She wanted the intimacy. Wanted *him*. She doubted she would ever feel differently.

But would anything really change when it came to the other aspects of their life? So often during their marriage she had felt he secretly hoped she would somehow transform into the childhood sweetheart he'd planned to grow old with. *Quiet* and *deferring* described the Patiences of the world, not the Tory Dewitts. What would happen after Heath was no longer a threat and she and Bran went back to the real world? Would they be able to deal any differently with each other when the problems of everyday life closed in and tempers ran short, as they were bound to?

Or would they wind up right back where they'd been? Each unable or unwilling to fit into a mold the other wanted them in, with bed the only arena where they were truly in synch?

She pulled her lower lip between her teeth. She and Bran were both headstrong. Each liked to have their hands on the controls. Run the show. She had to wonder if they could ever bend enough, compromise enough to find a happy medium, discover some way they could live in harmony. And if they had no more success than they'd had the first time around, what then?

She raked a hand through her hair. More time, she assured herself. Surely with more time they would be able to sort things out. Maybe find some answers.

Two days later, a swell of moody music flowing out of the surveillance equipment had Bran rolling his eyes while

he paced the motel room. The music told him that Leah
Quest had just tuned in to her usual noontime soap. He
knew that after the current program ended, two more were
on her list of regularly watched shows. Later, she would
surf to a shopping channel. After that came some talk
show where idiots showed up to tell the entire world what
moronic things they'd done.

In all the time she'd been at the motel, Quest hadn't so
much as poked her head out of her room. No one had
come to visit. She hadn't received a single phone call. The
only ones she'd made were to order meals from the truck
stop restaurant. She'd done nothing to make them suspect
she was waiting for Heath—or anyone else—to call or
show up.

Nate had reported that after Wynn Yale had left there,
he'd driven his Harley across town to his grandmother's
house. He'd spent some time in each of the past two nights
at Chappell's, but had left and returned to his grandmother's.

All of Bran's cop instincts told him he was standing in
the calm before the storm.

Another swell of music surged from the TV next door.

He jabbed his fingers into the back pocket of his jeans
and continued pacing. In truth, Leah Quest wasn't the only
woman troubling him. His wife was, too, in a far different
way.

He glanced at the bathroom's closed door. He could
hear water beating down, could picture Tory standing in
the shower, steamy water slicking down the endlessly long
length of her.

You're not making headway, he told himself. He paused
at the window, inched back the curtain and surveilled the
motel's parking lot. Not a soul in sight. Angling his head

allowed him a partial view of the truck stop where big rigs sat at the gas pumps. Business as usual.

He turned and stared at the bed. Granted, he and Tory were back to having scorch-the-hair-off-your-skin sex at frequent intervals, but he was gaining no ground in other areas.

He could see it in her eyes whenever she looked at him, the wariness, the uncertainty. The I-can't-quite-bring-myself-to-trust-you-to-stay look. No one had to tell him that love and trust couldn't be forced or coaxed out of a woman like Tory.

When the bathroom door opened, he glanced over in time to see her emerge in a billow of steam. She had one of the motel's white towels wrapped around her, and she'd bundled her hair up with a clip. Moisture glinted off smooth skin that still held a flush from the warm water.

She gave the equipment on the table a visual check. "Anything going on?"

"The usual."

A swell of music had her cocking her head. "Ah, 'Pride's Passion' again. Is Alice making any progress with Chuck today?"

Watching her, Bran felt the desire rise inside him. She looked dazzling in the sunlight that bled around the curtain. He knew if he reached for her, stripped off that towel, they could both lose themselves in the mindless heat they always brought to each other.

And that was the problem, he realized. They had always taken each other with an almost desperate intensity. Three days ago, they had simply reverted to the way things had always been between them.

Now, he could curse himself for having been so willing to shove their unresolved problems into the background while they fell into the same hot, boiling sex pattern that had begun nearly the first day they'd met. If he'd learned anything, it was that sex wasn't a relationship. It sure wasn't a marriage.

But that's what they'd based everything on.

So it wasn't hard for him to believe a part of Tory might wonder if steamy sex was all they could ever truly share. Maybe even all he was willing to give her. Hell, he'd walked out instead of staying and dealing with their problems. He could tell her a million times he would stay for the long haul, but he needed to show her.

He needed to make her understand that it was so much more than sex tugging at him as he stood looking at her. It was the woman herself. The way she smiled, her distinctive scent, her voice, the throaty sound she made when he filled her. And, yes, even her boneheaded stubbornness and prickly nature that so often scraped at his ego.

She had been his wife for nearly a year, and for all that time he'd loved her. Yet, only at this moment did he understand—*truly understand*—what she'd come to mean to him. And now that he knew, he needed to show her. But sex was the only way she had allowed him to get close so far. As a starting place it wasn't what he would have chosen, but until they got out of this room and back to their lives, it was all he had.

He gave the surveillance equipment a glance as he stepped to her. "Alice is never going to make headway with Chuck."

"Oh, and why is that?"

"He's an idiot." With a fingertip, he traced the soft swell of her breasts just above the towel and watched her eyes darken to green smoke. "He can't see what's right in front of him."

"So much for Chuck and Alice." Tory's mouth curved as she slid her hands up his arms. "I have this niggling fear that I'm already hooked on that soap. That I'll find myself watching the stupid thing after we get out of this place.''

His lips brushed hers, retreated. ''Think so?'' He cuffed his fingers around her wrists and drew her arms down to her sides, held them there.

''Yeah, I think—''

''Don't think.'' He dipped his head to nuzzle her long, slim throat and felt her hands flex against his hold.

Her skin was still moist from the shower and he took his time, savoring the warm, heated taste of her. She shuddered when his teeth nipped the curve between her neck and shoulder.

''Okay, no thinking,'' she murmured while angling her head to give him ample access to her throat. ''How about letting go of my arms so I can get those clothes off you?''

''No.'' He brushed his lips with hers once, twice. Then he kissed her lightly, casually. And lingered over it until she swayed against him.

She made a half-hearted attempt to free her wrists. ''I...really...need to get my hands on you, McCall.''

''Later.'' He shifted his mouth to her shoulder and trailed kisses along the hollow above her collarbone.

''Bran....'' Her voice was nothing more than a low, husky flow. ''What's going on?''

''Something that should have happened a long time ago. I'm seducing my wife.''

His mouth found hers again and he slipped his tongue through her parted lips to deepen the kiss. It went deeper, still deeper until he felt himself sinking into it along with her.

Tory couldn't get her breath, yet she could hear it. He had never kissed her like this before, with such unspeakable tenderness. Her limbs were weak, trembling. She felt as if something was slowly taking over her body. Her senses. Stripping her soul bare. But she was helpless to prevent it.

She hadn't realized his hands had released her wrists until he took the clip out of her hair. It drifted down while his mouth drank from hers.

"I left because you never acted like you needed me." His fingertips brushed across her shoulders, barely touching her. "And all along I never showed you how much I need you."

"Bran." She gripped his arms to steady herself while her heartbeat echoed slow and thick in her head. She seemed to be floating, clinging to him as she glided inches above the floor. His mouth remained gentle on hers, exploiting weaknesses, frailties she hadn't known were hidden inside her, weaknesses and frailties that she didn't want exposed.

Her heartbeat hitching, she tried to deepen the kiss to take them to more familiar, safer ground. He simply lightened it again.

"Slow." His fingers worked the towel loose, inch by inch, his knuckles grazing the swell of her breasts. "We're taking this slow." When the towel pooled onto the floor, his hands stroked her face, her shoulders, her back. He settled a palm against her heart. "For the first time we're both going to feel more than just the heat."

His words sent a frisson of panic through her. She *wanted* the fire, the flashing heat. It was familiar. Safe. But mixed with the fear was a dark, thrilling sense of anticipation at being taken slowly. Defenselessly.

And so she felt herself yield, knowing instinctively he would guide her to where neither of them had been before.

He eased back long enough to rid himself of his clothes, then drew her closer. There was no fevered embrace this time when he laid her on the bed, just inescapable possession.

"I need you, Tory." His mouth skimmed along the fragile skin just under her jaw. "Not just in bed. Everywhere."

Degree by torturous degree, his lips journeyed down her throat to retrace the long length of her collarbone.

The lingering taste of him, the faint scrape of stubble against her flesh, the background noise of the TV playing in the next room. All whirled in her head like a drug, both potent and possessing.

His hands patiently, languorously explored every hollow and curve of her body as if for the first time.

She murmured his name, heard the echo of it whisper through her head.

She saw the hot flash of desire that darkened his eyes to an electric blue. But his hands remained light, gliding along the curve of her breasts, then ranging down her ribs to the flat planes of her stomach.

He pressed a kiss to her cheek while his hand cupped her.

Staggered by his touch, his tenderness, her heart stuttered in her throat. Arousal clouded her mind, racked her breathing, transforming it into a moan. Never before had she felt the same glorious ache that now stirred deep inside her. Instinctively she arched against his palm, desperate for him to ease that ache.

She nearly moaned in relief when he levered himself over her and slipped inside her, iron into velvet.

"Slow." He used his weight to pin her as she moved restlessly beneath him. "This isn't going to be fast."

Her eyes fluttered shut, her breath was nothing but feverish little pants as he moved in her: long, slow strokes. She curled her arms around him. She felt helpless beneath him, open to any demand. His hips moved, a rhythmic rocking that ignited small fires across her heated flesh.

Time stretched, became fluid. She glided her hands over his bare back, wondering now why she'd never taken the time to truly explore all the intriguing ripples of sinew and muscle.

"Look at me." Fisting her hair in his hands, he tipped her head back. "Tory, look at me."

Her eyelids felt heavy, drugged, yet she forced them open. She stared into his intense, unwavering eyes while he continued moving, the pressure building inside her, gradually. Deliciously. Achingly.

He dipped his head, his breath hot against her jaw. "I'll never leave you again. I give you my word." The vow was as soft as a wish. "I'll stay with you for the rest of my life."

Beyond words, she felt her hands slide bonelessly off his shoulders.

Merged, they moved as one, him filling her, she surrounding him. And this time when they fell off the edge, they went together.

I'll never leave you again. Her skin still slicked with sweat, her heart racing, Tory lay curled on her side, Bran's arms around her.

How could he know for sure he would never leave when nothing had…?

She halted the thought that had become so automatic over the past days whenever her mind turned to their relationship. *Everything* had changed.

In one long, endless erotic sweep, Bran had changed everything.

With emotion avalanching down on her, she closed her

eyes, needing a minute to settle. To somehow get her bearings back now that her entire world had shifted.

She had never before been seduced. Never would have believed helplessness could be erotic. For a time, she'd had no will, no mind, no reason. No control. Where power had been concerned, she had been totally his.

Now here she was, independent, take-charge Tory McCall, glorying in having turned over the reins of control, at least for a time.

And having done that, she didn't feel needy or weak.

Her eyes opened slowly on the realization. On the knowledge that she was the same strong, confident woman she'd always been. A woman in love. *A wife* in love with the one man who satisfied her needs. The man whose needs she wanted to satisfy.

And, oh, why had it taken her so long to understand all that? Bran had left because she'd hurt him by not thinking of his needs, his pride. He had never tried to run her life, or change her. All he'd asked was that she share her burdens with him, turn to him. He hadn't wanted her to capitulate, merely compromise.

But she'd foolishly refused, in knee-jerk responses rooted in her upbringing. Why, oh why, had she let her parents' dysfunctional marriage serve as a guide for her own?

Well, she was no longer rooted in her past, her fears. Was no longer afraid to open her heart to him again and trust. Simply trust. This man whom she loved had pushed down her last wall of resistance.

Shifting, she echoed the gesture he'd made earlier by settling a palm over his heart. "Bran?"

His eyes were at half-mast, his mouth softened with a faint smile. He lifted a hand, brushed her hair away from her cheek. "Hmm?"

"We need to talk." Her tone, more serious than she'd intended, had his eyes opening, turning wary.

"About?"

"Us. I—"

Just then, the phone rang in Leah Quest's hotel room.

Chapter 15

Tory and Bran were up and off the bed in a heartbeat. She bounded into the chair at the table and turned up the volume on the surveillance equipment just as Leah Quest answered her phone on the second ring.

"Hello?"

"Waiting's almost over. I'll be there soon."

"Lover, be ready for something really hot."

"Countin' on it. We're gonna need us some food. Supplies."

"I'll take care of all that, lover," Quest cooed. "Just like I'm gonna take care of you."

The call ended. Tory looked across her shoulder. Bran stood just behind her, his face emotionless as a mask. *Cop face.* "You arrested Heath once. Can you tell if that was his voice?"

"It's him." He grabbed his jeans off the floor, jerked them on, then swept up the handheld radio Nate had left.

Bran was advising the cops in the surveillance van about

Heath's call when the door to Quest's room opened, then clicked shut.

Tory reached the window in time to see the redhead stroll past. She was dressed in the same laminated-on jeans, sweater and fake fur jacket she'd worn when she'd checked in three days ago. Her purse and oversized tote hung over one shoulder.

Tory swivelled. "She's got all her stuff with her. Heading down the stairs."

"There's no cab waiting to pick her up." Bran looked out the other side of the curtain while he spoke into the radio. "She's headed in the direction of the truck stop."

"Maybe Heath's picking her up there," Tory said when he signed off.

"Possible. There's a food store inside the truck stop. She might be going there to buy the supplies he mentioned, then pick up food at the restaurant. Maybe planning to stuff everything into her tote and bring it back. Meet up with Heath in her room." Bran grabbed his ice-blue sweater off the floor. "The surveillance van is in position to watch the room. You and I need to keep Quest in sight."

"Dammit," Tory muttered when she realized she was stark naked. "I need one minute!"

She dashed into the bathroom, hitched on jeans and her jade sweater. By the time she raced back, Bran had his black parka on and was stuffing his badge into its pocket.

"I'm hurrying, I'm hurrying." She dug her ankle boots from under the bed and shoved them on while he pulled his Glock out of the nightstand's drawer. He jacked a round into the automatic's chamber, a harsh, ratcheting noise in the small room. Shoving back his parka, he slid the Glock into the holster at the small of his back.

Her system revved with adrenaline, Tory whipped on

her leather jacket, then grabbed her Sig-Sauer out of the nightstand. She punched out the magazine, racked the shell out of the chamber, then went through the ritual of reloading.

"Ready." She slid the Sig into the pocket of her jacket.

"Since we don't have all our disguise stuff here," Bran said, tossing her baseball cap to her.

"Right." Scooping her hair into one hand, she tugged it ponytail style through the cap's back loop then pulled the bill down low. She snagged her sunglasses out of her tote, shoved them on. As an afterthought, she grabbed her cell phone, clipped it to her waistband.

Now wearing his own ball cap and sunglasses, Bran radioed the surveillance van to verify Quest hadn't changed her mind and started back to her room.

"We're clear." He slid the radio into the pocket with his badge at the same time as he pulled the door open.

Although the sun was out, the wind that slapped Tory in the face was as cold as a morgue freezer. Still, after having been shut in the motel room for three days, she ignored the frigid air and savored just being outdoors again.

They took the stairs at a hurried pace, then fast-walked across the motel's parking lot. When they neared the truck stop, the roar of idling diesels and the faint scent of fuel filled the air.

As if in silent agreement they slowed their steps, not wanting to snag attention. She knew with the wind so cold and sharp, they both looked natural with their chins down and the collars of their coats hiked up to camouflage a good portion of their faces.

"I don't see Quest," Bran said.

Tory glanced sideways; behind his dark glasses she saw his eyes sweep over the truck stop. An uncountable number of eighteen-wheelers were parked near the concrete fuel pad. Even more sat farther away near the steel building that housed the office, restaurant and store. A pair of hefty over-the-road drivers stood near a semi, conversing and sipping from foam cups.

"Let's hope she went inside to buy stuff," Tory said. "If Heath is in one of those trucks and Quest is already with him, we might not spot them."

"If either of them is in one of those trucks, I can't chance tipping them off by using the radio out here. The guys in the van have already called in black and whites and unmarked units. They'll form a perimeter around this place. If we don't spot Quest in the next few minutes, the uniforms will have to stop all trucks that pull out of here."

"So, we need to check the restaurant and store fast."

"Yeah. I'll find a place out of sight where I can use this radio."

Chins down against the cold wind, hands crammed in their pockets, they cut across the oil-stained concrete toward the steel building.

Inside, the store was on their left. Facing them was a set of rest rooms, a bank of phones and a locked suite of drivers-only showers. The restaurant sat on their right, emitting the smell of artery-clogging fried food.

"Quest might be in there." Bran pulled off his sunglasses and inclined his head at the women's rest room. "Step in and look around. Don't let the door shut behind you."

Tory nodded, knowing they were both thinking about what had happened to Drew Unsell in the airport rest room. She hooked one earpiece of her sunglasses into the neck of her sweater, then slid her hand into her pocket. Fingers locked around the Sig's grips, she pushed through the door.

The rest room was box-shaped, its floors and walls covered with pink tiles that had to have been mopped recently with pine disinfectant. Stalls lined one wall, a row of sinks marched along the opposite one. A woman who'd tip the scales in the three-hundred-pound range stood at a sink, washing her hands. Quest might be good at disguises, Tory thought, but not *that* good.

She swept her gaze back to the stalls. All the doors were partially open. No feet showed in the gap between the doors and floor. Just in case, she sent the heavyset woman a smile.

"Hi, my sister said she was coming in here, but it doesn't look like she made it. She's a redhead. Have you seen her?"

"Nope. Nobody in here but me."

"Thanks."

Tory reversed two steps, bumped into Bran. When it came to watching her back, he was doing it literally.

"I need to have a look in the men's room," he said. "If it's empty, I'll use the radio. Wait here."

He was back in a matter of seconds. "Couple of truckers, in there. No sign of Heath. I need to get someone to unlock this door to the showers."

"We don't have a lot of time. I can peek in the store while you check the showers and restaurant."

His eyes narrowed on her face and she could almost see his mind working in their blue depths. "All right. Turn around."

"Why?"

Instead of answering, he gripped her shoulder, spun her a half turn and stuffed her ponytail inside her leather jacket.

"If you spot Quest or Heath, just back out and find

me.'' For good measure, he tugged the bill of her cap down farther. ''There.''

''I've got to be able to see,'' she muttered, adjusting the brim.

''I don't want them to see *you*.''

''You think I want that?'' Reaching up, she tugged the bill of his cap down. ''I don't want them to see you, either.''

Grim-faced, he looked down at her, his eyes shadowed below the cap's bill. ''After we find them, you and I are going to finish things.''

She blinked. *''Finish?''*

Without answering, he turned and strode toward the restaurant. Tory forced back her confusion and headed for the store.

She paused just inside its doorway. The place was a cross between a convenience store and roadside gift shop, with ice cream bars, canned goods and shelves of munchies vying for space with T-shirts, miniature cars and fake red roses.

Several male customers milled in the aisles. She made a quick study of faces, height, weight. Heath wasn't among them.

To her left a short, silver-haired woman was handing money to the skinny male teenage clerk. Tory had started to leave when she spied the double doors at the rear of the store. For deliveries, she theorized.

The silver-haired customer moved off just as she stepped to the counter. She nudged up the bill of her cap so she wouldn't have to lean her head back when she talked to the clerk. When he met her gaze, his right eye drifted slightly toward his nose. She repeated her ''I lost my sister'' routine.

''Yeah, a redhead stocked up on sodas and junk food,

then left a couple of minutes ago.'' Looking halfway cross-eyed, he pointed toward the rear of the store. ''She asked to use the back door 'cause it's a shorter walk to get to her ride.''

''Thanks.''

Heart pounding, Tory hustled that way while punching Bran's number into her cell.

''McCall—''

''Quest went out the back of the store minutes ago. Told the clerk it was a short walk to her ride.''

''The restaurant has a rear door. I'll radio the surveillance team, then take a look.''

''I'll go out the back of the store and head your direction. One of us might spot Quest getting into a car or truck.''

''Be careful.''

''You, too.''

Easing out a breath, Tory inched open one of the doors. Bright sunlight, frigid air and the din of idling engines seeped in around her. An alley lined the back of the building, wide enough for delivery trucks but not big semis. Still, from the rumbling sounds of engines and hydraulic brakes, it was apparent some were nearby.

The portion of the alley she scanned was empty.

Leaning, she peered around the door in the opposite direction. An oversized Dumpster sitting at an angle to the building blocked her view of the direction Bran would come from.

She stepped out the door. It had no more than swung shut when a woman's voice coming from behind Tory said, ''...forgot to buy cigarettes.''

She swivelled as the man and woman stepped around the side of the building. Her mind registered a flash of red hair and dark, piercing eyes.

Quest and Heath.

His eyes locked on her face. And flickered with recognition.

"Hold it."

She froze, her hand halfway to her pocket. Heath's automatic had come up fast. Too fast. He'd had it already drawn, she realized, held inside his coat. An escaped killer, prepared to shoot.

"Keep your hands up where I can see 'em." His sharp-as-steel voice sliced through the cold air. "I've been staring at your picture for days. Got your face, the shape of your chin, branded in my head."

Her stomach began to churn, and she cursed her failure to put her sunglasses back on to help disguise her face. Heath looked identical to the mug shots she'd seen of him, tall with heavy shoulders, unkempt brown hair and those deep-set black eyes. Now, though, a shaggy beard covered his gaunt cheeks.

She lowered her gaze. A cast jutted from under his left coat sleeve, his fingers extending past the hard, white prison.

In the seconds it had taken her to raise her hands to shoulder level, she had considered and rejected the idea of going for the Sig. She stood in the V between the Dumpster and the building. Heath and Quest were in front of her. She had no place to take cover. No escape route. At this range, the hole Heath's Beretta would put in her would make a nasty impression.

"Who's she, lover?" One hip cocked, Quest had her purse and tote bag slung over one shoulder. A plastic bag dangled from each hand. Her expression as she examined Tory was one of vague curiosity.

"Wife of the cop who sent me to prison. He helped kill Andy and Kyle at the credit union."

Quest's kohl-lined eyes narrowed. "She the one who murdered Kerr at the library?"

"Yeah."

"Kill her," Quest hissed.

His eyes lit brilliantly. "That's the plan. Been looking for you a long time, Victoria McCall." His sharp tone had gone almost singsong. "Had that Invisible Man geek tryin' to track you. Couldn't." He stepped forward, keeping the automatic aimed at her heart. "Figure your old man had you hid. Where's he?"

"Who knows? We're divorced."

"If you'd been divorced, the Invisible Man would have found that out in all the databases he slipped in and out of before I put him out of his misery."

Carsen Irons, Tory thought. Another of Heath's kills.

"The cop had you hid so good, I decided me 'n Leah should take a break," Heath continued. "Hitch a ride to Mexico with a trucker pal. Come back in a couple of months when you felt safe. Kill you. All of a sudden, I walk around a corner, and here you are." His face contorted with hate like a rabid animal's. "Now I don't gotta wait."

"Lucky me." Despite the cold, Tory felt sweat trickle between her breasts.

"You won't be sayin' that when I get you in the back of my pal's semi. Four of four."

Cold fear prickled the back of her neck. If he got her in a semi, he could shoot her, cut her throat, *do anything.*

"My arms are getting tired. Mind if I put them down?"

"I mind like hell. You're a P.I., gotta figure you're packin'. Leah, search her."

"Sure thing, lover." Quest settled her purse, tote and the plastic bags on the ground.

"Keep to one side so I've got a clear shot." He kept his eyes on Tory's face. "Move, you're dead."

She knew if Bran had used the restaurant's rear door he had to be close by now. Had to have heard them talking. Would know she couldn't make a move until after she was out in the open and had an escape route.

"Got a gun, girlfriend?" Quest started the pat-down at Tory's shoulders. Seconds later, she had the Sig. "Won't need this phone, either," she said, jerking it off Tory's waistband.

Quest slid the Sig and phone into the pockets of her furry jacket. Then she plucked off Tory's ball cap. "I can use one of these." She put on the hat.

"Yeah, yeah," Heath grated. "Let's get out of here."

"Things are looking up all the time." Wearing the cap now, Quest sauntered away, collected her bags.

Heath gestured the gun's muzzle at Tory. "Walk to me."

Hands raised, she moved, her eyes locked on his face. Her thoughts, though, were on his left arm. The cast signified a break. Weakness.

"Stop." When he stepped behind her she felt the cold steel of the automatic's muzzle press against her scalp just behind her right ear. Her heart stopped beating.

"Walk." He used the barrel to nudge her forward. "Leah, keep watch for her old man."

"Got it, lover."

The instant they cleared the Dumpster Bran stepped into view.

"Police, freeze!" He held his Glock aimed in both hands, his feet slightly apart for balance. His face was fierce, his eyes hot enough to burn.

Heath whipped the cast up against Tory's throat, jerked

her against him. The Beretta's muzzle pressed into her flesh.

Bran's gaze flicked to Quest. "Keep the bags in your hands where I can see them."

"They're heavy."

"So is the lead I'll put in you if you make a move," he said. "Drop the gun, Heath."

"Drop yours, McCall." He tightened the pressure against Tory's throat. She could still breathe. Barely. "Do, 'n you might get your woman back alive."

"This place is surrounded by cops. Hurt her, you're dead."

"You son of a bitch, you killed my brother and cousin." The muzzle pressed into Tory's scalp. "I told you—gonna eat your heart out, McCall."

"Your brother and cousin died because they shot at cops," Bran countered, his voice calm. Emotionless. "They went down shooting. We didn't just fire for no reason. They could have surrendered."

"Bull. You'd have shot them anyway."

"These bags are getting heavier by the second," Quest whined.

"Shut up!" Bran barked.

"She's got—" The cast jerked against Tory's windpipe, strangling off the warning that Quest had her Sig. Stars swirled before her eyes just as Heath eased the pressure. Air surged back into her lungs.

For an instant she saw nothing but Bran's face—hard as rock, lit with eyes blue enough, sharp enough, to end a life in one vicious slice.

"Here's the deal, Heath. You've got the same choice Andy and Kyle had. Give up, or I'll kill you."

"Well now, seems your woman is standing in the way of you doin' that."

"Not for long."

For the space of a heartbeat, Bran's eyes met hers, a silent message passing between them. Tory knew as long as her body shielded Heath's, Bran couldn't take a shot.

She *had* to get herself out of the line of fire.

"Oh," she moaned. "I'm...going...to throw up."

"Puke on me, bitch, I'll kill you," Heath snarled.

"Can't help...." She shoved her hands under the cast at the same instant she bent her knees. The motion tipped Heath off balance, pulling the gun's muzzle away from her head. Despite the cast, his injured arm couldn't support her weight.

Her shoulder slammed into the pavement. She barely noticed the shock of the fall as the rapid coughing of automatic fire filled the air.

Heath cursed.

Quest screamed, "Die, cop!"

Rolling toward the scream, Tory came up in time to see Quest aim the Sig at Bran. "No!"

The shot blasted a half second before Tory sprang. Head low, she used the force of her body to topple Quest. They landed in a heap. Tory saw a flash of brilliant light as her cheek smacked against the pavement.

"I shot the cop! I shot the cop!" Quest screeched in glee. Tory clamped her hand over the wrist of Quest's gun hand, dug her short nails into her flesh and delivered a stiff-handed chop to her elbow. The Sig skittered across the alley.

Deflecting Quest's fingernails with a forearm, Tory straddled the howling woman, who bucked like a bronco. Tory grunted as a blow to her ribs stole her breath.

"Bitch!" she hissed, landing two hard punches to Quest's face. A third crunched cartilage. Blood fountained out of the woman's nose.

Quest gurgled a moan while her eyes rolled back in her head.

The wail of sirens pierced the air.

Coughing painfully, Tory slid off Quest onto her hands and knees. Struggling to breathe, fighting the now-genuine need to retch, she rolled the unconscious woman onto her side to keep her from drowning in her own blood.

Footsteps pounded toward her. "Tory!"

Nausea ebbed at the sound of Bran's voice.

"You okay?" Standing over her, he clamped a hand on her shoulder.

"Fine." Looking up, she blinked to bring him into focus. His face was pale, his mouth grim. His other hand clenched the Glock, aimed in the direction where she'd last seen Heath.

"Quest," she panted. "Quest screamed she shot you."

"Have to check Heath," he said and turned.

Tory frowned. There was an unnatural carefulness to the way he moved.

A few feet away, Heath lay on his side, dark eyes open and glassy. His right arm was stretched out as if reaching for the Beretta that lay an inch from his hand.

Leaning awkwardly, Bran snagged the automatic, then pressed two fingers to Heath's throat. "Dead."

He straightened and turned, his black parka gaping open. Tory's heart hitched when she saw a flash of crimson.

"You're hit!"

She shoved herself up, reached him in two wobbly steps. Pushing back his parka, she saw blood had completely soaked one side of his sweater.

"Oh, God."

"I've been shot before." He gritted his teeth. "I know when it's bad. This isn't bad."

"Shot anywhere is bad." While sirens grew louder, she tugged him toward the side of the building.

"Slug's not in me. Just grazed my side." He blew out a breath. Then another. "If it'd hit anything vital, I wouldn't be on my feet."

"Sit down. Sit down." She nudged him into a sitting position, prodding his shoulders back against the building. "I've got to slow the bleeding." For want of anything better, she pulled his ball cap off, pressed it against the wound.

He winced. "You've got blood all over the front of you."

She glanced down. Crimson spattered her sweater, jeans and leather jacket. "It's Quest's."

"*All* of it's hers?"

"Yeah. I broke her nose. Gave her one hell of a nose-bleed."

"Good."

The surveillance van and a black and white swung into the alley, sirens blaring.

"Ambulance!" Tory shouted to the first cop out of the van.

Nodding, he lifted a radio to his mouth as he bolted toward them, gun aimed low in the direction of the suspects.

"Heath's dead," Bran advised the cop. "Cuff the woman."

"Ambulance is thirty seconds out," the cop said, jerking a set of handcuffs off his belt.

Tory shoved back Bran's parka. Leaning in, she did a visual sweep until she spied a small hole in the black fabric.

"Okay, looks like you're right. The bullet's not in your side." Knowing that didn't make her hands any steadier.

"I told you it's a damn graze."

"Yeah, Dr. McCall, you told me."

Beneath her palm she felt the warmth of his blood already soaking through the cap. *Too fast. Too fast.*

She jammed her free hand into the parka's pockets, searching for gloves, *anything* to help absorb the blood. She came up with a handful of folded papers.

These'll do, she thought and pressed them hard against the cap.

Bran grunted. "Christ, woman."

"Sorry." She was shaking like a wet dog in a cold wind. "I'm sorry. I need to slow the bleeding. *Have* to slow it."

"I'm fine," he shouted over the advancing shriek of sirens.

"You're shot!" She looked across her shoulder, saw the ambulance, its overhead lights winking in rhythm. "They'll stop the bleeding." She nearly sobbed the words. "Get you to the hospital."

He gripped her chin, pulled her head back around. His expression was set in almost savage lines, his eyes so bright they seemed to burn her.

"I'm not going anywhere until you and I finish things."

Chapter 16

"Look, Lieutenant, you need to let us drive you to the hospital."

Sitting sweaterless on the edge of a gurney in the back of the idling ambulance, Bran gazed down at his right side. The bandage just above the waist of his jeans was a stark white slash against his flesh. "You stopped the bleeding, Handle."

"For now." The EMT crouched beside the gurney was middle-aged with thick black hair. The wide handlebar mustache that curled up to his cheeks had earned him his nickname.

"I cleaned the gash best I could." Handle pulled his latex gloves off with a snap and dumped them in a small hazardous materials bin. "But there's bound to be fibers off your sweater still in the wound. Plus, those butterflies I put on will hold only so long. You need stitches. Quite a few. You have to go to the ER for all that."

"Later," Bran said. "Right now I've got business to take care of."

That business was the image of Tory that had branded in his brain after he'd made love to her that morning. *Seduced her.* He had seen the same solemn look on her face only one other time—the day he walked out. What was she feeling? he wondered, as a skitter of panic crept up his spine. Dammit, what the hell was going on inside her?

"I don't think you've got any business to deal with, Lieutenant," Handle countered. "I stuck my head out of the ambulance a minute ago. The ME's doing his thing on the dead guy. Another ambulance transported the redhead with the broken nose who was squawking about some woman assaulting her. There's enough cops in the alley to contain a riot. As far as I can tell, there's not much for you to do." Handle grinned, sending the curled ends of the mustache creeping up his cheeks. "Except go to the ER."

"The business I need to take care of is personal." Leaving his bloody sweater for the hazmat bin, Bran grabbed his parka, pulled it on and hissed out a breath. The gash hurt like the devil. Gritting his teeth, he did his best to ease out of the ambulance without too much of a jolt to his side.

His gaze zeroed in on Tory. She stood across the alley with her back to him, talking to a uniformed cop who was writing purposefully on a notepad.

Nate, wearing a black overcoat, stepped to Bran's side. "We've got the trucker who drove Heath here. And some uniforms just picked up the professor for questioning." He frowned when the back door of the ambulance slammed shut. "Don't you have a date with the ER?"

"I'll go later."

Tory swiveled at the sound of his voice. Her eyes concerned and intense, she rushed to him.

"You're shot! What are you doing out here in the cold? The EMT said you need to go to the hospital. You have to get your wound cleaned. You need stitches."

His stomach tightened when he saw the purpling bruise along her cheekbone. The blood spattered across her leather jacket, sweater and jeans had dried to a rust color. Because the knuckles on her right hand were raw and swollen, he grabbed her left wrist.

"Let's go," he said, heading down the alley toward the restaurant.

"Go where?" She gripped his arm as she labored to keep up. "Have you lost your mind, McCall?"

He spared her a glance. "I told you, we're going to finish this."

"You keep saying that." A gust of cold wind tossed her hair in her face and she shoved it back. "What are you talking about? *Finish what?*"

Without answering, he pulled open the same door he'd dashed out of what seemed hours ago. "The restaurant's manager lent me his office when I was looking for a place to radio the surveillance van. We can use it."

The office was no more than a cubbyhole just inside the door. The short, burly manager working at his cluttered desk looked up at the sound of Bran's voice.

"I need to take over your space again."

When the man's gaze flicked to Tory, his eyes widened.

Bran figured her bloody clothes and bruises had the guy wondering if she was a suspect he'd taken a rubber hose to.

"Police business," Bran added sternly when the manager hesitated.

"Er, okay, Lieutenant, go ahead." The manager pushed

out of his chair and edged past them. The door closed behind him with a sharp snap.

"All right, McCall." Tory tugged her wrist from his grasp and crossed her arms over her chest. "You've dragged me down here and commandeered that man's office. Whatever it is you think you need to finish, go ahead."

She was standing under the office's bright lights, and for an instant all he could see were her bruises, the blood. He held up a hand. "First I need to know if you're really okay. Physically, I mean?"

"I landed on my cheek and my knuckles are scraped. Quest got in a lucky punch to my ribs, so I've got a saucer-size bruise on my left side. Other than that, I'm fine." She narrowed her eyes at him. "Physically."

"I'm going to see you with Heath, with that automatic against your head, for a long time." Reaching out, he brushed his fingertips along her jaw and realized his hand had gone unsteady. "I gave you my word I wouldn't let him get near you. I shouldn't have brought you over here with me. Dammit, he should never have gotten his hands on you."

"It's over now." Her voice and eyes softened. "I keep picturing Quest aiming my gun at you," she said, dropping her arms to her sides. "Pulling the trigger. Hearing the shot."

"We both have some bad images from today to deal with." Fighting the need to pull her into his arms, he moved to the desk, parked a hip gingerly onto its edge. "There's another image of you that I'm not sure I know how to deal with."

"What image?"

"This morning, in the motel room, what happened between us." He shoved a hand through his hair. "I gave you…everything. All of me. I've never given a woman that much. No other woman. Only you. Then afterwards, I saw the look in your eyes. Heard your tone when you said we need to talk. I've seen that look, heard that tone only one other time.''

She frowned. ''When?''

''The day I walked out. I've got to figure what you were getting ready to say today was bad.''

She took a step toward him. ''Bran—''

''No.'' He held up a hand. ''I'm going to get through this.''

She halted. ''All right.''

''You're your own woman, Tory. Intriguing. Strong and tough. Tough enough that you kept yourself alive when an escaped killer wanted you dead.''

''I kept myself alive at the library when Kerr attacked me.'' Her gaze flicked to the window that looked onto the alley. ''Not with Heath. If it wasn't for you, I'd be dead.''

''I can say the same thing about you. If you hadn't jumped Quest, she'd have probably gotten off another round. Maybe scored a direct hit.'' He raised a shoulder. ''We needed each other in that alley. I've tried to make you need me in other ways. That's another thing I realized in the motel room this morning. I can't force you to need me, to feel something like trust or love when you don't.''

''No, you can't,'' she said quietly.

''You say you want time to think things through. To figure out if you can ever trust me again. Trust me to stay.'' He shook his head. ''I've done everything I know to do to make you believe that I will. Time won't change how you feel. You're not going to wake up all of a sudden one morning trusting me when you don't now.''

''So, what are we doing here, Bran? Are you telling me

I'm out of time? That if I can't give you a definite answer right now, you're leaving again?''

''No. Hell, no.'' He came up off the desk, ignoring the pain that sizzled through his side when he grabbed her arms. ''Didn't you hear anything I said to you in bed? *I won't ever leave you again.* I mean that.'' He paused to steady himself. ''But meaning it doesn't do me a lot of good if you decide you want out. So if that's what you were going to tell me this morning, then just say it.''

''And if I do want out, you'll accept that?''

''No.'' He leaned in, his fingers tightening on her arms. ''I'll figure out a different way to come at you. To make you believe me. Get you back. I can't let you go, Tory. Three months ago I thought I could, but I can't. You're who I want. For now. For the future. Forever.''

''Bran, stop. Stop now.'' The hands she pressed against his chest trembled. ''You're in pain, I can see it in your eyes. Sit down before you fall down.''

''I'm not going to fall down.''

''That's right, because I won't let you. You've had your say. Just sit and let me have mine.''

With pain radiating straight up his side, he complied. ''All right.''

She took a step back, blew out a breath. ''Right before the phone rang in Quest's room, I was getting ready to say a lot of things. Starting out with the observation that it's no wonder our marriage wound up on the rocks since we started out with the odds against us. We never talked, never had a plan. We just acted. We ran off and eloped, then moved into the house you'd shared with another woman.''

''Looking back.... Dammit, I should have asked if that was what you wanted. Given you a say.''

''Yes. And when you didn't ask, I should have told you.

We never really talked, never sat the other down and just talked."

She shoved her hair behind her shoulders. "That's what I should have done when it came to Danny, too. Talked things over with you. Given you a chance to get involved. I just didn't want to burden you like my mother had my father. I was afraid you'd view me as needy and weak."

"I wouldn't have viewed your coming to me as a burden."

"I know that now." She dipped her hand into the pocket of her jacket. "I see a lot of things now that I didn't then."

He narrowed his eyes when she pulled out pink papers, folded and stained in places with blood. Then he remembered her desperately digging through the pockets of his parka, jerking out the papers and pressing them against his bleeding wound just as the ambulance arrived. He checked his pocket, found it empty. There'd been two sets of papers inside.

He lifted a brow. "You looked at those?"

"While I was pacing outside the ambulance." She opened them gingerly, stiff along the folds with dried blood. "They're hard to read because of the blood, but I could tell enough to know they're loan papers." She looked up slowly. "You cosigned a loan for Danny. Helped him buy a car."

"Kid's got a job, seems sincere about taking care of Jewell and the baby. He came to me about the loan after you were attacked. He said with Heath out there trying to kill you that you had enough to deal with. I agreed." Bran dipped his head. "You think the fact he came to me for this makes me feel like you're a burden? That you look weak and needy in my eyes?"

"Before all this, I probably would have." Her mouth

curved slightly as she refolded the papers and handed them to him. "Now, I'm just glad I didn't have to deal with another one of Danny's problems at the time. And your shouldering that didn't take anything away from me."

"You didn't know about the loan this morning," he pointed out, stuffing the papers back into his pocket. "So it's not what you were getting ready to talk about before Quest's phone rang."

"True." She moved toward him, stopping when only inches separated them. "After we started sleeping together again, I kept thinking how wonderful it was to be back with you in bed. But we never had problems in bed, so all we were doing was having glorious sex. Our problems were still there."

She looked away for a brief instant. When she remet his gaze, her eyes were darker. Smoky. "So, this morning when you took me to bed, everything was the same. And after, nothing was the same. Your tenderness touched me in places you'd never touched before. You took me to a place I'd never been. A place *we'd* never been."

She stepped closer, leaving a whisper of space between them. "You said you gave me everything that was inside you. You didn't have to tell me that. I *felt* it. And while you gave, you also took. Every ounce of my control. It didn't make me feel weak or needy to give it up willingly."

He closed his eyes. Opened them. "The way you looked at me after. The way you sounded. I thought it wasn't enough. I gave you all of me, and I thought it wasn't enough."

She cradled his cheek in her palm. "How could I not look and sound so serious after what we'd shared? You melted all my doubts. Showed me that being with you, surrendering to you, didn't make me less than what I am."

Needing to touch her, *hold* her, he slid his hands beneath her jacket, settled them at her waist. "What are you, Tory McCall?"

"A woman who needs one particular man to make her feel complete. Whole. I trust you with way more than just my life, Bran McCall. My heart and my soul are in your hands, too. I love you. I *need* you. I always have."

He tugged her into the wedge between his thighs, gathered her against him, kept her there, while relief swept through him. He pressed his face to her throat. "We've wasted a lot of time being at odds."

She held on, her arms around him. "Too much."

"We'll both probably forever keep reaching for the controls."

She laughed softly. "We'd be idiots to think anything else."

He held her away from him, brushed his lips over her brow, her cheeks. "Who winds up grabbing the controls is going to take some juggling. Compromise. As long as we end up heading in the same direction, we should be okay."

"We should be more than okay." She traced her fingertips along his jaw. "What we can't rebuild, we'll build new."

"Deal." Tenderness welled up inside him. She was precious to him. Vital to his life. "We both got a second chance today. In that motel room. Out in that alley."

"Speaking of out in that alley, there was another set of papers in your parka."

He smoothed a palm down her hair. "I wondered if you were going to mention them."

She pulled more folded, bloodstained pages from her pocket. "I didn't know you were carrying the divorce papers around."

"I stuck them in there the night I agreed to meet you at the library. Feels like a hundred years ago."

"At least." She angled her chin. "How about we start right now making the most of our second chance? Together."

"Works for me."

Her mouth curving, she held up the papers. He gripped one side. They ripped them down the center. Together.

"That's a good start," she said, dropping her half into the trash can beside the desk.

His half followed. "The best."

She pressed a hand to his chest. "Now, you hardheaded, macho Scotsman, will you please let me take you to the hospital?"

"Yeah." He lifted a hand to the one she held pressed to his heart. He could feel his own thundering beat. "So, Mrs. McCall, do you have a plan on where we go after my side gets stitched?"

"Home, Mr. McCall," she murmured, brushing her mouth against his. "I'm taking you home."

"I love you, Tory. Now...." Bran tightened his hold on her and turned her brushing kiss into a long, deep, slow one that had her swaying. "And forever."

She held him close, heartbeat to heartbeat. She felt love, trust, hope. There were second chances in life, and they'd found theirs.

* * * * *

Don't miss the next exciting book in Maggie Price's
LINE OF DUTY *miniseries:*
TRIGGER EFFECT
Coming in 2005 to
Silhouette Bombshell!
Available wherever Silhouette books are sold.

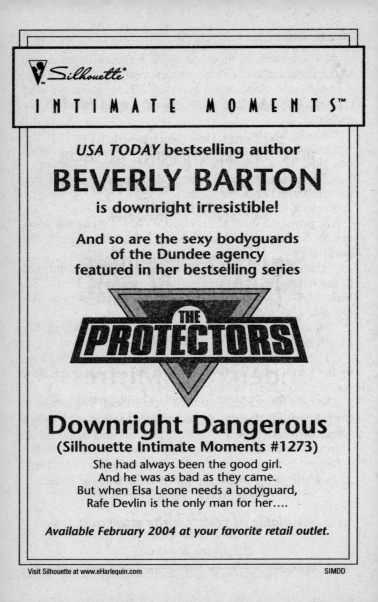

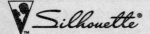

COMING NEXT MONTH

SIMCNM1204